LETHAL LUCK

The dice were loaded against Marc Dean from the start.

His landing craft were smashed to pieces by a storm before they even reached the African shore. Most of his men were missing. The arsenal of weapons he had carefully handpicked was at the bottom of the sea.

He had just twelve virtually unarmed men under him with whom to march through a country he did not know, and defeat a force that an entire army had not been able to budge.

He had a woman he could not trust—a woman who could not resist giving him too much too soon to be safe.

He had a ruthless, relentless enemy who seemed to know his every move in advance.

He had every reason to turn back . . . except that Marc Dean didn't believe that being lucky to be alive was enough when he still had a chance to go for the kill. . . .

THIRTEEN FOR THE KILL

THE MERCENARY #1

MARC DEAN
MERCENARY
THIRTEEN FOR THE KILL

#1

PETER BUCK

Ⓞ
A SIGNET BOOK
NEW AMERICAN LIBRARY
TIMES MIRROR

PUBLISHER'S NOTE

This novel is a work of fiction. Names, characters, places, and incidents are either the product of the author's imagination or are used fictitiously, and any resemblance to actual persons, living or dead, events, or locales is entirely coincidental.

NAL BOOKS ARE AVAILABLE AT QUANTITY DISCOUNTS WHEN USED TO PROMOTE PRODUCTS OR SERVICES. FOR INFORMATION PLEASE WRITE TO PREMIUM MARKETING DIVISION, THE NEW AMERICAN LIBRARY, INC., 1633 BROADWAY, NEW YORK, NEW YORK 10019.

Copyright © 1981 by The New American Library, Inc.

SIGNET TRADEMARK REG. U.S. PAT. OFF. AND FOREIGN COUNTRIES REGISTERED TRADEMARK—MARCA REGISTRADA
HECHO EN CHICAGO, U.S.A.

SIGNET, SIGNET CLASSICS, MENTOR, PLUME, MERIDIAN AND NAL BOOKS are published by The New American Library, Inc., 1633 Broadway, New York, New York 10019

First Printing, July, 1981

1   2   3   4   5   6   7   8   9

PRINTED IN THE UNITED STATES OF AMERICA

For George Kimball,
who knew the background.

In some "unclear situations" governments welcome a demonstrably private force which they can trust and if necessary direct, while at the same time disclaiming all responsibility for its activities.

There are occasions when situations need to be given a push in the right direction but when overt intervention may be hard to justify, either morally or politically.

—Patrick Seale and Maureen McConville,
The Hilton Assignment

Night Raid

1

The storm was at its most ferocious as darkness fell, although it was after midnight by the time the three landing craft were wrecked. A freak wind had fooled the forecasters, breaking free of the southeast trades to howl around the curve of West Africa and run up against the cold current that flows southwest between the Canaries and Morocco. In the forty-five-mile channel separating the island of Fuerteventura from Cape Juby, on the mainland, the collision scoured the surface of the ocean and built up huge seas that ravaged the coast all the way from Sidi Ifni to El Aaiùn in Spanish Sahara.

At Halakaz, a small port not far from the old frontier, the wild palms on the esplanade bent almost double under the relentless pressure of the gale and breakers roared white along the sands. Even the lights of freighters anchored in the lee of the harbor mole swung to and fro across heaving water that crumbled from time to time into whitecaps. On the far side of the town, a police captain climbed the steep streets of the Arab quarter on the promontory overlooking the bay. He was in plain clothes, although polished uniform boots still creaked beneath the trousers plastered to his legs by the rain. The captain held the collar of his trench coat closed as he leaned forward into the deluge—a spare man of middle height with a seamed brown face and a clipped mustache.

Flat-topped Arab houses leapfrogged the grade on either side of the rain-wet cobbles. No windows pierced the pale walls, but occasionally through an open doorway naked oil lamps revealed a tinsmith working late or

3

groups of old men drinking mint tea and smoking miniature pipes of *kif*. The captain strode up a final deserted slope toward the thrashing palm fronds surrounding the grand mosque. On the flat ground leveling the crest of the promontory, the full force of the southwesterly gale hit him as he battled his way across the Zocco Grande, a merchants' quarter based on an open-air market in Tangier. There were no bivouacs now between the cracked mud walls: a solitary Arab hurried splay-footed across the runnels of yellow water traversing the empty square, his slippers in one hand and his wet djellaba flapping in the wind.

Although it was twenty years since the last French troops had pulled out of Morocco, there were still notices and road signs at street corners in the French language. The captain himself had been born in Marseille. He passed a faded legend topped with a black triangle which warned: DANGER—PENTE ABRUPTE! And then the red circle on a white ground prohibiting all wheeled traffic. Beyond this the land dipped steeply toward the sea, the roofs of the houses dropped like a chaotic flight of steps, and the roadway finally zigzagged through a slant of rock and scrub to join a clifftop path circling the headland. Here the policeman paused in the shelter of a stone buttress to light a cigarette. Three times the wind snatched the flame from inside the stormguard of his lighter, but at last the red tip was glowing in the dark and a lungful of smoke whipped away into the night.

From this vantage point, at the head of the peninsula, the captain could look back at the lights of the port and the new town, glimmering through squalls of rain, or around to the south, where the Atlantic rollers marched uninterruptedly toward the blackness of an empty shore. Sixty feet below the path, waves exploded against a sheer cliff face, sending occasional sheets of spray hissing over the parapet.

The captain pitched away the stub of his cigarette and crouched down behind the buttress to light another.

4

White brilliance suddenly blinded his eyes. A man's voice exclaimed in astonishment, "Captain Ibanez! What brings you here at this time of night?"

Behind the powerful flashlight stood a bulky figure in sou'wester and streaming oilskins. The sound of approaching footsteps had been masked by the roar of waves and wind and the pelting of the rain. "What are you doing here?" the man asked again.

Ibanez shielded his eyes against the light with one hand. "Waiting for you," he said.

"For me? But . . . ? Why here? Why didn't you come up the steps from the dock area? Why not call by the coast-guard hut? At least it's dry and fairly warm in there. We could have had a tot of rum."

"Maybe I didn't want to be seen," Ibanez said.

In the reflected torchlight, water dripped like diamonds from the brim of the coast guard's sou'wester. "I don't understand," he said.

"I don't expect you to. Certain other things could happen—or not happen—tonight, and you wouldn't understand those either. It will be to your advantage not to mention that . . . incomprehension . . . to anybody else."

The coast guard was staring at him in bewilderment.

"Look, Benaud," the captain said. "You're just starting your first patrol, right?"

"Right enough. And two more to do before I'm relieved. In filthy weather like this, I wish more than ever that the damned Moroccans would take a little more responsibility for their—"

"Relax!" Ibanez cut in. "You don't have to do the other two . . . and you need not complete this one, either."

"Don't have . . . ? But I must, Captain. My report . . ."

"There will be nothing to report."

Benaud shook his head, splashing raindrops from side to side. "You're way ahead of me. I mean, on a night like this . . . Who says there won't be anything to report?"

"The telex."

"*What* did you say?" Benaud was forced to shout over the buffeting of the wind.

"The telex. Direct line from Fez. Acting on instructions from farther north."

The coast guard frowned. "Show me the message."

"I can't. Top-secret. Memorize and destroy," Ibanez quoted. "Not to be copied; not to be filed; not to appear on any cross-index."

Benaud's lips pursed into an inaudible whistle. His eyebrows raised beneath the wet brim of the rain hat. "You know my car," Ibanez said before he could speak. "The green Renault 16. It's parked behind the Customs House in the Place Lyautey. The trunk is unlocked. You'll find a case of liquor in there. Good stuff—a vintage Armagnac from the Marquis de Caussade's estate."

"You mean . . . ?"

"You'll find it a pleasant change from government-issue rum," the captain observed. "By the time you get it back to your lookout hut on the cliff, it'll just about coincide with the time you should be due back from patrol. All you have to do then is write 'Nothing to report' in the ledger . . . and have one on me."

"Yes, Captain. You're quite sure . . . ?"

"A night of bad weather with nothing to report," Ibanez repeated. He reached inside the pocket of his sodden trench coat and produced the dark blue pack of Gitanes. "Smoke?"

"Thank you, sir." The coast guard straightened up and dragged in a lungful of smoke. The rain had slackened off slightly. Somewhere above the hurrying storm clouds there was a moon. He stared out over the angry sea. "Good God Almighty!"

"What is it?"

"I thought for a moment . . ." Benaud strained his eyes, trying to peer through the almost-dark. "I could have sworn I saw some craft out there. It looked like a couple of—"

"You are mistaken," Ibanez said decidedly.

6

"But I'm sure! Look! Out there beyond the mole! It's hard to see with the moon hidden, but it looks like—"

"An optical illusion."

Benaud stared at the policeman for a moment and then nodded. "Very good, Captain," he said.

Ibanez walked to a corner from which he could watch the man stride past the lighted windows of the lookout hut and turn inland toward the Customs House below; then he retraced his steps and headed for the far side of the promontory, where the wind whistled above waves thundering on a deserted strand.

A mile offshore, three of the most unwieldy vessels ever conceived for rough-water navigation pitched and wallowed on the storm-tossed surface of the ocean. The two smaller ones—infantry landing craft dating from World War II, which had been refurbished for use in Korea and Suez, and finally auctioned by a Lebanese profiteer in the late sixties—each carried fifteen soldiers in full combat gear, together with a quantity of mortars, bazookas, and antitank guns. The third was a much-modified small-scale tank landing craft with ten more men, two M113-FS personnel carriers, and a Saladin armored car aboard.

The blunt-prowed, flat-bottomed craft were taking a terrible battering from the heavy seas. The storm had blown up out of nowhere, with no warning from the meteorological reports: most of the troops were miserably seasick, and the imperfectly secured vehicles behind the tall sides of the LCT threatened to break loose at any minute. In the wheelhouse above the starboard hold, a husky American with sandy hair and blue eyes stood behind the helmsman and stared through the streaming windshield. "Are we going to make it?" he asked tightly. "Don't give me any shit, Kurt: I want to know the truth."

The helmsman shrugged, spinning the wheel to bring the LCT head-on to an advancing wall of water. "You tell me," he shouted as the squared-off bows lifted high into the air and then smacked down into a trough with a concussion that shivered every plate in the vessel. "These babies were designed for a calm day in the English Channel or a quick dash across the Med. In a gale like this . . . in seas like these . . . we could go to the bottom in five minutes, we could last an hour—or we could still be afloat tomorrow morning. It's just a matter of luck, man."

"And skill, Kurt," the American said, clapping him on the shoulder. "I'm pinning my faith, every goddamn scrap I have, on that. I know you'll do all you can."

"So. That's maybe okay out here . . . given some luck as well. But . . ." The helmsman paused as a huge wave broke thunderously over the LCT's starboard quarter, splattering the windshield with foam. "It's when we get her in amongst those bastards that the real trouble begins!" he shouted, jerking his head at the distant shore.

The American had been thrown to the far side of the tiny wheelhouse by the impact of the last comber. Now he peered out the armored glass window at the lines of surf creaming against the dark coastline. "As bad as that?"

"On a shoaling shore? With this wind and this fucking current? As bad as you can imagine, man, and then bloody worse," Kurt said.

The American pulled the hood of his oilskin over his head and jerked open the door. Wind tore it from his grasp and slammed it back against the wheelhouse. The deck tilted alarmingly beneath his feet as the flat-bottomed craft tipped over the crest of a swell and slid down into the deep trough beyond. He grabbed the rail at one side of the catwalk and stared out over the whitecaps.

Moaning through the aerials, screeching past gaps in the upperworks, the wind whipped foam from the heaving surface of the ocean. As the clumsy craft surged and rolled, the lights of Halakaz rose and fell behind the waves. Through a gap in the clouds, stars swung wildly from one side of the sky to the other.

The girl who had been following Captain Ibanez earlier in the evening stood in the shadow of a warehouse with her back turned to the glare of the dockside floods. She had been unable to get close enough to overhear the policeman's exchange with the coast guard, but she knew the boats were coming. Facing away from the light, she was just able to make out the dim silhouettes of the three landing craft each time they were lifted up against the paler darkness immediately above the horizon. From where she stood, it was clear that the tide and the current were going to carry them way past the gap between the two breakwaters that stretched out to protect the entrance to the harbor. But the girl knew they weren't running for the port; they were supposed to drift past the headland and then put about and beach themselves along the deserted strand on the far side. The only problem was that the operation had been planned for fine weather. . . .

She watched until the boats were hidden by the bulk of the casbah sprawling over the promontory. Then she turned and glanced back at the brightly illuminated dockside. Empty railroad tracks gleamed along the shining asphalt. The derricks crouched motionless above hoppers of ore. From one of the freighters tied up on the far side of the basin, a gust of wind carried the faint strains of music, but apart from wisps of steam teased out from the smokestack of a parked shunting locomotive, nothing moved. Satisfied that she was unobserved, the girl walked quickly toward the stone stairway leading to the coast guard path. She tugged down her hat brim and began to climb.

Benaud was in his hut at the highest point of the path: through lookout windows pockmarked with rain, she could see him sitting on the edge of his desk. He held a bottle tilted to his lips, and his back was turned to the sea. The girl was short and slender, but she had to bend almost double to creep past the window below his line of vision. She turned a corner where the path rounded a shoulder jutting from the cliff face, and suddenly the full force of the wind was plucking at her clothes. It had begun to rain again, and the cold drops stung her cheeks. Wrapping her shapeless black cape more tightly around her, she bent her head and followed the route taken by Ibanez some time before.

Out at sea, the tall American with the blue eyes and the hard-bitten expression had returned to the wheelhouse of the LCT. They were, so far as he could judge, about a third of the way between the promontory sheltering Halakaz and the next headland two miles to the southwest. "All right, Kurt, that's it," he called above the hollow boom of waves thudding against the hull. "Hard aport, and we'll run in with the seas. The current should carry us far enough over to beach slap in the middle of the strand."

"There's a kind of a turbulence set up between these two capes," the helmsman began. "This Canary Current is—"

"Do as I say."

"You're the boss, Colonel," the helmsman said. He waited for two outsize rollers to sweep by toward the shore, then turned the wheel to ease the heavy craft slowly to port. She slid slowly, slowly back down the steep slant of water, and then suddenly rose like an elevator and careened forward as the next gigantic wave towered over her stern and stormed past with the wind whipping spume from its crest.

The man addressed as Colonel was working the shutter of an Aldiss lamp, signaling to the two LCI's. He was wearing olive-drab battle dress beneath his oilskins, but there were no flashes on the sleeves, and the shoulder tabs were minus insignia. With a frightening roar, white water broke over the stern of the LCT, sending cascades

10

of foam swirling among the men and vehicles in the open hold. "Jesus!" the colonel said. "Couple more like that and we could be pooped. What the hell goes on down there?"

There was a blur of movement and confused shouting below.

Kurt squinted through the windshield. "One of the M113's has broken loose," he reported.

"Holy Christ! As if we hadn't gotten enough . . ."

The American broke off in mid-sentence, staring horror-struck to his left. One of the smaller craft, riding a crest between them and the Halakaz promontory, had been caught by a huge wave speeding diagonally across the swell. They saw the wedge-shaped bow canted abruptly skyward. The whole boat seemed to rear up out of the water. Then the wave passed, and the vessel smashed down on its starboard beam, capsized, and sank like a stone before the next crest curled by.

Kurt gazed in disbelief at the place where it had disappeared. One moment the LCI had been there, a darker mass against the dark sky; the next, it had vanished as completely as though it had never existed, leaving a lacework of foam that was dissipated almost at once by the crosscurrent. "*Lieber Gott!*" he exclaimed. There wasn't even a collection of flotsam to mark the small craft's grave.

"Can you see the other one?" the colonel asked tautly.

Kurt shook his head. "She was a long way over, toward the other point. Did they answer your signal?"

"Yeah. But I lost them before they made the turn."

On the lower deck, the personnel carrier that had broken loose was charging this way and that like a wounded animal. Each time the boat heeled over, it slid to the lower side, scattering the men who were trying desperately to secure it, shifting the ballast weight, and making it harder for the vessel to right herself. "Run for the shore," the colonel ordered.

The helmsman glanced ahead. Beyond the rough

11

water that was giving them such a beating, a dozen rows of breakers seethed toward the strand. He could hear their sullen roar over the thudding of the ship's powerful diesels. "Are you quite sure . . . ?" he started dubiously.

"You have a better suggestion?"

"Stand off until the weather improves? This kind of freak stuff can die down as quick as it starts. Run in later on the ebb, when maybe that surf—"

"Be your age!" the colonel snapped. "We don't have any 'later'; you know that as well as I do. We have to be clear of that goddamn beach before dawn. We got no time for fancy sailing." He looked down quickly into the hold. "Besides, if we don't move our asses, that son-of-a-bitch APC's gonna punch a hole in the side of the ship."

"Sure. Only, in that kind of surf, we take a risk—"

"That's what we're paid for, isn't it?"

Once more Kurt shrugged. Threading the wheel a few degrees through his hands, he reached for the brass engine-room telegraph indicator and notched the lever into the "Full Ahead" position. The deck plates vibrated beneath their feet. The diesels roared as the twin screws were lifted momentarily from the water by a following swell. Every bulkhead and seam in the clumsy craft shuddered under the assault of the sea. Between the tall, armored sides shielding the hold, the rogue personnel carrier spun crazily as they surged toward the shore. It caromed off a steel catwalk, shot slantwise across the deck, and crashed into the rear of the Saladin reconnaissance car. The ten-ton six-wheeler, with its heavy 76-mm turret gun, broke free of its moorings as the bows of the LCT dipped sickeningly. Locked together, the two armored vehicles slid back toward the bridge when the vessel rose, and then hurtled forward the next time the bows burrowed into the water.

Whether the hydraulic locking jacks had been weakened by the constant pounding of the waves, or whether the structure itself wasn't strong enough to withstand the onslaught of a mass of metal with a combined

12

weight of more than twenty tons, nobody knew. Perhaps it was a combination of both. At all events, the massive sea doors which formed the prow of the ship—and which were let down to act as a disembarkation ramp once she was beached—burst open under the impact.

The great steel plates flapped in the gale like the wings of a wounded bird. One half buckled and broke away as an immense sea exploded over the starboard quarter. The armored car and the APC rocked on the brink and then dropped overboard. After that the water was everywhere.

With her hold suddenly awash, the tank landing craft yawed sluggishly, falling beam-on to the Atlantic rollers. She reeled, staggered, slid into a trough, and finally turned turtle when an outsize comber broke over the whole length of her from stem to stern.

The helmsman and his chief were just able to scramble from the diminutive wheelhouse before it was submerged in white water. The colonel grabbed a life belt from the guardrail. He was aware of shouts and screams. Then the whole world erupted into a tumult of icy blackness, pounding his muscles, numbing his brain. He struck out, fighting the dark.

And then the long cold silence.

2

His name was Marcus Matthew Dean. His mouth was full of sand, there was salt water up his nose, and the whole of his wet body was shivering.

He rolled over and sat up. It was dark. There was more sand beneath his hands. Flying grains of it, blown by a shrieking wind, stung his face. A steady crashing and roaring sound pulsed in his ears.

He stumbled to his feet, fell forward onto his knees, vomited, and collapsed facedown on the sand again.

A long time later he identified the noise. It wasn't inside his head at all: it was the sound of the sea. He opened his eyes. The sea was nearby; waves were breaking. Big waves—he could see line after line of them, rearing up one behind the other, pale against the blackness of the night. White froth, carried on water from a spent wave, touched his leg. What was Marcus Matthew Dean doing on a strange beach at night, half in and half out of the water? Who was Marcus Matthew Dean?

Returning consciousness opened the floodgates of memory. He was an American citizen. He was a WASP. He had a divorced wife he would still like to lay, a son that he was crazy about, and two small apartments in Europe. He was thirty-six years old. And he was what the world termed a mercenary, what the Americans called a soldier of fortune, and what he himself preferred to consider as a man with military skills for hire.

Military skills? With memory came recollection. The voyage, the storm, the wreck . . . *the mission!*

Jesus Christ! Marcus Matthew Dean should at this

moment be mustering forty armed men, three combat vehicles, and a quantity of sophisticated weaponry which had been disembarked from three landing craft, and here he was alone on the target beach half-drowned. Where was the fucking military skill in that?

Dean sat up again and spit the sand from his mouth. He scanned the long lines of breakers stretching away in either direction. There were no landing craft to be seen . . . and he could find no trace of a wreck, either. The LCT must have foundered in deep water. So okay, the sea had washed him ashore. But surely he couldn't be the sole survivor?

He remembered then. There had been contingency plans. He had made them himself. Military skills, okay? *At the southern end of the strand, there's a rock out-crop—kind of an overhang with a track beside it that leads up and away from the shore. If anything goes wrong, muster there.* He raised his head and listened. The wind—and the rain that it brought—was coming from the southern end of the beach. Over the thunder of surf, he thought that he could hear, faintly but unmis-takably, the sound of male voices.

He dragged himself to his feet, walked unsteadily to the soft sand above high-water mark, and began trudg-ing toward the far end of the strand.

He had gone less than fifty yards when suspicion be-came certainty: there were a number of men talking—ar-guing, by the sound of it—and they were speaking in English.

At once Dean's demeanor changed. He had been look-ing puzzled, slightly crushed even, by the disaster that had overtaken the expedition. Now his back stiffened, his shoulders straightened, his jaw set in a grim line of determination. There could be no doubt, as he strode more swiftly toward the scene of the dispute, that this was a leader, a man used to command—and accustomed to being obeyed.

Before the dark mass of the rock outcrop looming

above the dunes behind the beach, he could hear what some of the quarrel was about.

"What the hell's the use? With no fuckin' equipment—"

"I say we should scrub the whole deal."

"Wait a minute! Wait a minute! Who the hell are you to say what we should—?"

"Ah, piss off, Wassermann!"

"Any case, if the Cap'n bought it, how the fuck can we—?"

"Who says Dean's dead? Did any motherfucker check out the whole length of the shore?"

"Even if he ain't, what can we do? We're soaked to the goddamn skin; we got no irons; it's colder'n the North bloody Pole!"

"*Quel bordel!* You miss the point entirely, my friends . . ."

"The way I see it, we're bitched with no gear, Dean or no perishin' Dean. I say we should go on into town, tell 'em we was in a wreck, and let the wogs figure it out for—"

"Aw, shuddup, Molony! Trust a half-assed mick to—"

"Nobody's goin' to call me—"

"Look, the Colonel is with me when the ship capsizes. We both got out of the wheelhouse. I think he can be around somewhere."

The last interruption was from Kurt Schneider, Dean's German helmsman on the ill-fated LCT. Recognizing the voice with a twinge of relief—here at least was one man he knew he could trust—Dean stepped forward and spoke. His voice was quiet, but it was deep and forceful, and it carried a lot of weight. "All right, you guys, quit bellyaching and thank whatever gods you prayed to that you're the lucky bastards that were saved," he said. "Okay. Now, let's get organized."

He stilled the chorus of astonishment, relief, and what-did-I-tell-you's. "Quiet! Have you men forgotten we're not supposed to be here?"

16

"Most of us ain't!" someone said in the darkness.

"All right." Dean rode over the nervous laughter that followed the crack. "Just how many are we, for starters?"

"Thirteen, not counting you, Colonel," Kurt Schneider said. "But counting Van der Lee . . . and he got a broken leg."

"A lucky number already?" the man called Wassermann inquired.

"That's enough, Abe." Dean was in no mood for joking. "You get plenty of time for the funnies later on. Where is Van der Lee?"

"We propped him up against a rock. Farther down the beach."

"And that's all we have left? Out of forty guys? Jesus!"

"There's a couple down near the cliff, washed up by the tide. But we figure they was both drowned. One had his head bashed in. Hammer's down there now, checking them out."

Dean breathed a silent sigh of relief. Sean Hammer, a tough little Irish-American ex-con who had once saved Dean's life in Cambodia, was a friend as well as the best number-two in the business. He verified the identity of the survivors. Only three men had been lost from his own boat. "What the hell happened to the second LCI?" he asked one of the soldiers who had been on that craft.

"Hit a shoal," the man said briefly. "Smashed to pieces against those goddamn cliffs a coupla minutes later."

"And Mazzari?"

"Not a sign, Colonel."

Dean bit his lip. Edmond Mazzari was a huge black Congolese sergeant whose loss was as much of a disaster as Hammer's would have been. The three of them had fought together in Angola, and Dean's respect and regard for the supertough African—who had in fact majored in international law at Oxford University and spoke with a bizarrely English accent—was as strong as his affection for Hammer. Dean himself was sometimes addressed as Colonel by his men, sometimes as Captain,

17

and sometimes simply as Boss or Chief. But these titles were the result of no bullshit promotion list: they had to be earned; all of the men were free-lance volunteers, paid well, and at liberty to choose the leader under whose orders they risked their lives; their loyalty could only be bought at the expense of personal example and inborn authority. In the maintenance of that authority, Dean himself had always found the support of Hammer and the black sergeant invaluable.

With a mental discipline born of long practice, the mercenary leader dismissed his private chagrin from his mind and concentrated his thoughts on the dilemma facing them all. "All right, you guys," he said crisply. "We're wet, we're cold and we're shocked. Our collective ass is in one hell of a sling. But we have to get on with the job, and the first thing—"

"You're outta your mind!" someone interrupted. "With only a quarter of our effectives and no fuckin' arms, how can we? Get on with the job? That's crazy talk, boy!"

One or two voices murmured in what might have been agreement. Dean knew that this was a crisis moment: if he didn't show them who was boss now, it could screw the whole deal. He strode into the center of the group and grabbed the dissenter—a Canadian named Furneux—by the lapels of his sodden combat jacket. "The ships may have sunk," he grated, "but we can do without rats!" Lifting the man half 'off his feet, he smashed a hard and heavy fist into Furneux's face and sent him sprawling on the sand. "You lard-asses signed on to do a job," Dean yelled. "You already got paid half your loot in advance; the rest's waiting in a Swiss bank until I give the word. Okay, so we ran into trouble. Big trouble. But that's no reason to squeal and quit, for God's sake! Why the fuck do you think we're paid? To snivel and creep and crawl back under a stone? We'll do this goddamn job, and we'll do it good. Now, don't let me hear another word of this defeatist shit."

18

"But, Cap'n," someone began, "if we ain't got no arms—"

"We'll find some," Dean snapped. "And how we do that, you can leave to me. But inventories before plans." He gestured toward the water's edge, where dark blurs of floatsam from the wrecks were beginning to punctuate the seething foam. "First off, we'll check what's being washed up. There's waterproof bundles of tropical kit that could fix us some dry clothes. There may be arms and ammo." He glanced at the luminous dial of his Rolex. "Now, spread out and cover this whole strand. Dump anything you find here. You got exactly a half-hour."

Thirty minutes of wading knee-deep in the undertow, chilled to the marrow by a wind that lashed their faces with fine sand and rain, produced two RPG-7 bazookas, a mortar tube, three dismantled Armalite carbines, a large floating pack of the tropical gear that Dean had cited, and a few watertight boxes of ammunition. Each man, in addition, carried a holstered Dardick .38 pistol, but these lightweight, short-barreled automatics would need careful attention to counteract seawater damage, since they had not been polythene-sealed like the weapons carried as cargo.

Clearly, more would be washed up later, but police or coast guards could not remain in ignorance forever, and it was vital that the survivors quit the beach before they arrived and were obliged to ask questions.

Sean Hammer returned from the far end of the strand before the spoils had all been carried up and stacked beneath the rock overhang. He was a short, wiry, muscular man with a battered and pockmarked face that commanded instant respect. "Hellmer and Poliakov," he reported briefly. "Both dead." He handed Dean two automatics in waterlogged holsters.

"What did you do with the bodies?" Dean asked.

"Sure, I buried them in soft sand, the both of them." Hammer's parents had been Ulster Protestants, and the

Northern Irish in him showed most at times of stress. "The Dutchman's kind of poorly, but. His leg's paining him something terrible, and there's a quantity of blood has to be cleaned up."

"Van der Lee? We'll take him with us and attend to him as soon as we're out of this damned wind," Dean said.

"Just where did you have in mind, Marc?"

"Remember the sand-table model we trained on," said Dean. "The track beside this outcrop leads through the dunes to some kind of a minor road, doesn't it?"

"Oh, aye. That's right. So it does."

"And if we turn left in the direction of Halakaz, the first building we come to—it's about a quarter of a mile, I guess—is a lumberyard with a sawmill, right?"

"Right."

"Okay, I plan to leave the guys in the shelter of that mill while you and me go on into town and liberate us some transport. There'll be no watchman at the yard, and the guys can tend to Van der Lee and climb into dry tack while we're away. There's no sense changing while this fucking rain's being fired at us."

"Sounds good, Marc." It was obvious that the idea of abandoning the project had never occurred to Hammer. "And then?"

"Then we transport them some way into the interior. We find some place they can hide up. We leave them checking out the arms and cleaning up their own personal weapons . . . and we return to town after daylight to see what we can fix in the way of replacing the weapons we lost at sea. I understand," Dean said nonchalantly, "that there's some kind of a military depot on the far side of town."

"We?" Hammer queried. "Just you and me again, huh?"

"Yeah. Just the two of us." Dean sighed. "For a start, anyway."

"You don't by any chance have room for a third, old

chap?" a deep and mellifluous voice said from the shadows beneath the rock.

Dean and Hammer spun around. "Mazzari!" the Ulsterman exclaimed.

"Edmond! You son of a gun!" cried Dean joyfully. "We thought you'd gone to the bottom of the sea, for sure! Where the hell have you been?"

Dean stood six feet tall in his socks and he weighed 180 pounds, but the African who emerged from the darkness towered above him and dwarfed Hammer completely. "One of those seventh waves chucked me onto the beach immediately the LCI sank," he said. His teeth gleamed in the dark. "I thought I was the only survivor, you know. So I swanned around in the blasted dunes for a bit, looking for the track and the road it led to. Then I heard you fellows talking, and of course the old heart leaped in the chest. Mazzari wasn't the only man in this lunar bloody landscape! So . . ." He shrugged hugely. "Here I am, sir and Captain."

Dean punched him playfully on the shoulder. "You black bastard!" he enthused.

"Did you find the road?" Hammer asked.

"I did. It's a little farther than we thought. Damned near half a mile, I should say. But the track through the dunes isn't bad: it's been used often enough to pack the soft sand pretty solid."

"Great," said Dean. "All aboard for the sawmill, then."

It was a curious procession that wound in the darkness along the trail traversing the ridges of blown sand. Mazzari led the way, with the three Armalite carbines tucked beneath one great arm and the mortar tube cradled in the other. Dean marched with a bazooka on each shoulder. Wassermann, Schneider, and the Canadian Furneux—still sullen and muttering rebelliously— between them handled the ungainly plastic container filled with tropical kit. Molony and six other men carried the ammunition boxes, which were fitted with rope handles. At the rear, Sean Hammer and a former French

21

Foreign Legionnaire named Hervé Alphand made a crossed-hands seat to support the wounded Dutchman, who was still only half-conscious.

The rain had ceased for the moment, but it was penetratingly cold as the wind whistled through the dune grasses and plastered the men's sodden clothes to their bodies. When the thunder of surf along the shore had been reduced to a distant roar, Dean passed back the command for complete silence. It was, however, his own voice that intruded on the subdued clink of equipment, the squelching of wet shoes, and the labored breathing of the column. The trail had ended at the top of a steep bank. Dean had unclipped a waterproofed flashlight from his belt to check that the roadway ran below. He was about to switch off the shielded beam when something lying at the edge of the patched macadam caught his eye. He scrambled down the bank and picked it up. Bright blue in the thin ray of light, it was an empty Gitanes cigarette pack.

"That's odd," Dean said. "It's dry as a bone."

3

Dean, Hammer, and Mazzari lay facedown behind a stack of goatskins and cased the near side of the Halakaz docks. There were three ships berthed in the inner basin, rusty-hulled tramps trading along the West African coast in copra, lumber, chicken wire, vegetable oils, and anything else that would not be too badly contaminated by their evil-smelling holds. Beyond this was the outer harbor, where the larger freighters were moored—most of them waiting to load zinc ores mined in the interior. The rest of the men were back at the sawmill, where a roofed loading bay protected them from the worst of the wind and rain.

In the glaring overhead lights, the deserted dock looked like a movie set waiting for the actors to appear. Wind ruffled the pools of water along the asphalt quayside, shivering the reflection of the lights. By a small warehouse spiderwebbed with gantries for a traveling crane, a scarab-green Renault 16 stood by a line of empty boxcars.

"What do you say we get on with it?" Hammer whispered. The uncured goatskins smelled very bad. "Ain't nobody around—and look! There's a line of trucks parked beyond the yardmaster's cabin there!"

Dean glanced swiftly to right and left. In the harsh overhead lighting, his straw-colored hair became almost white, and the shadows hollowing his cheeks emphasized his strong nose and chin, lending his keen face a predatory look. There didn't seem the remotest chance that anyone would challenge them or even come into sight. "Okay, let's go," he murmured. "Close to the wire

23

fence and fast as you can until we get to the cabin. Then stroll in among those trucks like you owned one."

They rose to their feet and ran, rubber-soled sneakers splashing lightly on the wet macadam. In the shadow of the wooden hut, they stopped and surveyed the terrain once more. There were three long-distance artics in the parking lot, and half a dozen three-tonners. "What d'you say? The blue one with yon canvas top?" Hammer suggested.

Dean shook his head. "The little Estafette near the gate."

"But that's just a panel truck, Marc! There's fifteen of us and all that gear. She'll never—"

"So she'll be overloaded. But we only want her for ten miles of fairly good roads. And she has one advantage over all the others: the Estafette has no ignition key; she starts on a button."

"But, Christ, Mazzari can hot-wire any goddamn truck in—"

"I know it," Dean interrupted again. "But it takes time, and we *could* be seen. This way, nobody cares even if we *are* sighted." He gestured at the clothes they had changed into back at the sawmill—dun-colored bush jackets with lightweight denim pants in pale khaki. "We could pass for truckers making an early start in this gear . . . if anyone happened to be looking and if we just climbed in and started the motor. But fucking around with wires to bypass the key could lead to questions."

"Have it your way," said Hammer. "Anything to get clear of those son-of-a-bitch hides! Jesus, if we'd of stayed there another minnit, I'd of throwed up, I swear it!"

There was no problem getting into the panel truck: the sliding doors were unlocked. The difficulty was to get the truck itself *out*—of the parking lot. What they hadn't noticed before was that the lot was surrounded by a high curb, nicely gauged so that it was too high to drive over, and the only exit was between two concrete

24

posts closed off by a red-and-white-striped barrier. The barrier was machine-operated from a steel housing beside one of the posts. "Shit!" Hammer breathed. "One of them pay-as-you-enter deals: you feed in a punched card when you leave, and the barrier raises up to let you through. City Hall in Halakaz is like anyplace else: they make you pay for the space you use! I suppose they wouldn't be after usin' a wooden barrier?"

"Not on your life," Dean said. "I saw a Citroën run back over the operating mat on one of those in France. The motor stalled and the barrier came down on the roof like a karate chop. Broke the damned car in two! No—that baby's solid steel for sure."

"Why don't you chaps leave this to me?" Mazzari said quietly.

Dean looked questioningly at the big African. "You mean . . . ?"

"Get into the Estafette and start the engine. Rev her a little. Warming the thing up, you know. Then, when I give the sign, drive up to the barrier and wait by the machine. Pretend to shove a ticket in the slot, if you like. But leave the passenger door open."

"But what are you . . . ?"

"Just leave it to me," Mazzari said again.

Dean shrugged. With Hammer beside him, he emerged from the shelter of the hut and strolled toward the panel truck. Mazzari walked briskly to the barrier. It wasn't a pole but a flat length of metal, six feet long, a quarter of an inch thick, and tapering from a depth of six inches where it projected from the steel housing to three at the far end. Mazzari made a cursory examination of the ticket automat and the slot receiving the barrier. Then he ducked beneath the red-and-white-striped arm and backed up until it lay between his shoulder blades. Crouching with his hands pressing against his bent knees, he thrust upward against the steel bar with all his strength. Behind him he heard the

25

rasp of a metal door sliding, the whir of a starter, and then the rumble of the Estafette's motor.

Mazzari's forearms and biceps bulged. The muscles of his broad back rippled under the thin bush jacket and stood corded against the blue-black skin of calf and thigh. Huge beads of sweat started on his brow. But the bar was just that fraction too high off the ground to allow him the leverage he needed. Even the immense force he was able to summon was not enough to overcome the locking mechanism inside the steel housing and raise the barrier. Panting, he slid out from beneath it and squatted down to regain his breath.

The exhaust note of the panel truck had died down to a burble. Mazzari rose to his feet and wrapped his arms around the thinner end of the barrier bar. He braced one foot against the curb and heaved, flexing his calf muscles, pulling the bar toward him as he thrust with his foot, trying to shift the obstruction laterally if he couldn't move it in the vertical plane. Once more the visible areas of skin shone with perspiration in the brilliant light.

For seconds, as Mazzari's breath labored and grew hoarse, the motionless struggle between man and machine continued. And then suddenly he fell back a pace: the metal bar had begun to buckle at the end nearest the steel housing. Now he leaped around to the far side and began to push, straining with every sinew to increase the pressure on the weak point. Inexorably, the barrier bent out of true.

Mazzari waved the Estafette forward. It rolled to a halt by the automat, and Dean held an arm out the driver's window as if he were feeding a ticket into the machine. Mazzari thrust harder still. Red paint flaked off the bar at the point where the metal was crimped. Originally at right angles to the exit road, the bar now pointed outward at at angle of forty-five degrees. And then abruptly the metal gave. Mazzari bent it back until

26

it was parallel with the curb, and swung aboard through the open door of the cab as Dean accelerated.

Somewhere a bell was ringing shrilly. A red light above the door of the yardmaster's cabin flashed on and off, on and off. At the far end of the dock basin, light streamed from the interior of a long, low building as a door opened and men ran out into the night. Nearer, somebody was shouting.

The Estafette raced out of the parking lot, turned right in a wide circle with tires screaming, and headed for the shadows behind the warehouse. Gunning the motor, Dean steered between the boxcars and the loading bay. The green Renault had gone: there was nothing but a stretch of windswept asphalt between them and the unguarded side gate through which they had entered.

Out in the street, Dean made another right turn and drove past the Customs House and the steep alleyways leading to the Arab quarter. They were skirting a wide square with an ornamental fountain set among beds of withered flowers when Hammer spoke. "So far, so bloody good," he said. "And well done that sergeant there, by God! But what comes next, Marc?"

"Pick up the men and the gear, drive a dozen miles out of town, find a place where we can hole up, and then bring the jalopy a few miles back and abandon her, so they won't know just where we are," Dean said. In doorways around the square and stretched out on benches among the flowers, beggars slept like bundles of discarded rags.

"You don't think they'll follow us?" Hammer said. "They won't sic the gendarmerie onto us, but?"

Dean shook his head. "I was given certain assurances," he said. "Unofficial as hell, naturally. Provided the group was compact, disciplined, and landed on schedule, everyone'd be looking the other way. After all, we're only passing through the country at the narrowest part. Still, I guess a stack of . . . shall we say inducements? . . .

27

found their way to the right place first. But if we hung about, made ourselves conspicuous or fouled up in any way, then I was told that the Moroccan authorities would have to act. The guys in charge can stay blind only so long."

"And they still have their eyes shut? We didn't foul up, losing all our gear and leavin' a trail of wrecks all along the coast?"

"It's still dark, isn't it?" Dean said.

"You mean we're okay just so long as nobody sees us?"

"I guess so. That's the way *I* see it, anyway."

"And they'll not jump us for liftin' this buggy?"

"Not if we abandon it before daylight."

"Jolly good thing, too." Mazzari had recovered his breath and was looking out the rear window at the empty roadway shining beneath the streetlights. "We can't waste a lot of time dodging the fuzz, dammit: we've got a lot of fighting to do!"

The Estafette raced past a red light at an intersection and took the turnoff leading to the coast road and the sawmill. On the second floor of an apartment house at one side of the big square, the girl in the black raincape pulled a blind down over the window and reached for the telephone.

II

Secret Briefing

4

It was a long road that led Marcus Dean from the
northern borders of New York State, where he was born,
to the outskirts of Halakaz, in southern Morocco, some
thirty-six years later. And yet in some respects—given his
martial background and the accidents of his career—it
was a progression that could be seen as inevitable.

He was born on June 6, 1944, the day of the biggest
military invasion in history. His father had lied about his
age to become an aviator in World War I, subsequently
barnstorming in an air circus before he attended medical
school and then settled down as a country doctor in
Johnstown, New York. In the Second World War, Dean
senior was attached to the USAAF as a medic. When
Marcus, his youngest child, was thirteen, a small legacy
enabled the doctor to acquire a smarter practice in Wil-
mington, Delaware, and it was here that the teenage
Marcus Matthew Dean learned with other high-school
kids the skills of small-craft boating, on the Delaware
River and out in the bay. Encouraged by his father, he
joined a flying club and obtained a pilot's license at age
eighteen.

As a Yale freshman that same year, Dean was already
a young man with a character full of ambiguity. Births
in the early part of June, according to the astrologers,
are ruled by the sign of Gemini—those twins who so often want to go in opposite directions. And the year 1944,
in the age-old Chinese horoscope system, was the Year
of the Monkey, whose familiars again frequently show
apparently incompatible tendencies. On both scores,
then, Dean should have been subject to dichotomies in

31

his attitude to the world around him. If he was, the trait was exaggerated by his environment.

Since his father was a busy general practitioner and his mother a tireless social worker, he was left perhaps too much on his own as a child, at times an embarrassment to his elderly parents, feeling that he could never compete with a much older all-American brother and a socialite sister who had married into money. But this very isolation led to a special kind of independence: if he couldn't compete on their ground, he would damned well excel on his own.

It was such a drive for recognition—at least in his own eyes—that led to his mastery of light airplanes, small boats, and automobiles; it was this that stimulated a mania for physical fitness and stamina, a determination to subject his body to his mind. And it was this, allied to the basic polarity in his character, that allowed him to become at Yale both a brilliant student of languages and a champion boxer, that permitted him later to be a murderously accurate sharpshooter one day and a sensitive interpreter of Vivaldi at the harpsichord on another.

An enthusiastic member of the ROTC while he was reading for his bachelor's degree, Dean signed on for two years as an infantry lieutenant as soon as he graduated. The second of those years was spent in Vietnam, where he was twice decorated for bravery and initiative repelling a Vietcong attack during the Tet offensive.

Back in the United States in 1969, he took a graduate course at USC and obtained a master's degree in political science, which brought him a job on the secretariat of a senatorial committee on international relations. But studying reports and drafting minutes and preparing speeches for other men to deliver on subjects of which they had no personal experience was too boring a life for Dean: he wanted to be out where the action was, where the international relations took place. After a few months in Washington, he applied for an overseas post with the Peace Corps.

He was sent to Central Africa, and there, in 1970 and 1971, his experience of guerrilla activity was broadened—on the receiving end in Biafra, the Central African Republic, and Uganda at the start of the Idi Amin tyranny.

This much of his background was encapsulated on the first two pages of a dossier delivered by special messenger to a first-floor suite at the Hotel Doelen in Amsterdam one day early in 1980. The man who received the dossier was Belgian—a short, fat man wearing a vicuña cardigan over a vest and trousers in gray pinstripe. He sat behind a heavy carved oak desk and read the material aloud to a thin German with a beaky face and deep lines etched into his forehead. "The Peace Corps," the German said. "They only did two-year tours, did they not? What happened when he returned to the United States?"

The fat man turned a page of the dossier. "'At the end of the tour, subject reapplied immediately for overseas work with AID,'" he quoted. "'After a period of specialized training, he was sent back to Vietnam as part of a pacification program.'"

"Pacification?"

"A euphemism coined by our American friends," the fat man explained. "Theoretically, the idea was to resettle villagers who had been dispossessed by the Vietcong in new areas under American protection. It was hoped that in this way a substantial part of the population would become firm allies of the West."

"I find that both simplistic and naive," the German said.

"The Americans are often accused of being both. The accusation would be justified if that had been the only aim of the program. But I was speaking simply of the theory. In fact—as Dean found out soon enough—his 'specialization' was the training of guerrilla bands to infiltrate across the Cambodian border and attack Vi-

33

etcong supply convoys using the so-called Ho Chi Minh Trail."

"Ah. This begins to sound interesting."

"Dean," the Belgian continued, "was one of the undercover men supplying information to Westmoreland's headquarters which was used to brief B-52 pilots flying seek-and-destroy bombing missions over Cambodia."

"The raids they swore never took place at all?"

"Exactly. Even when the press got hold of the story some years later, Dean's part in the operation never came out."

"Discretion is an essential factor in the project we envisage," the German observed. "What did he do when the war was over?"

The fat man sprang open the clips of the dossier, carefully extracted a single sheet, and passed it over. The German read:

Repatriated after the termination of hostilities early in 1973, Subject married Samantha Hurok, daughter of an Air Force colonel, and obtained employment through a veterans' association with a multinational electronics corporation. In the opinion of various sources, Subject was unsuited characterwise to a post that was territorially fixed. The word "restless" occurs in several reports. In 1974, Subject resigned the post and became an arms salesman for an international consortium. His territory was Africa and the Middle East.

1975. Son Patrick born. Subject is believed to have accepted proposition from Portuguese entrepreneur (a client of arms company) to train small band of volunteers to fight against Soviet- and Cuban-trained guerrillas in Angola.

1976–77. Subject's parents killed in auto accident. Through Peace Corps knowledge of Central African Republic and reputation gained in Vietnam and Angola, Subject was hired, with band of French mercenaries, to "pacify" certain tribes in order that Bokassa could be proclaimed emperor (12/77). Dean's company supplied arms for this operation.

1978. Subject successfully led group of irregulars fighting with French and Belgians in Katanga at request of President Mobutu.

1979. Subject divorced. Decided to become full-time mercenary.

"That report becomes a trifle laconic at the end," the German said dryly, handing the paper back. "What exactly happened in Katanga?"

"Rebels fighting from communist Angola invaded the Congo that year," the fat man replied. "Remember?"

"Naturally. Several of my companies lost a great deal of money while they were there."

"Their aim was to provoke the secession of Katanga, economically the only valid part of the Congo—or Zaire, as I suppose we must call it now. They occupied Kolwezi, the richest of the copper-mining towns."

"My bankers in Zurich have reason to remember that too," the German said. "What had the man Dean to do with all this?"

"In certain areas he represented the FN armaments concern in my country. When Mobutu sent out his SOS for French and Belgian troops to be flown in, the FN people supplied most of the weapons; they also suggested that Dean's little private army be included because he knew the terrain so well. As you know, they succeeded in liberating Kolwezi and throwing out the invaders."

The German rose to his feet and walked to the window. On the far side of the cobbled street below, February winds had piled drifts of yellow leaves against the wheels of parked cars. "And this divorce?" he asked. "Do we have any information on that?"

"I'm afraid not. The agency who prepared the dossier were unable to discover the reasons behind the suit. Why, does it matter?"

35

"It might. Psychological instability would obviously be a grave disadvantage in the kind of operation we have in mind. What were the official grounds for the divorce?"

"Mental cruelty. It was the wife who sued."

"That is another American euphemism—or rather the opposite. It can mean anything from sadistic violence to the fact that each of the people involved wished simply to change partners. Is this man promiscuous?"

"Not more than usual. In fact, judging from the little we could find out about his private life, he seems singularly discreet."

"No matter." The German had been staring through the bare branches of trees at the tall, narrow houses on the far side of the canal. Now he turned back into the room. "None of the companies of which I am president would wish in any way to be associated publicly with this venture," he began. "I assume . . . ?"

"Nor would my French and British associates," the Belgian said. "I think we are all agreed on that. The money will be subscribed according to our share of the prospective market. But all negotiations will be conducted through an intermediary; not even Dean, if we decide to use him, will know the true identity of his employers."

"You have such an intermediary in mind?"

"Certainly. An Englishman named Saul Jarvys. He is experienced in such matters and completely reliable."

"And his fee?"

"Five percent of all sums disbursed. Off the top. But he has sufficient confidence in his judgment not to demand payment on the end money if this should be withheld—through failure of the operation or for any other reason."

"Very well." The German fished an old-fashioned fob watch from the pocket of his vest and sprang open the lid. "I will agree with your choice. It remains for us to convince our French and English colleagues that it was the right one."

"You have made the rendezvous?"

"I have. I ventured to make it outside, as inconspicuous as possible. You know how sensitive the market is at the moment. If the four of us should be seen together—in a place like this, for instance—the stock quotations could be affected overnight."

"Very wise," said the Belgian, reaching for his jacket. "Let's go, then."

They met as if by chance, sitting at adjacent tables in a sidewalk café off the Sint Pieterstraat. Later they strolled to the bridge spanning the junction of the Prinsengracht and the Leidsegracht, and stopped to lean on the parapet and watch the glassed-in tourist boats on their way to the Lido and the Amstel River. The Englishman carried a rolled umbrella, with which he fastidiously flicked wet leaves from the spaces between the pillars of the balustrade.

"Since he is a full-time mercenary," the Frenchman said when the information in the dossier had been briefly resumed, "how has this fellow employed his time?"

"Professionally?" The fat man cleared his throat. "One does not announce one's services in the small-ads, of course; such matters are almost entirely a question of personal recommendation. But according to my information, he has successfully concluded two missions since he made that decision."

"In addition to the three he carried out when he was an arms salesman?" This was the Englishman.

"Precisely. It seems that an old Vietnam comrade, now employed by the CIA, suggested him—very unofficially, of course—as the leader of an airborne raid on a Palestinian refugee camp in Syria. A certain terrorist leader was kidnapped and turned over to the Israelis, who are

37

to put the man on trial for murder. So far, the story has never got into the papers."

"And the second mission?"

"He trained and led a small sabotage and infiltration group, helping the Christians during the civil war in the Lebanon—at least, that is what I understand."

The wash sweeping outward from the sightseers' launches had died down and the water was still again. The Englishman flicked a pebble over the parapet and watched the ripples widen until they disturbed the reflection of the canalside houses and the gray sky above. "Does the bloke have any political affiliations?" he asked. "I mean to say, my chaps wouldn't want to get involved in that sort of thing, even indirectly."

"So far as we know, he has none," the Belgian replied. "It is, however, said that he will refuse any assignment which might be against the interests of the United States."

"Quite right, too. The only thing is, if a man works for money . . ."

"You mean his loyalty can be bought? But do we not all work for money?" the Frenchman queried. "Much money, if it is possible. And are we not all loyal to our principles, each in his own way?"

"Perhaps I should make it clear," said the fat man, "that this Dean is no ordinary soldier of fortune, with a trigger finger anyone can hire if they pay the price. He is above all a man whose *skills* and *experience* are for hire—as much a planner, a trainer, and a commander of assault groups as a simple fighter."

Large drops of rain had begun to fall, pitting the surface of the canal. The Englishman unfurled his umbrella and put it up. "Well, I vote we call in this contact man and give Dean a chance," he said. "After all, what can we lose but our companies' money?"

There was a general murmur of agreement as topcoats were buttoned and collars turned up. The rain was falling quite heavily now. Striding into the roadway
38

among passing cyclists, the Englishman made for a tramway stop at the center of the bridge. "Just so long," he called over his shoulder, "as none of us are tied up with the action."

5

Dean's briefing was not complicated. "We want you to organize and train a small operational task force," Saul Jarvys told him, "and then use it to destroy the military capability of the garrison and liquidate this agitator who's leading them. Don't destroy the town if you can help it: we may need that later."

They were talking on the first floor of a restaurant overlooking the Grand Place in Brussels. On the far side of the slanting, cobbled square, the intricately gilded turrets and spires of the fifteenth-century Hôtel de Ville stood against a clear but wintry sky. "It sounds feasible," Dean said. "Depending on the sophistication of their weaponry, of course. Getting there will be the headache."

"Provided a few simple rules are kept, that can be arranged," the contact man said smoothly. Everything about Jarvys was smooth, from the hand stitching on his suede ankle boots to the cut of his iron-gray hair, which curled just enough at the nape to be chic. He was wearing lightweight heather tweeds with a suede vest that matched his boots, and a Sulka foulard. If I hit him just once, Dean thought, eyeing the smooth pink face, he'd fall over and never get up again. Aloud he said, "All right, squire. But I'd want to know a hell of a lot more about the deal—from every possible angle—before I even discuss it."

"My dear chap! Of course." Jarvys had the classic PR man's knack of never disagreeing with the person he was trying to promote. "I'll fill you in one hundred per. Starting from the very top. But first, a spot more lubricant for

40

the works, don't you think?" He raised a peremptory finger. One of the waiters in long white aprons who were handing around huge platters of cold meat and salad hurried across. "Another carafe of the same," Jarvys ordered.

Dean sniffed appreciatively when the wine was served. "Sancerre!" he said. "It's not often you can get that *en carafe.*"

"That's one of the reasons one comes here," said Jarvys. He glanced with a proprietary air around the oak-beamed room, with its mullioned windows and the log fire burning beneath the vast open chimney. The place was sufficiently crowded—and sufficiently noisy—for a conversation to remain private. He leaned across the table, glass in hand.

"To get to the point," he said. "The northern part of West Africa. Opposite the Canaries. Where the border between Morocco and Spanish Sahara used to be. You know what happened to that, of course?"

Dean sighed. "Sure. The Spanish looked after it from '58 to '76 and then they quit. Since then the country—which is ninety-nine percent desert—has been split between Morocco and Mauritania. Except of course there's the Front Polisario, the left-wing guerrillas who want to make the place an independent state, God knows why."

"They're not the only ones."

"No kidding!" Dean's blue eyes opened wide in astonishment. "You mean . . . ?"

Satisfied that he'd made an impression, Jarvys leaned back in his chair. He sipped his wine. "There's a place called Halakaz," he said. "Small port between Tarfaya and Cape Juby. Couple of hundred miles inland from there—two hundred and five, to be precise—just where Morocco's at its narrowest, there's a mountainous region on the border of the Sahara's Erg Iguidi. Are you with me?"

"The Erg Iguidi. Yeah, that's the westernmost of the great dune deserts, isn't it?"

41

"So they tell me. Never been near the place myself."

"They're incredible, *all* those Ergs," Dean said. "With no vegetation to keep the surface in place, the dunes can build up to six or seven hundred feet high!"

"Jolly good luck to them. Well, this region does have some vegetation: part of it's pretty dense forest; the rest is mountains. It's quite small, something like a hundred square miles—but it's where the borders of Algeria, Morocco, and Mauritania meet. You know, like the three spokes of a steering wheel. And this area's slap in the middle, right where the horn button would be." Jarvys laughed, pleased with his simile. "The thing is, the bloody button's being pressed . . . and the horn'll make the devil of a row if we don't take care!"

"And you're asking me to . . . ?"

"Shove the finger off the button, old boy. Take it away, take it away, like the finger in the blackbird's hole. Re-move it."

Dean said nothing.

"Perhaps I'd better explain," Jarvys added hastily.

"I guess it might be a good idea."

"Yes. Well." The contact man coughed. He took another sip of wine. "As I was saying, there's only one town of any size in this area. It's an ancient Berber walled city called Gabotomi—one of those mud-colored fortress towns you get in the Atlas. The point is . . ." Jarvys leaned forward again. ". . . your actual Berbers have been turfed out, shown the bally door, made into a subject race in their own back garden, as it were."

"Oh?" Dean looked surprised. "When? And who by?"

"A very rum lot called the Nya Nyerere. They're a non-Muslim tribe thought to have migrated westward from southern Sudan sometime in the last century. They were originally of nomad stock; they've got no ethnic claim to this area at all. Not a shred of a claim. But they do have this fire-eating boss man, Anya-Kutu. You know the kind of thing: studied at Moscow University,

42

Cuban-trained, very well in with the comrades in Angola."

"Yes," Dean said. "I know the kind of thing."

"So anyway, whoever put him up to it, this lad's begun to make a right nuisance of himself. He's in cahoots with the Polisario, of course—and with a bit of encouragement from them, and a lot of loot from Angola, he's chucked out the Berbers and now he's making territorial claims on the three surrounding countries. With a claim for the establishment of an independent state thrown in, if you please!"

"He's out of his skull. There never was a separate kingdom in that area."

"I know it. I know it. Everybody knows it, old boy. And the whole thing would be dismissed as preposterous—it wouldn't even get as far as the United Nations—it'd be nothing more than a political embarrassment for Morocco, Algeria, and Mauritania . . . if it wasn't for one fact."

Jarvys paused for effect. The man's flat, pale eyes were almost lashless, Dean observed with astonishment. Perhaps that was why everything he said seemed to be so soulless and considered. Or maybe it was just that the interests he was plugging were only indirectly his own. The American shrugged. "All right," he said, "I'll buy it. Put me out of my misery."

Jarvys remained silent while a waiter ministered to them from a copious cheeseboard, and then continued, "It's just this. Gabotomi stands on a granite outcrop, and somewhere in that granite there's an ancient silver mine. You know what's happened to the silver market, of course?"

"Sure. Blew the top off the bottle. World demand, I guess."

"Exactly. Gold's become too expensive, and nobody trusts currencies anymore. But that's not all. The rocks around the granite are all folded and contorted—"

"The Canaries are volcanic," Dean could not help interposing. "Presumably your granite is a post-Cambrian extrusion, a boss, that metamorphosed an existing shield of Paleozoic sedimentaries?"

Jarvys only looked disconcerted for a moment. And then: "I'm glad you realized that," he said. "It saves me having to explain."

Dean laughed. "Can't win, can you?"

"I beg your pardon? Never mind. Anyway, recent surveys—carried out in secret, I may say—among these other rocks have uncovered deposits of garnierite, molybdenite and chalcopyrite. I'm sure I don't have to tell you," Jarvys said in a brave comeback attempt, "that those are the principal ores of nickel, molybdenum, and copper."

This time Dean was genuinely surprised. "Jesus!" he said. "Hardening special steels. Lightweight alloys. Copper tubing in electronics and nuclear generators. Cupronickel for rocketry. With the silver thrown in, that's quite a property there!"

"Isn't it?" The PR man resumed his role, the professor pleased with a bright pupil. "Now, none of the governments concerned wants to risk stirring up an international storm, especially criticism from the Eastern bloc, by suppressing the Nya Nyerere forcibly. On the other hand, there could be rich rewards for all three of them . . . if a certain international consortium interested in the mineral rights could be assured, absolutely assured, of peaceful, undisturbed access to the lodes."

"You mean they'd cut Morocco, Mauritania, and Algeria in for a piece of the action, a percentage, the way they do with oil?"

"The way they *did* with oil."

"Sure. And these guys, the Nya Nyerere, with their stupid little squawks for independence, are lousing up the deal? They're all that stands in the way of a happy ending?"

Jarvys nodded. "If the Berbers got their city back, they'd play ball, as you say. But nobody would dream of

44

acquiring the rights if the Nya Nyerere were still there: they're a warrior tribe; they're well-armed; and they'd make trouble. They've got to be . . . eliminated."

"I think 'pacified' is the word you want," said Dean. "But none of the principals dare take the risk of doing it—or to be seen doing it—so they figure it's time to call in the hired help? Is that it?"

Jarvys held up a finger to call for the bill. "Precisely," he said.

They walked out into the winter sunshine. The gold decorations on the facade of the King's Palace glittered in the clear, cold air. "My God," Jarvys said, "that Brabant Gothic really *is* flamboyant, isn't it? Do you know Brussels well?"

"So-so," Dean replied. In fact he had a small studio apartment at the top of a glass-and-concrete building behind the central railroad station. There was another one like it in the rue Cavalotti near the Paris Opera, for it was in these two cities that the shadow men who commissioned mercenaries were most likely to congregate. But Dean's meetings were always in public places, and none of his contacts knew of the two apartments. Like a jungle cat, he kept the location of his lair a secret. "If I was to accept this assignment," he said, "any combat team I trained would have to cross a couple of hundred miles of Moroccan territory before it reached the target area, wouldn't it? You don't think that'd stir up more problems than the assault itself?"

Jarvys shook his head. "I told you. Nobody's prepared to be associated with this project *openly*. But there'll be plenty of people secretly wishing you luck . . . and most of them can be persuaded to look the other way when it's necessary."

Strolling down a pedestrian precinct toward Jarvys' hotel, they passed display windows crammed with sable and mink, shelves laden with electronics and hi-fi gear, women in suede suits and Ferragamo shoes standing in line to buy airline grips from Gucci. "This is a rich

45

town," Dean said. "It seems as good a time as any to tell you that this operation would cost a hell of a lot of money."

"There's a hell of a lot of money at stake," Jarvys said. "And my clients are prepared to spend quite a lot to save it."

"These clients, now: just who would I be working for? A government? A multinational? A trade association? Or this international consortium you mentioned?"

"Let's just say that certain friends of mine are anxious to see you gainfully employed," Jarvys said lightly.

Dean grinned. "Have it your way," he said. "I'll think it over."

6

A week later, Marc Dean alighted from the eight-car Brussels *rapide* at the railroad station in Mons, southern Belgium, and began walking toward the city center. It was four-thirty in the afternoon, and judging by the rain clouds massing in the west, it would soon be dark. He crossed the Place Leopold, climbed the hill skirting the chunky Gothic cathedral, and hurried along the Rue des Clercs.

In the four days since he had called Saul Jarvys to say that he would undertake the assignment, a great deal of the groundwork had been finalized. That is to say that financial terms had been agreed between Dean and the shadowy figures represented by Jarvys: all that remained before the operation was actually mounted were the three R's of the mercenary world—recruitment, routine, and rehearsal. Plus of course the selection of suitable arms that fell within the overall budget. Dean himself was to be paid $100,000—half on the conclusion of the agreement and the remainder when the job had been successfully done. The forty men he calculated would be required were each to receive $1,000 a week during the three weeks necessary for briefing, training, rehearsal, and the activation of the assault, with a bonus of $5,000 per man if it was successful. Dean's end money and the forty bonuses were to be in the form of bank-certified checks, paid into a Swiss safe-deposit before the operation started. Allowing $40,000 each for Hammer and Mazzari, this costing fell neatly within the half-million dollars allowed by Jarvys for wages. A similar sum was to be made available for weapons and transport,

47

and it was agreed that regardless of the outcome, the bonus of any man killed in the action would be paid to his dependents. Jarvys' principals had offered to provide a suitable "mother ship" from which the assault craft could be launched, but Dean himself was to choose the vessels used in the landing—and the weapons and vehicles they would carry. It was to arrange for the supply of these that he had come to Mons.

The Rue des Clercs climbs to the summit of the hill that gives Mons its name and then drops steeply to the Grand Place, which lies just below the crest. On the corner is the Excelsior café, a long, dark establishment with a wooden, glassed-in extension built out over the sidewalk. Gaston Jammot was sitting at a table in the window on one side of the steps leading to the entrance. He was a small, bespectacled, gray-haired man with a wizened face and laugh lines around his eyes. He looked—Dean thought, pushing through the swing doors into the aromatic heat of the café—rather like a Swiss watchmaker in a Disney movie. Jammot had never been featured in a Disney movie, but he had in fact worked as a watchmaker in Switzerland when he was a young man. After World War II he had directed his talents toward larger-scale, less complex mechanisms, and it was as a gunsmith that he had immigrated to the Congo in 1950. Twenty years later, homeless after the Belgian withdrawal from the country, he had been acting as an adviser in Biafra when Dean had met him during his Peace Corps tour. Jammot had taught the young American almost all he knew about firearms, and the two men, so different in age and background, had become firm friends. It was through Dean's influence that Jammot had been able to set up in business as adviser, armorer, and supplier of clandestine arms to half the private armies in Europe. He had chosen Mons as his base because it was near enough to Brussels to be convenient, yet small enough to be anonymous and discreet.

"Well, my boy," the old man said when they had exchanged greetings, "what brings you to this part of the world in winter? Do you have another shopping list for me to fill?"

"Yeah," Dean said. "One that'll need a sizable basket to carry away the merchandise. I want two armored personnel carriers, a Saladin six-wheeler, an LCT to carry them, and a couple of landing craft with assorted ironmongery."

Jammot was nursing a tall glass of beer. He took a sip before replying. "Ironmongery, all right," he said. "But I am not in the shipping business or the retailing of panzer supplies. You know that."

"You have the contacts."

"Perhaps. I will see. A few telephone calls maybe. But I can promise nothing: it is very difficult, what you ask."

"You old bastard, you always play hard-to-get at first!" Dean said. "You know damned well you can swing it . . . and you will if the order for weaponry is interesting enough!"

The Belgian's eyes twinkled behind his gold-rimmed glasses. "We shall see," he repeated.

A waiter in a white linen jacket was standing by the table. "Coffee," Dean said. "And another beer for my friend, please."

The coffee was served on a small oval silver tray. It was accompanied by a miniature beaker of cream, a tiny bowl containing two oblong sugar lumps, and a wrapped chocolate lozenge and a cookie sheathed in cellophane. "They make it best and they serve it best," Dean said, sipping appreciatively. "That's one thing they can't take away from the Belgians." He looked over his shoulder. Red leather bench seats with marble-topped tables in front of them ran up each side of the long narrow room. A heavyset man with a mustache sat behind a cash register at a raised desk spanning the far end. Otherwise, except for a couple of housewives exchanging confidences over a pot of tea, the place was empty.

"I need to arm forty men," Dean said in a low voice.

49

He produced aerial photographs of Gabotomi that Jarvys had supplied, with maps of the surrounding area and estimates of the firepower available to the garrison. "I aim to soften them up at long range and then go in to take out the rest at close quarters. What do you think?"

"So you'll need automatic rifles and bazookas, with SMG's or machine pistols for the close work, eh? You hadn't thought of a drop instead of this seaborne landing? If you could get hold of a Chinook or a couple of Huey choppers, you could float down much heavier stuff along with your troops and finish the job more quickly, no?

Dean shook his head. "My principals are sold on the overland raid. It's only a couple of hundred miles, well within the range of the vehicles, and it seems the local law is being paid to look the other way. Besides, my guys have access to a mother ship that can take us there, and the right kind of aircraft are hard to come by."

"Very well," Jammot said. "Now for the rifles: Armalites or our good Belgian FAL's that they use in NATO?"

"I'd rather use the Kalashnikov AKM."

Jammot pursed his lips. "Very difficult. The comrades would never release AKM's. Even if I could get you AK47's, they would be very expensive. The Armalite has a longer range, a quicker rate of fire, and it weighs a little less."

"But the Russian gun's five inches shorter, there are ten more rounds in the magazine, and it uses standard 7.62-caliber cartridges that you can pick up anywhere."

"The 5.56mm rounds in the Armalite have a better stopping power because the bullets tumble as soon as they hit the target."

Dean laughed. "Have it your way. Submachine guns, now. And here there's only one possible choice for me—the Uzi."

"My dear boy!" Jammot looked scandalized. "Surely you must know that is impossible? Impossible? The Israelis make the most *exhaustive* inquiries before they will accept an order."

"They don't have to be new."

"The secondhand market does not exist. Now, I could get you as many MP-40's as you want—at a very reasonable price, too."

"The good old Schmeisser? No thanks. I'm not making a TV drama about World War II. The damned things are twenty-five inches long without the stock, and they weigh ten pounds. The Uzi's only that long *with* the stock, and you can lop off another ten inches if you detach that and use the gun as a machine pistol. Weighs three pounds less than a Schmeisser, too."

"Well, I'm telling you I cannot do it." The old man looked up over his glasses. "What is the size of the order, by the way?"

"Two dozen automatic rifles, two dozen SMG's, I guess, to be on the safe side and cover every angle."

"It's a very small order." Jammot drained his glass, wiped the froth from his lips with a silk handkerchief, and set the glass carefully on the table. He leaned toward Dean. "I tell you what I could do. If you'd accept the Czech VZ-61, I could put the order through Omnipol in Prague. They're always happy to lay their hands on Western currency. We could get the bazookas, grenades, mortars, and any explosives you wanted through them too. Then, if I get to the right man, I might even be able to coax half a dozen Kalashnikovs out of him, as a favor. What do you say?"

Dean thought it over. The VZ-61—Eastern-bloc countries called it the Skorpion—was a useful-enough little weapon. It weighed only three pounds and was ten inches long, with a ten-inch wire stock that could be extended if necessary. Its drawbacks were nonstandard (7.65mm) ammunition and a very rapid (700rpm) rate of fire, due to the lightness of the moving parts. This made it somewhat inaccurate because of the excessive recoil action. Nevertheless . . .

He made up his mind. "Okay, Gaston, it's a deal," he said. "Do what you can about the Kalashnikovs. I'll take the balance in Armalites, as you suggest."

"Good. And the sidearms?"

"We'll talk about that back at your place," said Dean, "and I can list the explosives and other stuff at the same time." They left the café and walked past the city hall. It was dark now, a cold wind was blowing, and late shoppers hurried home past the lighted windows of pastry shops and bars. Jammot veered toward the city-hall entrance, where the cast-iron effigy of a marmoset perched on the blackened stone. He passed his hand over the creature's skull, worn silver-smooth by the touch of countless palms. "Excuse me," he said. "A tradition of the town since hundreds of years. For good luck, you know."

Dean stretched out an arm in his turn and caressed the tiny metal head. "I could use all the help I can get on this deal," he said.

Gaston Jammot lived at one end of a street behind the jail—a row of prewar terrace houses facing a twenty-foot wall half-hidden by trees under which the residents parked their cars. At the far end of the narrow entrance hallway, a door led into a walled backyard which had been glassed over, and it was here that Jammot carried on the legal side of his business as a gunsmith. Drills, punches, tapping machines, and lathes were clamped to workbenches along each wall. Shotguns, sporting rifles, and target pistols lay among the litter of tools and cartridge cases. At one side of a padded booth where the old man carried out ballistics tests for the police, a beautiful Mannlicher elephant gun was held in a double vise. "Repairs, repairs!" he grumbled, indicating an elegantly chased sideplate that was buckled and torn. "They pay out huge sums of money for a work of art, and then they complain of the cost when they have to employ a skilled craftsman to make good their own carelessness." He bent

52

down to unlock a cupboard beneath the bench and took out a canvas satchel.

"There's nothing artistic about this baby," he said, unwrapping an oiled silk package from the interior of the satchel. "It's functional and it's cheap and it's ugly—but, by God, it works!"

Dean hefted the little Czech machine pistol in his right hand and then his left. He pulled back the overhung bolt, examined the breech face, and fingered the extractor. The wire frame that served as stock was folded forward over the muzzle. He pulled it back so that the gun was extended to its maximum length, then squinted along the absurdly short three-inch barrel. "It comes with a wash-leather holster and straps," Jammot said.

Dean closed his right hand around the near-circular pistol grip and grasped the curved twenty-round magazine with his left. "It seems a handy little weapon," he said.

"My dear boy! How many times do I have to tell you? A gun is not a weapon; it is—"

"All right, all right." Dean interrupted. "I know. It's not a weapon; it's a method of transport."

"Exactly. The shell or the bullet is the weapon; the gun is simply the means of delivering it to its target. Now, talking of sidearms . . ." He dived down and produced another satchel.

"We weren't," Dean said. "But *once* a salesman . . ."

"You know, the Dardick pistol was invented in 1949," Jammot said. "There was some talk of the U.S. Air Force taking it up, but the deal fell through. There were, however, a number of units made. As it happens, I can lay my hands right away on fifty—at a knockdown price: only one hundred dollars each."

"There's that crazy triangular cartridge case, and—"

"I can get as much ammunition as you need. And the guns come complete with holster and magazine."

"Forty will do me; I don't need fifty," Dean said, picking up the curious pistol, with its heavy stock and butt and its short, slender barrel.

"Unfortunately, the lot cannot be broken up. The seller, you understand, wishes to sell out and cut his losses."

"Then the most I can pay is eighty bucks a unit. Take it or leave it." He laid the gun down on the greased wrapping paper.

Jammot sighed. "You are a hard man to deal with. I will see if I can persuade him to agree. Now, if you could use half a dozen Gyrojet rocket pistols . . . ?"

"Later," Dean said. Jammot's plump blond wife, Dagmar, was standing by the armory door. "There's a *blanquette de veau*," she said. "With salsify *beignets* and a bottle of Muscadet. If you don't come now, the sauce will thicken . . ."

"How is Samantha?" Jammot asked as he ushered the American into the dining room.

Dean's face stiffened. "She divorced me last year," he said.

"I am so sorry, my friend. I did not know. I hope that it was not too . . . Such things are painful. I hope you were not too badly wounded."

"Would you like me to sit here?" Dean said. "Shall I open the wine?"

Soon after midnight, emerging from the central station at Brussels with the crowd from the last train, he saw a blond girl in a raincoat waiting by the cab rank. For a moment his heart almost stopped beating: except for the red-heeled boots, it could have been Samantha herself. "Buy me a drink?" the girl said.

In a brightly lit bar behind the Sabena building, she looked him up and down appreciatively. "You!" she said. "For a moment I thought I was talking to James Coburn!"

"James Coburn?"

"The movie star. You're American, aren't you?"

"I'm afraid I don't get to see the movies too much," Dean said.

The girl's slumberous eyes were weighed down with blue shadow, caged behind artificial lashes. "Now that I look," she said, "you're younger. And tougher, too."

"Have another cognac," Dean said. Freed from the constriction of any foundation garment, her breasts lay easily beneath a black silk blouse.

"My apartment's quite near," she told him later. "Only five minutes in a cab. I can promise you that we'd have fun."

"I've got a flat just up the road," Dean said angrily. "I want to go to my place. Do you hear: I want to take you to my place."

III

Surprise Attack

7

Dean's plan to attack the military depot at Halakaz was formed less from a sense of desperation than from a cool appraisal of the facts and the certain knowledge that there was no place else he could find the weapons he needed.

Inland, the twenty-mile coastal strip rose gradually through increasingly barren areas of cultivation to the foothills at the southern extremity of the Atlas Mountains. It was here, in a disused stone quarry, that the remaining members of the expedition hid out while Hammer and Dean himself returned the stolen Estafette, abandoning it on the outskirts of town and continuing their journey on foot. Soon after daylight, they were on the esplanade leading from the docks to the city center.

The storm had blown itself out, although there was still a big sea running and scattered cloud formations sailing up from the south. By eleven o'clock these had disappeared and the sun shone fiercely from an empty sky. Dean and Hammer drank at a sidewalk café on the Place Glouai. There were sailors around everywhere, but their story that they were off one of the larger boats in the outer harbor would nevertheless be easier to maintain here than it would in a crowded waterfront bar: here in the commercial center, miners from up-country, French businessmen, dockers, shopkeepers, and an occasional prospector mingled with the throng of Moroccans in Western and Arab dress, and there was a much better chance of two strangers passing unnoticed.

Most of the *souks* were in the casbah on the promontory, but here and there in the side streets below, tinners, leatherworkers, and the vendors of fruit, vegetables, and local delicacies cried their wares in open-air markets. Once Dean and his lieutenant had soaked up, as it were, the atmosphere characterizing the town, they started to move around, behaving like any travelers ashore in a foreign country. Dean's first priority was to find provisions for his team; enough food to satisfy fifteen men for several days was quite a tall order. Dean solved the problem with typical directness. He went to the railroad station, flipped through the pages of a directory in a phone booth, and made one call. Fifteen minutes later and three blocks away, he was peeling bills from a wad of Moroccan currency and handing them across the counter of the Halakaz branch of a European rent-a-car agency. The girl who filled in the forms and made out the receipt for Dean's deposit was slender and manicured, with a cap of short dark hair and a wide smile. "How long will you be wanting the car for, sir?" she asked. "There are special rates for a weekly—"

"Just today and tomorrow," Dean interrupted. "We don't have too much time, but we'd like to take a look at the backcountry while we're here."

"Just as you wish, sir." The girl wrote busily. "And the address in Halakaz?"

"We're off the *Esmeralda*," Dean said easily. "The big freighter in the outer harbor."

She wrote again, and then asked: "Your name and passport numbers, if you please?"

"Is that really necessary?"

"A local police regulation," the girl said. "Sometimes tourists are foolish and venture too far into the interior. If they get lost or something happens to them, it assists the authorities if they can be properly identified."

"Don't worry: we don't aim to leave the regular highways," Dean assured her. "We get enough empty spaces at sea without needing to repeat the dose in the desert!" He reached into his pocket. Like the rest of the team, he had carried papers and money in a sealed waterproof packet, so they had remained undamaged by the sea.

"Americans?" the girl said, copying down the details. "You speak very good French, sir."

"If you want to hear bad French, talk to my friend!" Dean joked, slapping Hammer on the shoulder.

"Do you find modern Greek equally easy?"

"Modern Greek?"

"Talking with the rest of the crew on the *Esmeralda*."

"Oh. Well . . . We get by. Most of them speak some French or German," Dean said vaguely. In fact he knew no Greek, and he dared not pretend he did, in case the girl should prove to be multilingual.

She handed back the passports, together with a plastic folder containing the car papers, receipts, insurance certificates, and a map of the region. "I hope you enjoy your trip," she said politely. "Barbuz, a hill village about twenty-five miles to the northeast, is very picturesque. Or if you prefer coastal scenery, the cliffs at Sidi Marsuq . . ."

"We thought we might take a look at Gabotomi. They say that's a classic Berber fortress town."

"Oh, but that's almost four hundred kilometers! You'd never make it there and back in two days—not on our roads! Besides, it's a dangerous area for tourists . . . there are nomad tribes . . . it would be most ill-advised. If you wanted to go there, you should have taken our special weekend rates and gone with a guide."

"Maybe we'll just stay closer to the coast, then," Dean said.

The car was a small Renault with a rear door that made it into a miniature station wagon. "We'll load it up with supplies, drive out to the quarry after dark, and then come back to check out the arms tomorrow," Dean said.

"What arms?" Hammer asked. "We don't know nothin'—"

"You've seen the town, Sean. By now, you must know

61

as well as I do that it's not the kind of dump where you can run across black-market arms dealers in every café. Even if we had time to wait for them to be delivered. No, this is a thriving, small commercial city, living off the dock trade. The only place we can get weapons is from the army camp. We'll case the joint this afternoon and come back to plan some kind of raid tomorrow, like I said."

"I thought we was supposed to keep our noses clean in this town?" Hammer objected.

"That's right."

"This is one hell of a way to keep your nose clean, boyo, raidin' an army barracks!"

"If the raid's quick enough and clean enough, our noses will stay clean, too," Dean said cheerfully. "That's why we're going to look the place over—to make it that way and keep it that way."

"Yeah, but . . ."

"Look, Sean, keeping our noses clean means staying out of sight and running into no trouble. It doesn't mean *doing* nothing. Not necessarily."

Hammer shook his head. "I don't know. . . . I thought . . ."

"Don't think, you Irish bum. Listen!"

"All right, Mr. Ivy League," Hammer said good-naturedly. "Explain it to the colonials."

"It's like justice in reverse," Dean explained.

Hammer stared blankly.

"Justice must not only be done: it must be seen to be done," Dean quoted inaccurately. "With us, the mission must *not* be seen to be done. The Moroccans want it to *be* done, just like everyone else. But they don't want it pinned on them. Which means they don't want the whole damned world to know there's a band of mercs roving about unchecked on their territory. The authorities are keeping their eyes shut; if nobody else sees us either, we're in the clear. A little nighttime assault on an army depot . . . well, that could be the Polisario, couldn't it? Or some band of Arab terrorists hoping to hijack a plane."

"But, Christ, *they'll* know it's us! S'posin' we kill some of their fellers? They'll not look the other way on that one, but!"

"We'll fire into the air," Dean said.

They stopped the car in a residential street on the far side of town from the docks. In a *place* nearby, stall-holders beneath striped awnings sold foodstuffs to a motley crowd. Moroccans and Algerians in European suits; *fellahin* in robes and fezzes; white-gowned bedouin from the desert, with fierce, proud eyes; Berbers and Tuareg with black burnooses and brightly colored shifts milled around between the soft-footed Arab women bargaining behind their veils. Dean and Hammer bought dried figs, bananas, apricots, raisins—anything that was nourishing, nonperishable, and not too bulky. The only fresh produce Dean allowed himself was oranges and lemons, and they dared not buy too many of those in case they attracted unwelcome attention.

They loaded their purchases into the back of the Renault and covered them with a strip of parachute nylon Hammer had found at a clothing stall. At another market farther out of town, they repeated the process. Then they had a lucky break. A little way out along the coastal highway leading to Tarfaya and Sidi Ifni, an enterprising Lebanese had started a Western-style supermart. Surrounded by a huge beaten-earth parking lot, it was housed in a hangarlike building that must have covered almost a quarter of an acre. Dean saw the signs and the arrows just as he was turning to go back through town and out the other side toward the quarry. "Man," he enthused, "that's just what we need!"

The owner had chosen his site well. Lying between the outer ring of suburban villas and the shantytowns where the poorer Arabs lived, the big store was convenient for workers on their way into the city—and attractive to the suburbanites because they could do their marketing there without going into town at all. Even at four o'clock in the afternoon the narrow aisles between the stacks of merchandise were crowded. Dean and Hammer loaded the car with canned foods, biscuits, rice, *couscous*, and two whole legs of lamb. In the hardware section they bought pots, pans, skillets, and a couple of campers' cooking rings fueled by small plastic bottles of butane gas. Finally Dean wheeled out a quantity of liquor—not sufficient to cause trouble if it fell into the wrong hands but enough to stifle the craving of fighters who were hard drinkers to a man when they were not actually operating a mission.

As they were threading their way to the Renault through ranks of beat-up 1950s' Simcas and Chevrolets owned by the *fellahin*, Hammer saw an exit sign at the back of the lot and grabbed Dean by the arm. "Hey, Marc, look!" he said excitedly, pointing at the legend. "There's a road that runs into the interior by Wadi El-mira and Insalah. An' if I read my map right, Insalah's on the high ground north of the town. Maybe if we went that way we could case this army camp of yours today; at least get us an eyeful of the layout, huh?"

"You're right," Dean said, staring at the sign. "And then we could cut across and hit the road to the quarry without going back through Halakaz at all."

The stocky Irish-American was not mistaken. At dusk they pulled off the road just below the crest of a ridge and looked down on the suburb of Sidi Marsuq, much of which was covered by the camp. Past a stretch of hillside scrub and a terraced orange grove they could see the geometric lines and squares of the hutted complex. Lamps marking the graveled pathways and parade grounds had just been switched on, printing the layout of the depot against the oncoming night. By the time

64

darkness fell, Dean had sketched a map of the place on the back of the envelope containing the car documents, paying special attention to the contours of a gulch that formed the southern boundary of the camp. A fast-flowing stream wound along the floor of the steep-sided valley and gashed the cliffs fronting the shore.

"We may need to use that valley," Dean said.

"How come? It's too steep, sure, for any kind of attack—at least with the forces we have."

"Not for an attack," Dean explained. "For a recce. If we're going to lift these arms, it's got to be done but *quick*—in like a streak of lightning, grab the merchandise, and out. But before we do it, we have to have complete and detailed information on the location of key areas: guardhouse, motor pool, mess halls, officers' quarters, and above all, the armory." He shook his head. "No way can I pinpoint them from here."

"So?"

"So I'll go on in there and find out before we plan the assault."

Hammer clapped him on the shoulder. "That's my boy! Bully for you, Marc! Now, what do you say we make tracks for the quarry—and roast lamb with a tot of Martinique rum? It's the last meat meal the guys will have for several days, so we might as well make it into a party!"

Ninety minutes later, the lamb was turning on an improvised spit, and Hammer and Mazzari were stowing the supplies in a cave as Dean briefed the men on their roles in the attack he planned for the following day.

They were happy to be moving before dawn: the nights were cold and their sleeping bags had gone down with the invasion craft. Dean made three trips to the outskirts of town, taking three men with him each time and leaving them to find their own way to the center and the rendezvous he planned for dusk. There were five in the car on the final run—Hammer, Mazzari, Wassermann, Kurt Schneider, and Dean himself. The nylon sheeting covered the three Armalite rifles, the mortar tube, and a limited amount of ammunition. The bazookas, too clumsy to hide and too valuable to risk anyway, had been left at the quarry in care of the wounded Dutchman. Van der Lee's condition had improved after he had been given a shot of antibiotics and his broken leg set in splints by the Frenchman, Hervé Alphand, who had medical experience with the Foreign Legion.

This time, Dean turned off the direct route to Halakaz and took the track he had followed with Hammer the previous evening. When they arrived at the vantage point from which the camp could so clearly be seen, Mazzari and Schneider were offloaded with the arms and ammunition. "Remember the signals, Edmond," Dean said. "Furneux and Molony will climb up and join you guys sometime after noon. And don't forget—this is a *raid*, not a regular assault! I don't want any of their men killed. The only purpose of the operation is to grab us some arms. And keep them quiet while we do it. Okay?"

"Understood, old chap. Over and out." Mazzari raised a large black hand in farewell and then led the German through the scrub toward the orange groves.

Below the ridge, on the trail leading to the supermart, Dean ran into a roadblock. A blue gendarmerie wagon with a flashing amber light on its roof was drawn up at the side of the road, and three men in uniform waved the Renault to a halt. They were carrying submachine guns slung over their shoulders. An officer stepped up to the car and saluted. Dean rolled down the driver's window.

"Your papers, please?" the gendarme said.

"What's up?" Dean asked, reaching for his passport. "Bank robbery in town?"

"Just a routine check, sir."

Scanning the three sets of ID papers, the officer said, "May I ask what brings you gentlemen to Halakaz?"

"Sure, we're off the *Esmeralda*," Hammer said. "Seein' a spot of the country before we sail."

"Strangely early to be coming *into* town, Monsieur Hammer. And yet strangely late, too . . . in the circumstances."

"What circumstances, then?" Hammer asked rashly.

"The *Esmeralda* sailed with the floodtide at daybreak."

"All right, Captain, we confess," Dean said. "The three of us are jumping ship." He looked the man straight in the eye. "We don't get on too well with the Greeks."

"And what do you propose to do now, messieurs?"

"Make our way north to Tangier, maybe. Or south through Mauritania. Find another ship, in any case."

"I see." The officer handed the papers back. "I must caution you, nevertheless, that you may not stay more than a week in Halakaz without a special *permit de séjour*—a visa obtainable from the commissariat. But then only if you can furnish proof that you have a valid reason for remaining."

"I thought three months was the usual time for tourists?"

"Elsewhere perhaps. Not here. We are on the fringe of a disturbed area, and special regulations are in force."

Dean shrugged his acknowledgment of the warning. One of the armed men was moving toward the back of the Renault with the aim of opening the rear door and taking a look inside, but the officer waved him away and signaled them to drive on.

"How d'you like that?" Wassermann breathed as they picked up speed. "Just a couple miles farther back and they'd of grabbed us with the weapons already!"

"The point," said Dean, "is that the roadblock *wasn't* a couple of miles farther back. Scaring yourself thinking what *could* have happened, that's negative thinking, Abe."

Wassermann was a chunky, fresh-faced man who had a business in the garment trade on New York's Seventh Avenue. He shook his head. "I like a leader who

67

lives dangerously," he said in mournful tones. "It adds kind of a spice to that fear of being dead, don't you think?"

Hammer laughed. "Wait till he sends you attackin' that army camp with orders just to fire into the air!" he said.

There was scarcely any traffic on the road. It was already very hot. The sun shone once more from a cloudless sky, barring the blacktop with shadow as they approached the first flat-roofed buildings on the outskirts of town. Dean drove past the camp twice, then parked in a street at one side of the depot and strolled up to the main gates a couple of times. When he was satisfied that his observations of the previous day had been confirmed, he rejoined Hammer and Wassermann and drove them back to the center.

They were sitting over cool beers at a sidewalk café near the railroad station when the girl spoke to Dean. "So you didn't get very far, then?" she said.

Dean looked over his shoulder. She was slim, dark, and trimly built. Behind her, the shadows of stone lions guarding a fountain lay iron-hard across the parched grass of a small square. It was not until she smiled that he recognized the clerk from the agency where he had rented the car. "Hi! Since our time was limited, we figured it'd be better to make several short trips, using Halakaz as our base," he said. "Why don't you join us? May we buy you a drink, mademoiselle . . . ?"

"Hradec," the girl said. "Rada Hradec. Yes, thank you, I should be pleased to join you. But only for a few minutes."

"Hradec," Dean said when she was seated at their tables and introductions had been made. "That sounds like a Czech name."

"It is. I was born at Klatowy in the Bohmerwald. My mother and I managed to get out just before the Russians came. My father is still there in prison—if he is still

68

alive. First, I worked at Linz, in Austria. Then Tangier. And now here."

"Isn't that . . . something of a comedown, but?" Hammer asked.

"Not if it means you become a bureau chief." She smiled. She had very even, very white teeth. She looked cool and self-possessed in a pleated white skirt and a sleeveless flowered silk blouse. "So where did you go finally, Monsieur Dean?"

Dean was prepared for that one and repeated some names and descriptions he had gleaned from a tourist guide. Presently Rada Hradec smoothed down her skirt and said she must get back to the office. Dean asked could she join them later for lunch: there might be useful information she could give them, he figured, on police or troop routines in the city. She laughed. "That *was* my lunch hour that just finished!" she said.

He looked at his watch. "So early in the day?"

"Other folks' lunch hour is our busiest time," she explained. She looked at him approvingly. "Perhaps another day . . . ? In any case, you have to check in the automobile later, don't you?"

When she had gone, they moved to Dean and Hammer's original café on the Place Glouai. It was almost noon, and the tables, shielded by awnings from the blazing sun, were crowded and noisy. At midday exactly, Hervé Alphand, the ex-Foreign Legionnaire, strode past the café and stopped to light a cigarette by the main entrance—the agreed signal to tip off Deán that everything was going according to plan with the other members of the party. A few minutes later, a lean man with a lined face and a clipped mustache slid into an empty seat next to the mercenary leader. "A word in private, if you please," he said.

Dean stared. The man was wearing a short-sleeved blue shirt with dark slacks and espadrilles. Large sunglass lenses hid his eyes. It was a moment before Dean realized: this was the officer who had stopped them at the roadblock earlier that morning. "Paul Ibanez, captain of gendarmerie," he introduced himself. "What I say now is said in a private capacity and not officially. But I have to warn you that the time limit quoted to you this morning is unalterable. One week—not a minute longer—and you must be out of the country." He looked meaningfully at Dean, then glanced at the others. "All of you."

"We don't aim to stay long, Captain," Dean replied. "I told you our plans this morning."

"Quite. It is to be hoped that nothing untoward occurs—nothing that could . . . delay them. That would be embarrassing for everybody."

Once more Dean gazed at the seamed brown face. Ibanez's eyes were invisible behind the smoked lenses of his sunglasses. Was this simply a policeman doing his job, or was it one of the authorities who had been "persuaded," an official reminding them of their undertaking to keep their noses clean? Were they being given a veiled warning that the Moroccans could look the other way for only so long?

There was no way of telling: the captain's expression remained inscrutable. "It must be a hard life, full of danger, a seaman's," he said conversationally. "Especially for sailors without ships." He laid a folded copy of the local paper on the table. Halfway down the front page they could see a headline: "STORM WRECKAGE WASHED ASHORE." And then, in smaller type: "A Foreign Warship Founders Off Halakaz?"

"A soldier's life, sometimes, must be equally . . . unexpected," Ibanez said. "Our goums here, for example—I expect you have noticed the barracks on the way out of town to the north?"

"Goums?" Hammer said. "What's that, then? It sounds like something out of a strip cartoon!"

"I use the old French term—from the Arabic word gūm, meaning a troop. In colonial days it implied locally recruited units which acted as auxiliaries to the regular

70

army. Now, of course, our local regiments *are* the regular army of independent Morocco. Nevertheless . . . as a military man myself, somehow I don't see them as being totally professional. You know what I mean? I hesitate to think, for instance, what the garrison here would do in the case of a surprise attack. I am sure they would be very slow to react." The captain rose to his feet. "Well, I must not detain you gentlemen any longer. I have a great deal to do—and I am sure you must have also."

They watched him thread his way between the tightly packed tables, pausing here and there to shake hands or exchange a greeting. Finally he crossed the square and drove away in a gray Mercedes sedan which had been parked by a fireplug. "And what, for fuck's sake, do the gentlemen assembled here make of *that*?" Wassermann asked. "You do not for one moment imagine, I suppose, that our *flic* friend was trying to communicate some kind of message?"

Dean grinned. "Search me. Your guess is as good as mine."

"A fly-boy, that one," Hammer said. "A person would think he was warnin' us off and invitin' us to raid the bloody barracks at one and the same time!"

"Whatever he meant," Dean said, "the raid goes ahead as planned."

Later that afternoon, Dean dropped his two companions near the army camp and then drove back and turned the Renault in at the rental agency. A Berber in Arab dress was leaving as Dean made his way to the office to hand back the car papers and receive his returned deposit. The man was as tall and muscular as the American, with flashing eyes, a drooping mustache, and vivid robes in electric blue and citron.

Rada Hradec looked vivid too. She was more brightly made-up than she had been in the morning. Her flowered silk blouse was more tightly tucked into the waistband of her skirt. Dean could have sworn that she had

71

changed her brassiere for one that gave greater emphasis to the uplift and separation of her small pointed breasts. "You must allow me to associate myself with the Arab tradition of hospitality," she said when the transaction was completed. "In a few minutes my relief arrives and I am free to leave. Now that you are on your own, why not let *me* offer *you* a drink?"

"Why, sure . . . that'd be swell. I mean . . ." He was for a moment at a loss.

"Around the corner in the next street—the first on the right—there is a little bar called the Blue Bird. It is cool and it is quiet. I will meet you there in ten minutes," the girl said.

Dean's rendezvous with Hammer was not for another hour and a half. Why not? he thought. He might even learn something: the town was too full of enigmatic behavior for his liking.

The street was narrow and crowded. Marketeers trundled barrows between the double line of parked cars and Arabs on mo-peds buzzed in and out of the snarled traffic. It took Dean some minutes to cross over, and then he had to jump back hastily to avoid being run into by a swarthy youth delivering panniers of fruit on a tricycle. "Watch your step, Mr. Dean," a voice said genially at his elbow. "I should hate to see you incapacitated through carelessness—especially while you are a visitor to Morocco."

Dean looked down. A gray Mercedes was parked at the curb. A figure lolling in the front seat. Dark glasses glinting above seamed cheeks. "I aim to take all the precautions necessary, Captain," he said evenly.

Ibanez nodded as if satisfied, and rolled up the big car's window.

The Blue Bird was indeed very cool. It was also dimly lit, with padded leather booths, palm trees in brass-bound tubs, and a clientele altogether too smooth for an outpost town like Halakaz. Two large-bladed fans like the rotors of idling helicopters stirred the filtered air beneath the low ceiling.

The booths were all taken, so Dean hitched one foot onto a stainless-steel rail and leaned against the polished acajou bar. He ordered a whiskey sour.

There were no bottles on view behind the bar. The space where they would have been was occupied by a tropical aquarium set into the wall, from which most of the light in the place derived. Rada Hradec still looked pretty in the blue-green radiance. And sexy as all get-out, Dean thought to himself with a quickening pulse. She was standing very close to him, with the points of her breasts almost touching his bush jacket. "Tall blond men are rare in Halakaz," she said.

He allowed his thoughts to wander. The banal phrases they were exchanging had nothing to do with the real conversation that was going on between them anyway. Was this girl simply a nymph, a piece of ass with hot pants? Certainly the invitation in her voice, her eyes, had been unmistakable—almost blatant—ever since she had joined them at the café during her lunch hour. On the other hand, if she was a refugee from the East, could she possibly be something to do with security? Did the Moroccans hire beautiful foreign chicks as spies? Was she in cahoots with the enigmatic Captain Ibanez—or was *he* keeping an eye on *her?* Had he been tailing Dean, or was his presence outside the agency a coincidence? Some fucking coincidence! Dean thought to himself.

Rada laid a hand on his arm. Her fingers were cool. "After all, three-fourths of the American people come from central Europe," she said. Brightly colored fish moving in the aquarium cast changing patterns of light across her face.

The barmaid was a half-caste in a low-cut blue dress. A bouncer in a blue linen jacket stood by the door. Dean ordered two more drinks. "Lucky I could pick up that cash deposit on the car!" he said. Why didn't she

73

ask how come he didn't sail with the *Esmeralda*? She must have known the ship had gone; in a small town like Halakaz, everybody knew.

What did it matter anyway? The point was, here was a girl making it as clear as she possibly could that she wanted to get laid. She wasn't a business girl, like the one in Brussels: if she had been, the question of money would have been raised before now. Whatever the reason, she wanted him in the sack. *Now that you are on your own,* she had said. Well, why the hell not? He stole a glance at his watch. He still had almost an hour. It wouldn't be one of those long-winded, sophisticated seductions, that was for sure. But the urgency of Rada's desire made nonsense of that approach in any case: if she was all set for a quickie, who was he to complain?

Dean was always like this just before the action started—keyed up, tuned tight as a drumhead, tense as a coiled spring. He was like a match ready to flare, bursting with suppressed energy at the thought of the excitement, the danger, just around the corner. But the cold intelligence that ruled his professional life was still in command. He was objectively aware of the opposing pulls from the poles of his Gemini personality, the one warning *Are you crazy?* and the other saying simply *I want her!* He was able to rationalize, to weigh the pros and cons, to decide: Okay, I'll take what's offered, it will relax me before the fight; the questions and answers can come later; and in any case, I might find out something. "Rada," he asked abruptly, "where do you live?"

"Haven't I just told you? Half a block from here, on the corner of the big square with the ornamental fountain."

It was a typical hot-country apartment—and surprisingly anonymous: tile floor, cane chairs, a glass-topped table, and Gauguin reproductions on the walls. The drapes, on the other hand, were heavy and expensive, the bed was wide, and there was a complex stereo deck beside it.

74

Dean was taking no chances. The drink she fixed him ended up among the roots of a potted houseplant; he parried the questions with lies or evasions. What did he do? Why was he here? He hadn't really jumped ship, had he? Did he know West Africa well? Even if there was a bug hidden among the hi-fi gear, tape spools slowly turning in some hidden place, there would be nothing to learn from his replies. In any case (Dean thought), anybody who would go to the length of setting a honey-trap for this particular foreigner would probably know why he was here in the first place.

He went into her, deep as a sword wound, as the trembling calves scissored over his back. She gripped him fiercely with her thighs. Her nails raked his shoulders. "Yes," she moaned against his lips. "Yes!" And again: "Yes!"

She couldn't have faked that, Dean thought as the small cries died away, the jerking of her hips subsided. He was almost sure that her disappointment—her anger even—when he refused to stay longer was genuine. Maybe she really did want to see him again.

"A seaman, a stranger, a tourist—why would a man like you want to carry a gun?" she asked, seeing the Dardick pistol in its holster as he dressed.

"Because there's violence all over. A guy who travels a lot can run into a stack of trouble if he's not smart. A gun at least helps him to *feel* smarter than the next jerk. The psychologists call it an extension of the penis."

"I should have thought that was one thing you didn't need to worry about," Rada Hradec said.

8

Marc Dean's rendezvous with Hammer was half a mile along the side road that led to the ravine forming the army post's southern boundary. The main gates to the barracks fronted the coastal highway, but there was a secondary entrance beyond the half-completed villas that lined the upper side of this road, and Dean hoped that he might be able to penetrate the compound somewhere near that.

The hope was a forlorn one. At the far end of the incomplete development, the blacktop degenerated into a dirt road herringboned with tire marks and the tracks made by tanks. Before this section spiraled down to lose itself among the brushwood scattered over the sides of the ravine, a group of officers stood by the gateway studying the terrain below through field glasses. Dean could see figures in camouflaged fatigues moving among the scrub; a couple of three-ton army trucks were parked halfway down the slope, and there were half-tracks fording the lower reaches of the stream. Clearly the valley was being used as a battle course or for some kind of maneuvers.

Worse still—a detail Dean could not have seen from the ridge in the dusk—the camp perimeter on either side of the gateway was guarded by a chain fence that was all of ten feet high.

"Shit!" Dean said under his breath. "I figured there'd be *some* way—bluffing the sentries, climbing a wall, something. But with all that brass and this goddamn wire . . ." He looked along the perimeter: occasional stumps showed where trees that might have helped an intruder to get in had been felled. He shook his head. "No way!"

"What're you gonna do?" Hammer's nutcracker face was creased in concern. They were already cutting it fine so far as the timing of the raid was concerned. Dean wanted the group to go in at dusk, and his own reconnaissance had been left as late as possible in the hope that he could hit a period when most of the camp effectives would be terminating an exercise, changing duties, or preparing for chow. In less than an hour the Frenchman, Alphand, would have hot-wired a delivery truck somewhere in town and driven it to the main gates. Another merc would have hired a pushcart, loaded it with fruit, and taken the same route. A Pole named Novotny and four other men would be admiring the view from a clifftop public garden. Wassermann and Hammer were scheduled to play the role of prospective buyers at a brassware stall opposite the gates. None of them could stay around for long without attracting the wrong kind of attention.

"And they can't do a damned thing until I show, loaded with details of the camp layout," Dean said bitterly. "Every man knows what he has to do, but I still have to tell him where he does it!"

"So what do you think?" Hammer asked again.

Dean sighed. "I guess I'll have to go in with the boys"—he nodded toward the ravine—"when they come home from the exercise."

"You must be joking!"

"Never more serious, Sean boy. Up to this point, we could be two guys maybe interested in purchasing one of these lots. Any nearer the soldiers, and they'll figure us for spies or something. So why don't you go on back there and liaise with Abe Wassermann?"

"But what will you—?"

"Don't worry about me," Dean said. "Go back and check out the dispositions—and that's an order. See you by the main gate at sunset."

When the little Ulsterman had reluctantly departed, Dean sauntered up to the last unfinished villa and circled the building, staring at the empty window embrasures and the roofless rafters of the terrace. Finally he walked up a slanting plank and vanished inside through the open doorway.

Thirty seconds later, he was lying flat on his face behind a stack of lumber in the backyard. He crawled slowly forward, worming his way toward a line of stunted bushes on the lip of the ravine. On the far side of the bushes, the land dropped away, plunging down to scoop up the tiny figures of the soldiers and their vehicles on either side of the stream. Dean glanced back at the group of officers: they were still engrossed in their war game. The sentries behind them stood rigidly at attention, staring woodenly ahead. He rose to his feet, bent double, and raced for a thicket farther down the hillside.

Dean's guerrilla experience in Cambodia and Central Africa had made him a master in the art of cover. Using every subtlest undulation of the surface, each fleeting patch of shadow, he could—given light coming from the right direction—traverse undetected a stretch of open country that most people would swear was flat. Compared to Dean, the *goums* engaged in their ritualistic maneuvers below were beginners.

He gained his first objective—the remains of a ruined shack some way down the slope—in a series of halts and dashes: crouch . . . run . . . flat on the face . . . crawl . . . rise, run, fall . . . slide . . . run again, always with an eye on the officers above, watching for the telltale flash of light that would signal binoculars turned his way.

The shack was evidently serving as some kind of pretend headquarters in the exercise: he had noticed, talking to Hammer, that there was a single soldier on guard there, a tall Moroccan about his own height. Dean waited at the rear of the ruin for the man to make his routine circuit. When he rounded the angle of desiccated stonework, out of sight of the officers, Dean attacked.

Since university days he had scorned the stylized techniques of judo, karate, and kung-fu. "You can do it more efficiently," he often told his men, "more quickly, and more quietly with a sharpened pencil aimed at the eye, pressure on a nerve center behind the ear, or a simple rabbit punch well-directed. All that jumping about wastes energy you may need."

The soldier was carrying a carbine at the trail. Dean leaped at him from low down. His left hand fastened around the wrist of the man's gun arm, smashing it back against the wall so that the fingers opened and the gun dropped. One knee jerked upward into the Moroccan's groin. At the same time, Dean jammed his right forearm beneath the man's jaw, cracking his head against the stones. The soldier gargled, fighting for air. Dean released him, stepped back, and hit him twice before he could shout, once in the solar plexus, once, with the edge of the hand, at the side of the neck. The soldier dropped to the ground.

It was the work of only a moment to unzip his camouflaged fatigue coverall, shrug into the garment, pick up the weapon, and resume the round. Dean made two more circuits of the shack, and then, hearing a whistle shrill somewhere below, he quit the post and began working his way under cover toward the stream, as though in obedience to a prearranged plan.

Nearer the valley floor, he was obliged to deploy all his expertise to avoid running into one or other of the *goum* squads moving around on the hillside. Over the whirring of caterpillar tracks and the whine of gears, he could hear shouted commands, and then the stutter of a machine gun firing blanks on the far side of the water. Keeping the sentry's steel helmet lowered sufficiently to hide his face, Dean crawled toward the parked three-tonners.

Beneath the first of the two trucks, he realized how

79

hot the day still was: cool, gasoline-tainted air played refreshingly over the sweat dewing his forehead, gathering on the nape of his neck, and rolling between his shoulder blades. Beyond the stony bay housing the vehicles he could see a blue sparkle of sea in the wedge carved from the coastal cliff by the ravine.

Somewhere near the bridge that carried the highway over the valley, he knew, Hammer would be waiting. He looked at his watch. Three-quarters of an hour.

The exercise was ending. More whistles blew. The noise of tanks and half-tracks was temporarily stilled. Dean heard voices, footsteps, the clink of equipment approaching the trucks. He prepared himself for the ordeal he had selected as a means of getting into the camp unobserved.

He was lying on his back. Reaching up, he grasped a chassis cross-member and lifted his shoulders experimentally from the ground. For a moment his fingers slid in the thick coating of grease and grime; then they hooked around the steel strut and held firm. He raised a foot, feeling for a purchase, a ledge or the lip of a former where he could rest his heel . . . and froze as the advancing soldiers surrounded the truck.

Twelve or more men climbed aboard. The springs creaked. The motor started with a roar, shaking the whole fabric of the vehicle.

It was a four-wheel-drive Tatra, made in Czechoslovakia. Dean saw with a pang of anxiety that he was positioned too far forward to cling on as securely as he had hoped: his head was just behind the gearbox, only a few inches from the bolster-shaped muffler; exhaust gases jetted from the stubby exit tube, almost choking him. He saw that the only safe place for his feet would be the axle casing on either side of the differential—but he could reach that only if his arms were at full stretch, and while it would be hellishly difficult to keep himself off the ground with his elbows bent, at full stretch he would have to be a superman.

80

Dean had to be that superman.

He gripped the cross-member hard and pushed, shoving his shoulders along the ground toward the rear of the truck. Raising his left leg, he rested the heel on the tubular axle housing. Before he could lift the right, gear selectors thumped into place behind his head and the propeller shaft began to rotate as the driver engaged the clutch. With a jerk and a shudder, the truck moved forward.

Dean's heel slipped and his foot plunged from the casing. He cursed, straining his arm muscles to keep his shoulders off the ground as the truck accelerated down the slope. He had to lift up his feet, too: if he allowed his heels to drag, the stony surface would wear away his boots and pulverize the flesh in no time. Kicking frantically upward, he found the axle casing again and lodged his left foot there.

The truck driver shifted into second, the vehicle lurching and bouncing over the rough terrain as it careered toward the stream. About to try for the other side of the axle casing with his right foot, Dean saw with a thrill of horror that the propeller shaft was open, spinning at several thousand rpm's just above his hip; the universal joint was dangerously near his head. If he centered his body beneath the spine of the truck, the bolts on the joint would slice into him like a circular saw and at every bump he would risk a fatal burn from the shaft. Tensing his leg muscles, he searched for a second foothold on the same side of the chassis, found a brake rod, felt it bend under his weight, and finally crossed the free foot over his own left ankle.

Only a fitness freak with Dean's abnormal stamina could have kept his body off the ground in those conditions. Fingers, biceps, calves, and belly muscles were on fire with the strain. Dust clogged his nostrils and filled his mouth. Oil dripped onto his face, welling from the eye socket down to the ear. Breathing in shallow gasps to keep carbon-monoxide fumes from the exhaust out of

81

his lungs, he found that he was starving his muscles of oxygen . . . and the tonus of his limbs was slackening. He forced himself then to take deep breaths, fighting to keep his mind clear, concentrating on the rigidity of his body, willing himself to overcome the soporific effect of the deadly gas. He remembered reading a spy novel once in which the hero, clinging in the same way beneath a bus that would take him out of Soviet Russia, hypnotized himself into the belief that his fingers were steel hooks that could not break, could not break, could not break . . .

Cold water drenched him with the force of a blow; mud sluiced his back and shoulders; he was hammered with pebbles thrown up by the front wheels. The truck was plowing through the ford at the bottom of the valley.

Dean shook his head, gasping with the shock. Every nerve in him was throbbing, burning, but he was still clear of the ground. All he had to do now was hang in there until the truck had climbed the far side of the ravine, driven through the gates, and parked in the motor pool. He was deafened by the low-gear vibration as they crawled upward.

The journey seemed ten times longer than the initial section. His muscles almost gave out on him and dropped him to the ground when the driver halted to exchange pleasantries with the guards at the camp entrance. But finally it was over; the engine was switched off, the troops de-bused, the driver slammed the door of the cab and walked away. Dean lay sweating on the smooth macadam. After a while he thumbed the drying mud from the face of his watch.

Twenty-eight minutes.

He stared out from beneath the truck. He could hear voices, but they were some way off. Around him, cooling metal from the motor and exhaust system ticked into the silence.

He crawled out and stood stiffly upright, massaging

his tortured limbs. He was in the center of a line of parked trucks. Beyond them were light tanks, personnel carriers, and then the first of a row of wooden huts. He could see nobody. A bugle blew somewhere on the far side of the camp. It was followed by shouted commands and the tramp of feet as men marched to the mess hall.

Dean was filthy—the steel helmet had protected his hair, but the rest of him was soaking wet, fouled with mud and oil, blackened with grease. He stripped off the sodden fatigues: beneath them, his own clothes were equally wet. He shrugged, walking warily toward the line of huts. At the far end there was an ablutions block. Stepping quietly, he approached the entrance and peered inside. The place was empty. With the harsh soap provided, he cleaned his face and hands as best he could, wadding paper towels to dab at the dirt marking his bush jacket and pants. He went back outside.

Nineteen minutes.

Dean had still seen nobody. He walked swiftly up toward the camp entrance, behind the line of huts. Most of the buildings were of wood construction, but the headquarters block, the officers' quarters, and the armory were brick. Carefully he noted the relative positions of each on a damp message pad salvaged from his pocket.

Behind the officers' quarters, he had a piece of luck. Through an open window on the ground floor he saw a freshly pressed uniform hanging behind a door. The room was empty. With no hesitation Dean vaulted over the sill and approached his prize. He had to sacrifice his bush jacket, but the high-collared Moroccan tunic buttoned easily over his shirt, and the pants, though a trifle short, fitted well enough. He retained his own safari boots. And then, taking a gold-leafed *kepi* from a table beside the bed, he scrambled back out into the open air. The sun had set, and there were eight minutes to go.

Dean pulled the peak of the *kepi* as low down over his eyes as he could. There was still enough grime on his

83

face to give his skin a swarthy appearance, but—except at a distance—no way could he be mistaken for a Moroccan officer. Stepping cautiously out from the shelter of the block, he looked across a wide parade ground at what was evidently one of the men's mess halls. The singsong of many Arab voices and the clatter of plates carried clearly across the graveled square. Beyond the hall, a group of men stood around the steps leading to the officers' commissary. Two more emerged from the guardhouse and headed for the main gate, where sentries stood one on either side of a striped barrier pole beneath the parasol pines.

At that moment, Dean had his second lucky break. A stores truck turned off the highway and stopped on the far side of the pole. The sentries moved up to the cab to check the driver's papers. The two officers walked past the barrier. One raised a hand in a languid salute, but the sentries barely glanced at him. He and his companion turned and strolled toward the town.

Dean made up his mind instantly. He already had noted all the information he needed. And while, as a civilian, he might have been able to bluff his way out of trouble if he was discovered in the camp, the theft of a uniform and the impersonation of an officer were serious offenses which would result in his immediate transfer to the glasshouse if he was caught. The important thing now was to get out.

Skirting the parade ground, he walked behind the guardhouse and then marched briskly toward the gate. His boots crunching on the gravel sounded alarmingly loud over the thumping of his heart. Two *goums* carrying a trash can from behind the mess hall stared at him curiously but said nothing. He turned his head away and stared up into the trees as if he were watching a bird. From the corner of his eye he saw that the striped pole was rising and the truck was being waved through. Increasing his pace slightly, he walked out the gateway as the truck moved in.

He crossed the road, still looking away, giving a nonchalant salute as the officer had done. It was as easy as that.

As he gained the far sidewalk, he glanced back. One of the guards had his back to him; the other was lowering the pole. Clearly neither suspected anything untoward. Far off along the highway, Dean could see a handcart laden with fruit being pushed in the direction of the army post. A hundred yards away, Alphand leaned in beneath the open hood of a panel truck.

Hammer and Wassermann were behind the brassware stall. "Get *you*!" Hammer said. "A rehearsal for Halloween, is it?"

"Jokes later," Dean said tersely. "Into the garden and make copies of this plan to hand out to the others. We don't have much time."

They found an empty bench among the yuccas and phoenix palms, transferring the notations from his neatly drawn map to sheets of paper from his still-damp message pad. Breakers no longer thundered on the shore below the clifftop garden. Above the western horizon, a thin line of orange shading into green separated the ocean from the darkening sky. When they had made four copies, Hammer took two to Novotny and his men, and one to Alphand. Wassermann walked toward the fruit barrow with the last. "The armory is the important building," Dean said. "Third alley on the right, behind the drill hall."

His plan, such as it was, relied on three different types of surprise: surprise that there should be a raid at all; surprise that the attack should apparently come—thanks to Mazzari—from the ridge above the orange grove, the most difficult way to approach the post; and surprise, finally, that the actual snatch of weapons should be made by relatively unarmed men entering via the main gate. Those three factors plus the circumstances that there had been half a dozen antiterrorist grenades among the ammunition boxes washed up from the wreck of the

LCT. Even so, Dean's chances of success would have been dubious if it hadn't been for the arrival of two MICV's a few minutes before zero hour. They rattled along the highway, wheeled in through the gate, and parked just beyond the guardhouse while their crews fell out and marched to the mess hall.

"MICV's? I should be so lucky someone would explain the term," Wassermann said. "They're just jumbo-size Bren carriers to me."

"Mechanized Infantry Combat Vehicles," Hammer said severely. "Your normal armored personnel carrier, like the M113's we lost in the storm, it will simply ferry men across the battlefield or transport them from one place to another. But these babies are something else: they will let you fight from *inside* the vehicle, using firing ports cut from the hull."

"Those are British-made BMP-1's," Dean said. "Twelve tons, three hundred and eighty horsepower, and a range of more than three hundred miles." The two armored vehicles were less than a hundred yards away, their six-cylinder diesel motors still idling. "I would be very happy," he added reflectively, "if we could somehow add them to our strength. . . ."

The fruit barrow had arrived on the graveled sweep leading to the camp entrance, and the merc pushing it paused, ostensibly to regain his breath. He began talking to Wassermann. Suddenly a dispute arose. Voices were raised. Fists flew. In the struggle, the handcart overturned and oranges, lemons, pineapples, eggplants, and peppers bounced and rolled in front of the gate. The sentries left their posts and ran forward to remonstrate with the fighting men. Dean hurried officiously across the road, an officer determined that no scandal attach itself to his barracks. Behind him, Novotny and his quartet ran out of the garden as if to aid the soldiers.

In back of the brassware stall, Hammer struck a match. A child's Fourth of July fireworks rocket sputtered, emitted a trail of sparks, and hissed into the sky to burst in a shower of blue sparks over the depot.

On the ridge above the orange grove, Mazzari was waiting with a primed mortar bomb. The moment the signal rocket burst, he dropped the bomb into the tube and gave the command to fire to Schneider and the two other men who had joined him during the afternoon. The projectile whined through the air and exploded with a shattering detonation on a stretch of waste ground just short of the camp perimeter. At the same time, the three men loosed off short bursts from the Armalite rifles. Mazzari dropped in a second bomb and then a third. These too were calculated to burst harmlessly just outside the camp.

This maneuver was designed to draw the Moroccan guard to the rear of the depot while Dean and his men made a lightning raid at the front. Even so, Mazzari was astonished at the rapidity with which the Moroccans responded. Alarm bells were already shrilling, orders being shouted into the dark, feet pounding toward the perimeter fence. Before the echoes of the third mortar burst had died away, flames from the muzzles of automatic weapons were twinkling in the darkness below. "By Jove, it's almost as though the buggers were expecting us!" the big Congolese sergeant said. "Come on, chaps: let's move to Position Two before they get the range!"

At the main gate, things happened fast too. The struggle around the handcart was short and sharp. When it was over, the two sentries, minus their weapons, were lying unconscious beneath the overturned barrow, half-covered in spilled fruit. Novotny took one of the rifles and handed the other to Wassermann. There were now nine men to follow Dean through the unguarded camp entrance: Novotny and his quartet, Hammer, Wassermann, Alphand, and the merc who had been pushing the barrow.

Dean raced for the guardhouse. He knew that, whatever the imagined strength of the attack from the rear, the officers in command would never leave the main gates undefended. They had dealt with the sentries; now it was up to him to silence the rest. Two or three soldiers were already turning out, unslinging their rifles as they ran. Seeing Dean in a senior officer's uniform, they hesitated. He fired several rounds from the Dardick pistol over their heads, and they ducked hastily back inside, their faces a picture of bewilderment.

He dashed to the doorway, holding one of the concussion grenades. These were of the type perfected by Britain's Special Air Service, designed to immobilize captors and victims alike in hijacked planes or any other confined space where hostages were held; they brought instant loss of consciousness with no bodily damage. Dean lobbed the grenade through the open doorway. There was a loud yet curiously flat explosion. One of the guardhouse windows blew out, and glass tinkled to the ground.

Dean paused, listened, and then ran on. The alarm bells set off by Mazzari's feint attack were still ringing all over the camp. He heard the sound of automatic fire in the distance, and the shouting of orders in Arabic as shell bursts from the mortar shook the ground once more. The men from the mess hall had all been sent out to the perimeter, but there were officers and orderlies in the headquarters building, a number of *goums* on various duties around the huts, and more officers inside the commissary block. A crowd of them was pouring down the steps leading to the entrance now.

Hammer, Novotny, and Alphand had been given a grenade each, with specific targets to attack. Dean himself retained the other two; Wassermann and the others had been told to fan out and enfilade anyone threatening him and his grenadiers. They fired over the heads of the officers as Dean noted the thumping detonations of concussion devices exploding in mess hall, duty office, and headquarters block. There were about a dozen officers at first, but some scurried back inside as soon as the shooting began. The remainder, however, made for Dean and the other three bombers, who were racing back from their targets. A tall man ran at Dean, drawing a revolver from his unflapped holster. Dean sprang forward and closed with him before the Moroccan could fire, reversing his own pistol in his hand as he did so. "Pardon," he said in French. "Tu m'excuses, hein?" The Dardick's heavy butt struck the officer behind the ear and he crumpled to the ground.

The men attacking Hammer, Alphand, and the Pole were not so easily taken care of. There were four of them. Realizing that Wassermann and his group would be unable to fire, for fear of hitting their own people, if they were at close quarters, the senior officer barked an order. A moment later the seven of them were grappling fiercely at the foot of the steps. Hammer rolled on the ground, trying to protect his head from a rain of blows aimed at him by the two heaviest officers; Novotny was trading punches with the senior man; Alphand had wrapped gorilla arms around a lean young lieutenant who had tried to pistol-whip him.

Dean leaped to Hammer's rescue. He rabbit-punched one of the aggressors, kicked the side of his head, and then dragged him upright by his uniform collar and landed a jarring short-arm right to the man's jaw. The Moroccan staggered, and then ran at Dean with his head down. Dean reached out with both hands, shoved the head down farther, and brought one knee sharply up. The officer dropped like a felled tree, with blood spraying from his fractured nose.

Alphand broke his hold, scooped up Novotny's stolen rifle, and used it two-handed like a quarterstaff, blocking the lieutenant's blows and then swinging the butt to stun him with a savage clip behind the ear. At the same time, Novotny knocked out his opponent with a karate blow to the throat, and Dean and Hammer between them accounted for the remaining heavy.

There was a confused shouting from inside the building. Dean ran up the steps, kicked open the door, and emptied the magazine of his Dardick into the ceiling of the hallway. He saw two unarmed men dart through a doorway at the far end, and then shots splintered another door on his right, the slugs passing uncomfortably close to his chest. He flattened himself against the wall, waited a moment, and then swiftly kicked that door open too. An impression of shocked faces, a crowd of men, three or four smoking revolvers . . . and then he had tossed in the last two grenades. After that there was no more shouting.

So far, the raid had gone according to plan. The next step was to have been for Dean's men to re-form and rush the armory while Mazzari kept the rest of the garrison occupied at the farthest end of the compound. But Dean was not entirely happy. He was amazed, like Mazzari, at the speed with which troops had arrived at the perimeter to deal with the pretense attack: it was almost as if the Moroccans had been forewarned, were in fact prepared for an assault and waiting only to find out from which direction it came. If this were true—if there had been a leak or a betrayal somewhere along the line—there was no telling what contingency plans the *goums* might have made; they would have no time to batter down armory doors; the sooner they were out, the better. Apart from that, Mazzari had very few shells: it would not take an acute commander long to realize that mortar fire injuring nobody and fire from three automatic rifles hardly constituted a threat requiring the attention of the whole garrison.

And there were those two MICV's, their motors still astonishingly idling, less than eighty yards away. He made a snap decision. "All right, you guys," he yelled. "Back here at the double: there's been a change of plan."

He was in his element. This was the way he liked to work, off the cuff, with the odds stacked against him, playing the cards as they were dealt. Nothing excited him more than this kind of challenge—improvising in the face of danger. "Sean, can you drive one of these things?" he called to Hammer, pointing at the MICV's.

"Sure I can," the stocky little Irish-American yelled. "Didn't I spend me holidays in Belfast one time?"

"Right! Too good an opportunity to miss . . . and if the local law don't like it, they can catch up with us and say so!"

"What about the truck that Alphand hot-wired? It's—"

"Forget it. Each of these heaps will take eight men and a crew of three." Dean panted out fresh instructions as the ten of them raced back to the armored vehicles. Each had a shallow turret equipped with a machine gun and a 73mm automatic-loading cannon—and the flat hull behind the turret was pierced by four hatchways beneath which the infantrymen sat. Dean swung up onto the track shield of the first and dropped down into the driving seat. The idling diesel opened up with a roar. He juggled the levers to bring the machine skidding around so that it faced the interior of the camp. Novotny and Alphand climbed into the turret, and two more mercs lowered themselves through the hatches. Hammer, Wassermann, and the others piled into the second carrier.

Dean waved his hand, and the two vehicles, each of them twenty-feet long and ten-feet wide, rocketed down the graveled driveway, wheeled right, and took the alley leading to the armory. Desultory shots were fired at them from some of the goums' huts as they passed, but no troops appeared to offer them genuine resistance.

The strategy now was uncomplex. Dean simply drove the twelve-ton carrier straight at the armory entrance. The wooden doors, set above a single low step, burst inward with a splintering crash, carrying some of the brickwork with them, as the machine smashed through. Men swarmed out of the two MICV's and rushed inside as Dean backed up out of the wreckage and yanked the

91

levers into neutral. "Take my place," he ordered Novotny, "and be prepared to go like hell!" Pistol in hand, he followed the mercs into the ravaged building.

Two storekeepers in white coveralls cowered behind a counter on the far side of the entrance. "Facedown on the floor . . . hands on your heads . . . and nobody will hurt you," Dean rapped. He swept his hand across a battery of switches as the men dropped obediently from sight. Lights blazed down on the sweating mercenaries. They pillaged racks and shelves, passing the lighter weapons straight out to the MICV's, stacking heavier ammunition boxes near the broken doors. Dean shouted, "You know what we got; you know what we need. You've been told what to do, and you got less than two minutes to do it—so move your asses, okay?"

The sounds of shifting equipment were broken only occasionally by a muttered comment.

"Hey, lookit that! These fit our fuckin' bazookas!"

"Jesus! A gen-u-ine Uzi, still in the maker's wrapping!"

"Not that one, you *schmuck!* The AK-47 takes 7.62-caliber . . ."

Outside, there were no more mortar bursts, and only sporadic shots came from the ridge above the orange grove. Soldiers were now firing at the armory, however, from all over the compound. Windows shattered, a light went out, slugs spanged off the armor plate sheathing the carriers. "All right, men, this is it!" Dean yelled. "Everybody out!"

The last weapon and a final ammunition box were passed out to the waiting carriers. Novotny and Hammer sat at the controls, gunning the motors, ready for a quick takeoff. The mercs hurled themselves aboard and dropped through the open hatches. "That way! Take 'em by surprise!" Dean waved toward the interior of the depot, calling back to Hammer, "And hold your fire. They may think . . ."

It was good advice. As the carriers surged forward and sped down the quarter-mile driveway leading to the sector under fire from Mazzari, they were met with a scene of utter confusion. Clearly, not all the officers in the camp had been incapacitated, and orders must have been transmitted to the perimeter troops, informing them that there was a second assault at the main entrance; it might even have been realized that the attack in the rear was only a diversion. On the other hand, there *was* still firing from the hillside above the orange grove: it could be that the action around the *gates* was a feint—with the men on the hillside deliberately reducing their rate of fire to fool the defenders, hoping that most of them would withdraw and rush back to the entrance. . . .

The indecision that these opposing views provoked worked in the intruders' favor. Some of the Moroccans piled into jeeps and careered toward the guardhouse and the headquarters block; some ran with guns at the ready; some milled around awaiting orders; others went on firing at the orange grove from behind their sandbagged emplacements. Almost all of them, seeing two of their own MICV's race down the main driveway, assumed that the machines had been sent to support the perimeter defense. The guns were not firing; the hatches were closed, so the crews were invisible. And those soldiers who had witnessed the sacking of the armory were too far behind to warn their companions. Some of them in fact fired after the fleeing carriers . . . and troops returning to the main entrance mistook them for attackers, scattering to fire back at them.

The machines had reached their top speed of between thirty-five and forty miles per hour. The *goums* along the perimeter raised a cheer as they approached. Dean was studying his original map under the turret light. "Straight ahead," he told Novotny. "Don't slack off. You'll find there's a track runs along the lip of the ravine and then climbs to the left of the grove."

The Moroccans realized that something was wrong only when the carriers, instead of reducing speed, bucketed straight for the chain fence marking the perimeter. They fell back with cries of alarm as the leading MICV smashed into the wire and flattened it, with Hammer's vehicle bursting through the gap immediately afterward. By the time they had recovered enough to aim and fire after them, the two stolen carriers were churning up the rough ground on the way to the orange trees.

Wassermann looked out through a slit in the armor at the rear of Hammer's machine. They were plowing their way upward to the road where Mazzari and his three men would be waiting. Behind, there was an indescribable chaos of shouts and whistles and alarm bells, punctuated by shots fired blindly into the night. "And this," Wassermann said over the threshing of the caterpillar tracks, "is what he means by keeping our noses clean?"

9

Nobody followed them. This did not surprise Dean at first: only fully tracked vehicles could have made the steep slope of scrub above the orange grove, and it would take some time to get those organized and under way. But he had noticed a number of half-tracks and Soviet-built BRDM-2 armored reconnaissance trucks along with the light tanks and carriers in the motor pool. Since the road traversing the scrub could only take them back to the northern outskirts of Halakaz or on through Wadi Elmira and Insalah to the highway leading to the interior, he was astonished that none of these appeared to have been detailed to race through the town and intercept them: the Russian trucks were capable of over sixty miles an hour—more than twice the speed of the stolen carriers—and the jeeps he had seen at the camp were faster still. But there was no roadblock where the trail joined the highway; no hooded lights appeared in the rearview mirrors, closing fast; no voice through a bullhorn ordered them to halt.

"I don't get it," Dean said to Mazzari, who had swung aboard with his men as soon as they reached the ridge. "It seemed like they'd been tipped off that we were coming and did their best to clout us; yet they practically sent us a printed invitation to grab these carriers, leaving them empty with the motors running—as if they knew we were on our way! It doesn't make sense."

"How do you figure the cop, Colonel?" Novotny asked over his shoulder. Dean was sitting behind with his head and shoulders in the turret.

"I'm damned if I know. I don't—"

"How do you read a *flic* who drives a five-year-old Renault 16 when he is in uniform, and a 1980 Mercedes sedan when he is in plain clothes?" Alphand interrupted from the seat next to Novotny.

"A five-year-old . . . ?"

"A green Renault. A little beat-up. He was waiting in her at the side of the garden where Novotny and his men are walking. Brass buttons and *kepi* and all."

"I only saw him in the Mercedes. You're sure it was the same guy?"

"Of course I am sure," Alphand said. "I see him with you at the café this morning. What do you think this means?"

"I should think it means, almost certainly, that he's on the take," Dean replied thoughtfully. "But from whom? And for what? The way it looks to me, he's being paid to lead us on, to encourage us to attack that dump, so that we walk into a fucking trap because we're like expected . . . and at the same time, in his private capacity, he's trying to warn us off." He shook his head. "I'd give a hell of a lot to know just what part he's playing in all this ruckus." Dean would very much like to have known also what role, if any, had been assigned to the mysterious Rada Hradec, but this wish he kept to himself.

The two carriers racketed on across the darkened landscape, their low-slung, shielded lamps casting long shadows dancing beyond the imperfections in the road surface. The moon would not rise for another two hours, and most of the villages they passed through were already in darkness. The few lights they saw were half-hidden by screens of cypress trees, on the big estates where olives and vines and fruit were farmed. There was no traffic at all on the road.

"I still don't understand," Dean said. "There are telephones here. Police posts are built every few miles: we passed at least two already. Even if they were primed to gang up on us, it seems like they want us to get away with our stolen loot!"

"Talking of which, old chap, it might be an idea to check just what we do have, don't you think?" Mazzari said. "It's only a couple of miles to the quarry now: do you plan to lie up there for the night and count our ill-gotten gains?"

"Not on your life," Dean said decisively. "There are no choppers based on Halakaz, but there's a heliport outside Agdz-el-Skira and a military airfield at Barbuz—they could call one up and spot these buggies in a half-hour, once they knew what they were looking for."

"If they are looking."

"Sure. But we can't afford to take chances. We got a hell of a way to go, and we've been delayed enough already. By daybreak, I want us to be on the fringe of the Anti-Atlas, where there are no more metaled roads and even the desert trails are hidden in gulches."

"You're the boss," Mazzari said.

One of the carriers waited outside the entrance to the old quarry while the other rumbled inside to load the wounded Van der Lee and the remainder of their salvaged supplies. Then they were on their way again, climbing higher and higher as the villages became more scattered and the vegetation sparser.

Soon after nine o'clock, the darkness ahead of them thinned, became translucent and silvered over. A sudden flowering of golden light limned in the jagged crest of a range of hills to the east. And then a three-quarter moon, amber and splendid and magnified by the thickened air, hoisted itself into the sky. Fifteen minutes later, far away to the north and immeasurably high, the snowcapped peaks of the Atlas appeared gleaming in its ghostly radiance.

There was no snow in the region known as the Anti-Atlas, which separated the coastal plain from the desert. But the mountains were barren and steep, the precipitous zigzag trail barely discernible in the milky light.

Their speed was reduced to a crawl. It was not, nevertheless, until midnight that Dean called a halt. They
were on the edge of an upland plateau, itself a near-lunar
landscape, with huge boulders studding a forest of thorn
trees that rattled in the wind. Dean snapped shut his
pocket compass and folded his map. "In this light, with
no landmarks visible, we could be forty degrees out by
morning," he said. "We'll rest up here and check our
position at dawn."

They parked the two MICV's between the graveled
slopes of a wadi. Then, with the aid of flashlights that
Hammer and Dean had bought at the supermart, they
checked out the spoils gained in the raid.

Considering the pressure under which they had
worked and the lack of time at their disposal, they
hadn't done too badly. The Moroccan Army—or at least
its southern command—had clearly placed orders for its
weapons both with Warsaw Pact countries and with the
West. The two rifles taken from the sentries were the
Kalashnikovs that Dean had craved—not the newest
AKM's, but AK-47's made under license in Czechoslovakia. A rack in the armory had yielded a batch of
six more. Like the PKT machine guns in the carriers,
they fired standard 7.62mm rounds as used also by
NATO, and apart from the salvaged supplies, Dean's
men now had several dozen 250-round belts fitted with
this caliber ammunition and a further two boxes carrying 2,500 rounds each. The Kalashnikovs taken from the
armory were fitted with British Trilux telescopic sights.

There had been no 5.56mm short-cartridge slugs
suitable for the three Armalite rifles in the armory: they
would have to make do with the single box salvaged
from the wreck. The raiders had, on the other hand,
found a dozen five-pound rocket grenades which could
be fired from their bazooka-style RPG-7 antitank
weapon, a small quantity of mortar shells, and a padded
case containing two NSP-2 infrared night sights. These
too could be adapted to the RPG-7.

Without doubt, though, the find that pleased Dean the most was the consignment of six Uzi submachine guns—still, as one of the mercs had pointed out, in the maker's greased wrappings. The stubby, lightweight weapons, with their pistol grips, short barrels, and "overhung" bolts, were not wooden-stock originals made in Israel but examples of the model made under license in Belgium by FN at Herstal, which had a retractable wire stock. Several unopened boxes of 9mm ammunition had been passed out with the guns.

Dean decided to apportion the weapons right away. "And when you've been given your gun, or whatever," he told the men, "it's your own personal responsibility to keep it safe, clean, and in good order. In the French *maquis* in World War II, any man who abandoned or lost his gun was shot. It's just possible that I might not go that far—but I'll beat the shit out of any son of a bitch who does the same!"

One of the Uzis was given to Van der Lee, who would normally be left in charge of supplies, because it was the easiest for him to manage. The others went to Schneider, Novotny, Hammer, Mazzari, and Dean himself, who would together form the spearhead of any close-quarters attack. Wassermann, who was a crack shot, was detailed to be the unit sniper, equipped with an Armalite and an infrared sight. Schneider and Novotny took the remaining two Armalites, while Alphand, Furneux, and Molony between them handled the mortar and the RPG-7. Since Schneider and Novoty had also been given submachine guns, their rifles were likely to be less used, and the limited amount of Armalite ammunition could therefore be channeled mainly to Wassermann in his specialized role.

The other five members of the team were issued with Kalashnikovs. This left three of the Russian guns available either for Dean and his two henchmen or for the antitank crew when they were not working the larger weapons. There were twelve 73mm rounds in the automatic loaders of each carrier.

At dawn Dean called the men around him for a briefing. "I didn't tell you guys too much about the target so far," he began. "There didn't seem any point until there was at least a fair chance we could make it. But I guess it's time now to wise you up some."

He drew a circle in the dust with the point of a stick. "Gabotomi's a hilltop fortress, with pretty tough, mountainous country all around. We have to attack straight up the valley from the west . . . and that'll be tough too, because the town commands the approach." The stick traced a line that touched the circumference of the circle.

"Couldn't we make a detour and take the place out from the rear, or from one of the sides?" one of the mercs asked.

Dean shook his head. "Country's pretty well impassable on both sides. Those Berbers chose their site well. And to get around to the rear, we'd have to detour into Algerian territory."

"So what?" the Irishman, Molony, demanded.

"So that wouldn't be smart. All three of the countries surrounding this region would like to see the Nya Nyerere eliminated; none of them want to cede territory that may be rich in minerals to the tribe. But Algeria is believed to support the Polisario, down in what used to be Spanish Morocco. And the Polisario are allies of the guys we have to smash. Okay?"

"You mean the Algerians would try to stop us?" Novotny asked.

"Not necessarily. But they might kick up a stink. I mean like internationally. And we're being paid to avoid it. We've been told the Moroccans might look the other way; not the Algerians."

"What the hell! Smash the niggers and get the hell out—isn't that the aim of the fuckin' operation?" Furneux said.

100

A large black hand reached out and grabbed the Canadian by the collar, lifting him eighteen inches off the ground. "I'd watch that mouth if I were you, old son," Mazzari said gently.

"Shit! No offense to you, Ed! I only meant . . ." Furneux squirmed in the big man's grasp.

"We know what you meant," Mazzari said, releasing his grasp. "Many of your best friends, and so on and so forth. Just watch it, that's all."

"Yeah, just watch it," Dean echoed. "Now, talking of the Polisario, we have a problem." His stick drew a series of sinuous curves some way from the circle representing Gabotomi. "Around fifteen miles south of the town, the mountains give way to a patch of rain forest. It's what they call a micro-climate. Fifty square miles of vegetation fed by a river that rises in the last range before the Sahara and runs toward the sea. And I don't mean a dried-up wadi like this, but a regular river with water flowing the whole year."

The stick gouged a short, straight line crossing one of the curves. "The river used to be the border between French and Spanish Morocco. The far side of it's Polisario territory. Now, here . . ." He pointed at the straight line. "Here, the river has cut a gorge into the forest floor. The gorge is steep-sided, almost a thousand feet deep, and it's crossed by a viaduct, a narrow single-span arch that's the only way help could come to the garrison at Gabotomi from the Polisario or from Angola farther south."

"You really think these tribesmen could call up the comrades?" someone asked. "And the comrades would come?"

"Listen," Dean said somberly. "This is no piece of cake. The Nya Nyerere have pretty sophisticated defenses. This guy Anya-Kutu isn't one of the original fuzzy-wuzzies armed with a spear and a flintlock musket. He has Moscow's ear, or he certainly did have. He's probably in with Castro's pals in Angola. He'll have radio con-

101

tacts. And while I don't rate the chances of an airlift from Angola high, it's in the cards that the Polisario would rally around."

"So we blow the fuckin' bridge," said the merc who had spoken before.

"Sure we blow the bridge. If we had the full complement I planned," Dean said, "I aimed to detail a small squad to do that while the rest of us attacked the town simultaneously. But since there's so few of us left now, we have to play it another way."

"Meaning?"

"Meaning we have to make certain the tribe gets no reinforcements before we can risk an attack. Meaning we blow the bridge first." Now the point of Dean's stick was making arabesques in the dust. "And to do that, we have to make a detour into the forest before we get near the town . . . along this valley here . . . over a pass here . . . and then on to the ravine around here." He looked around the circle of hard-bitten, experienced men. "So far as the territory is surveyed at all, I'm giving you photocopies of what maps we have." He nodded to Hammer, who handed around folded eight-by-ten duplicated sheets from a waterproofed plastic wallet.

There was a temporary silence as the men studied the maps. A puff of hot wind stirred the dust at their feet and half-obliterated Dean's diagram. Above the rim of the wadi, the branches of the thorn bushes rattled again.

"Shit, that's a hell of a detour!" Molony said finally. "If we did it the other way around, sure, it'd be straight ahead for the town and then turn right for the bridge after we'd taken it out. Why don't we do that, for God's sake, instead of fuckin' around over half of Africa?"

"I thought I'd explained why. If we'd taken out the town, there'd be no need to blow the bridge."

"Well, I think—"

"I'm not interested in what you think, Molony," Dean said tightly. "Only in the way you obey orders. Now, any other questions?"

102

"Yeah. How long's it gonna take us?" another man asked.

Dean glanced at his map. "We're between seventy and eighty miles from the coast here. There's another hundred and twenty, hundred and thirty to go, as the crow flies. And it's tough going, too. We'll be lucky to make the rain forest by dusk. Tomorrow we'll stake out the bridge *and* the town. Then maybe we can blow the bridge after dark and move into position to attack the town the following dawn."

To avoid wasting their limited butane supply, they made a small smokeless fire from the dry branches of the thorn bushes and brewed coffee which they drank with a handful of raisins and a couple of dried apricots. By seven o'clock, with the sun already scorching down from a cloudless sky, the two MICV's had scrabbled up the stony side of the wadi and headed east.

It was two hours later that Novotny saw the helicopter. They were traversing a great slant of shale that ran down to a dried-up riverbed between two limestone bluffs. At first the machine was just a speck in the sky, and when the Pole drew his attention to it, Dean figured it for a buzzard. Then they lost sight of it against the dark wall of the cliff. When it sailed into view once more, sunlight glinted on the perspex bubble over the cabin and they could make out the movement of its rotors. Dean frowned. It was fifty minutes since they had passed any sign of human habitation—and that had been simply a group of Berber tents high up on a hill beside the ruins of a mud-walled fort that had probably served once as a Foreign Legion outpost. It was inconceivable that the helicopter could be there for any civil or military reason: it wasn't on the direct route between any two towns; there was no army camp within fifty miles; and this sterile wilderness was hardly a tourist paradise. It must have been sent to spy on them, to check out their position. He glanced quickly around from the open

103

turret. As far as he could see along the rock-strewn, twisting ravine, there wasn't an inch of cover; the desiccated scrub on either side of the trail was no more than waist-high.

Dean shrugged. There was nothing they could do. He leaned down and spoke to Novotny. "Keep going. Let's hope it's no gunship but just a recce." Privately, he didn't believe the machine would attack them in any way. If the Moroccans had wanted to do that, there had been plenty of opportunities, better ones, the previous night. Nevertheless, just to be sure, he motioned Mazzari to take up station by the machine gun and slapped a full magazine into his own Uzi.

The helicopter sank below the rim of the gorge again. They could see its shadow racing over the rocky undulations of the mountainside. Then the clatter of its rotors was directly overhead, drowning the roar of the carrier's six-cylinder diesel.

Dean looked up, gripping his gun. It was a small machine, a two- or three-seater, he thought. But the sunlight reflected from the perspex nose was too blinding for him to make out any details.

The helicopter flew past the two MICV's, soared above the bluff on an updraft of warm air, turned, and then settled down only fifty feet above the trail for a second pass. This time the nose was partly in shadow and Dean could see that the machine was painted a dull brown, that it carried no identification marks, and that there appeared to be only two people beneath the transparent blister. The ports were closed and he could see no trace of any offensive weapons.

He turned around and gestured to Hammer, in the turret of the second carrier, spreading his arms in the universal "Search me!" signal. Hammer shrugged and pointed ahead.

The winged shadow sped along the trail, leapfrogged down a boulder-strewn slope, and then, together with the ship casting it, was lost to sight among the dark, sunless cliffs on the shadowed side of the ravine. When it returned for the third time, it hovered high above the speeding vehicles until they reached a double hairpin taking the trail to a lower level, and then it flew away to the west. "Leery!" Dean commented sardonically. "I guess they were shooting pictures and were too scared to come lower in case *we* fired at *them!*"

Novotny shifted gears to take the second hairpin. The MICV skidded around the turn in a shower of dust and small stones. "How do you figure it, Colonel?" he asked.

"Pinpointing our position, obviously," Dean said. "Either as a recce, just to keep tabs on us. Or as a range-finding operation, with the aim of calling up combat ships to strafe us."

"Yeah, but who? I thought them Moroccans were lettin' us through."

"That's what I was told. If that chopper was Moroccan Army, I'd figure it was just a checking-out mission—unless they're so hopping mad that we stole these carriers, it made them forget their promises! In that case, they could have stopped us before . . . and they'd hardly want to blow their own machinery to hell!"

"That's logical," Mazzari said. "And if it wasn't the Moroccans?"

"Christ knows! It's just possible that it might have been a Mauritanian or an Algerian ship on long-range patrol—illegally over Moroccan air space because they'd gotten wind of our mission. That would account for the lack of markings. I was told that Nya Nyerere had no air support, but I guess that's just possible too, if somebody had leaked something somewhere along the line and they knew we were coming." Dean shook his head. He was in fact more worried about the possibility of a leak than he cared to admit. Contradictory evidence—the veiled encouragement to raid the depot on one hand, the readiness of the *goums* for an attack on the other—made the problem more puzzling still. But the fact that the helicopter carried no identification he found the most disturbing of all. "In any case, we'll find out pretty soon," he said to Mazzari. "The first reasonable cover we find, we'll lay up and see what happens. If they're aiming to call up pursuit ships, they should be overhead in less than half an hour."

Ten minutes later, around a curve in the ravine, they found the kind of cover they needed. The trail was down to the level of the river here, and the gorge narrowed to a point where, over thousands of centuries, the torrent had gouged out a near-vertical *clue*—a cleft between the tortured strata where the towering cliff faces were little farther apart than the width of the stream itself. And since the *clue* was on a bend in the river, in the millennia when the waters were higher, the swirling current had worn away the rock to make a huge overhang beneath which the trail ran.

Dean told Novotny to stop, and waved Hammer's vehicle down behind them. In the shadow of this enormous outcrop, they would be completely invisible from the air.

He ordered the men out from the roasting metal interiors of the MICV's. The air beneath the overhang was dank and chill: it would be a refreshing change from the sweaty oven heat of the carriers. "We'll wait here an hour," he told them. "If no pursuit planes have showed by then, I guess we can reckon the chopper was here just for a look-see. In the meantime, I want every weapon taken out, checked, loaded, and readied for firing, okay?"

Watching the men as they offloaded automatic rifles, grenades, submachine guns, magazines, and boxes of ammunition, sorting the rounds into calibers suitable for the various weapons they had, Dean wondered, not for the first time, how much he could rely on the team under his command. Hammer and Mazzari were his regular aides; Schneider, Wassermann, and Novotny he had worked with before. But of the others he knew very little. Recruiting a sizable body of mercenaries isn't a

106

chore that can be accomplished through discreet use of classified ads in newspapers. Although the international merc community is relatively small and tightly knit, there are nevertheless far too many soldiers-for-hire for any one commander to be able to pick his entire complement personally. Even when a man is known, there are many factors to consider before he can be officially added to the strength of a unit in formation. Of these the primary one is of course availability: mercenary operations tend to be of short duration, so the men involved move often from one part of the world to another. This apart, a man's fighting history, reliability, honesty, loyalty, and moral fiber have to be judged. His willpower and determination are important, and so is his expertise with firearms. Lastly his prejudices and his temperament must be considered. Does he show any proclivity for drinking? For whoring? For looting? Sometimes it is important; sometimes it isn't. Certain missions require lone wolves with plenty of initiative, used to working on their own; others demand gregarious men, content to obey orders. For these reasons almost all mercenary recruitment is a matter of word-of-mouth recommendation. Somebody in on the operation has to decide on the right men for the job.

Most of Dean's original effective had been supplied through contacts of Hammer's in Paris and Brussels. He had recruited Van der Lee himself in Amsterdam, and Dennis, an older man who had fought in Korea, he had known Stateside. Of those that remained, the Frenchman, Hervé Alphand, was a friend of Hammer's. But of the others he knew very little.

He had learned on the beach that the Canadian, Furneux, was a defeatist. It seemed also that he was something of a racist, as was Molony, the barrack-room lawyer who always figured he knew better than anyone else. That left four men who were completely unknown quantities—Goldsmith and Kent, two Vietnam veterans recruited by Hammer; a Swiss named Weisenberger;

and Daler, who said he was Norwegian but whom Dean suspected of being a British ex-commando.

He watched them servicing the weapons under the supervision of Hammer and Mazzari. At least they seemed to know their job: they worked quickly and efficiently, talking only occasionally in low voices barely audible over the rushing of the stream, whose yellow-brown waters creamed over the jumble of rocks at the foot of the *clue*. Dean glanced at his Rolex. He looked up beyond the moist, dripping curve of rock shielding them from view. The bright blue strip of sky separating the two sheer faces of the cleft was empty. No snarl of aircraft engines had echoed from the cliffs since they arrived. He beckoned Hammer over and said, "I guess that's it, Sean. There won't be any strafe now. Christ knows who sent it, but the chopper must have been nothing more than a lookout of some kind."

"You want we should be on our way?" Hammer asked.

"Sure. But this time I'll ride in the second carrier with you. Alphand can drive the first, with Novotny in the turret; Kurt Schneider can take over the control of ours." Dean took the plastic map wallet from his pocket and added, "There's some stuff I'd like to go over with you and Edmond."

A few miles beyond the *clue*, the gorge broadened into a shallow valley which gave way to a lifeless, dust-colored plain. On the far side of the plain—perhaps twenty miles away—a range of flat-topped hills rose above the heat haze.

The sun-baked earth powdered and rose in choking clouds, penetrating the slits in the armor, clogging eyes and mouths and nostrils, as the caterpillar tracks churned them onward toward the hills. The sky turned the color of molten lead. The river curved away to the south and vanished beneath a wasteland of stones and gravel. The temperature rose inexorably under the battering of the sun.

Horizontal strata colored rose and ocher and brown
108

topped the range, whose crests were as flat as if they had been ruled across the sky. But the decomposition of these sedimentary rocks by sun and wind erosion had clearly resulted in a slightly richer subsoil than that covering the barren region they had crossed. The trail wound up to the plateau surmounting the range, and now in the valleys below they could see an occasional palmery with patches of cultivation and sometimes a mud-walled Arab village beside the stream. Here and there, nomad tents dotted a hillside, surrounded by camels and mules and flocks of goats. The tribesmen stood and stared at the two machines as they rattled past, but it was impossible to tell from their faces if they were hostile, welcoming, or indifferent.

In the early afternoon the track led down again, into a depression where erosion had left the harder rock in strange-shaped columns and towers. "My God," Dennis said to Alphand in front of the leading MICV, "it's like the back lot at Universal or the buttes of Montana!"

"*Pardon?*"

"Before your time, boy. I mean like enter the redskins at any minute. Send Tonto for the paleface braves. Pronto, Tonto!"

"Oh," Alphand said blankly. "Yes?"

They passed the wheelless skeleton of a military truck, with the American Army star still painted on its hood. Beyond, around a shoulder of the hillside, was another village, abandoned and deserted this time. The outer walls of the casbah had crumbled away and were scattered down the slope; red sand silted up the broken arcades of the *souks*. Across the road, on the far side of a wadi, the ruins of an old fort, with a square tower at each corner, surmounted one of the buttes.

"So why the hell do they call it a casbah?" Wassermann turned around in the front of the second carrier and spoke to Mazzari, who was installed in the turret. "I thought a casbah it should be the Arab quarter of a city?"

109

The big man leaned forward. "Quite right, old boy," he called down. "In places like Algiers and Casablanca, the Casbah *is* the name for the whole Arab quarter. *The* Casbah, with a big C. But *a* casbah—small C—is just the Arabic word for a stronghold, the castle of a *caid* or chieftain."

"And a *souk?*"

"An Arab market. In villages like this, the *souks* are often roofed in against the sun, with different alleys for different trades. You can see . . ." Mazzari leaned farther forward and gestured at the broken arcades. The movement saved his life. The slug that had been aimed at his head struck the rear of the turret and screamed off into the overheated air.

Alphand, in the leading vehicle, was not so lucky. As Mazzari, bewildered, was registering the small puff of smoke above the nearest watchtower of the ruined fort, a second bullet passed through the open hatch of the Frenchman's carrier and struck him in the chest. He slumped forward across the controls, knocking one of the levers forward.

The offside track spun wildly, spraying sand and gravel across the trail. The carrier slewed to the right, balanced for a moment on the edge of the wadi, and then tilted over and dropped from view. Seconds later, a cloud of dust ballooned up over the rim of the depression and hung against the sky.

10

The second MICV shuddered to a halt. Mazzari slid down into the interior and pulled the hatchway closed after him. Schneider and Wassermann slammed the forward hatches shut. The hull of the vehicle reverberated like a gong as bullets ricocheted off the armor plate. Dean had been thrown forward as Schneider braked. "What the hell's going on?" he demanded.

"Snipers, old man," Mazzari panted. "Up in the old fort on the right. Bloody nearly got me, too. I'm afraid Alphand may have bought it. His carrier's gone into the wadi."

"Jesus!" Dean and Hammer closed the two hatchways behind the MICV's turret. They were alone in the rear compartment with Van der Lee. Apart from Mazzari, Wassermann, and Schneider, all the other mercs had been in Alphand's machine. Dean crawled forward, pushed Schneider aside, and peered out through the driver's windshield slit. Small-arms fire was being directed at them now from both sides of the trail. Flame stabbed the shadows in the crumbling embrasures of the old fort, and there were shots coming from behind every wall and buttress of the ruined village on the opposite slope.

"A fucking ambush! And we walked right into it with our eyes open," Dean said bitterly.

"What say I take her forward at full revs?" Schneider suggested. "And then we try to enfilade them from behind?"

Dean shook his head. "I have to find out what happened to the others first," he said. "We can't afford to

111

junk nine guys in a wrecked MICV when there's only five of us fit to fight." He turned to Mazzari. "I'm going on down in that wadi and find out the score. Feed a belt in the machine gun and give me covering fire. Make the bastards keep their heads down while I cross the trail."

"You don't think it would be more . . . persuasive . . . to give them a taste of the old bazooka?" Mazzari nodded at the three-and-a-half-foot rocket launcher stacked with the other weapons in the center of the rear compartment.

"Uh-uh. We can't spare the grenades. Fire a couple of short bursts while I get out. Then, when I give the word, a longer one to cover me across the road, okay?"

"Or the turret gun?"

"Later. And for Christ's sake don't use too many rounds!" Dean opened the armored flap at the rear of the carrier, waited for Mazzari to fire a short burst from the PKT machine gun in the turret, and then, as the Congolese sergeant aimed a second burst at the fort, scrambled out onto the trail with one of the Uzi SMG's.

Crouched behind the square tail of the carrier, he was safe for the moment. The sun beat fiercely down on his back. He was aware of the smell of his own sweat, of the odor of hot oil and diesel fumes and dust from the road. He crawled to the offside of the vehicle and peered over the track shield. The ambushers, whoever they were, had chosen their site well. Stalled in the center of the trail, the mercs were dominated from above on both sides. If they hadn't been in an armored vehicle, they would have been dead ducks. The attackers, moreover, had the advantage of perfect cover, with communication between the firing points. Beneath the haze of cordite smoke, which lay like a canopy in the windless air over the ruins, he could see robed figures flitting from wall to wall. The wadi was ten yards away on his right. "*Right!*" Dean shouted.

The harsh stammer of Mazzari's machine gun split the silence. Dean hurled himself across the intervening space, his boots skidding on the stony rubble of the trail as a fresh outburst of firing from the fort sent bullets scuffing the dirt around his feet. He reached the lip of the wadi and slid frantically down the steep twenty-foot slope in a miniature landslide of pebbles and dust and fragments of decomposed rock.

Alphand's MICV had bounced once and then landed on its back. The armor plate was buckled and the turret smashed. The nearside rear sprocket had sheared off and the track was broken. Even if they could have towed it somehow out of the wadi, the carrier was evidently a write-off. There were three men—white-faced and shaken, their hair powdered with the dust that was only now settling—in the lee of the wrecked machine.

Novotny, Daler, and Goldsmith. "What about the others?" Dean asked as he came breathlessly to a halt beside them.

"The Frenchie's had it," Novotny replied. "Dennis is out cold, but I think he'll pull through. I was lucky: I saw it coming and was able to duck out of the turret in time."

"The fellows in the back should be okay," Daler said in his curious half-cockney, half-European accent. "Weisenberger had the sense to slam down the hatches before we went over. They're shaken up, but I don't think any bones are broken."

They leaned in through one of the distorted hatches and helped out Furneux, Molony, Kent, and the Swiss. All of them had suffered cuts and bruises, but as Daler had surmised, were otherwise undamaged. In the stifling interior of the carrier, the sweet and sickly stench of blood and feces overlaid the engine smell of diesel. There was nothing they could do for Hervé Alphand: the dum-dum bullet had torn open his chest, and from the way he was slumped below the inverted controls, it looked as though his neck had been broken as well. Dennis was crumpled against the aluminum-magnesium plating of the hull. His cheek was lacerated and there

113

was a large swelling on one temple, but his breathing was regular and his pulse not too shallow. "The skull's not cracked," Dean said. "We'll come back for him later. Right now it's more important to gun these bastards down."

Outside the doomed MICV, the hard, dry heat of the sun was almost refreshing. "Bring the AK-47's and a hundred-round bandolier, each of you," Dean ordered. "We're going to have to flush these characters out."

His pulses were racing. Even the sick regret he felt at the loss of the Frenchman was swamped now in the tingling excitement of the chase, the thrill of pitting his wits against an adversary when the odds were against him, in that heart-stopping moment when the distinction between the hunter and the hunted hung in the balance. "First we have to drive them out of that fort," he told the seven men sheltering behind the wreck. "We'll go that way." He nodded toward the butte, where the wadi curved away from the road and there would be a dead area immediately below the tower. "But we have to have one hell of a spread of covering fire, or we'll never make it."

Furneux looked uneasy. "Wouldn't it be better—?" he began.

"All right, Furneux, you can cool it," Dean said curtly. "I guess it'd be safer to leave you as part of the covering fire. You stay here and shoot as fast as you fucking can at the embrasures in that tower." He turned toward the bank of the wadi and cupped his hands around his mouth. "Hammer! . . . Can you hear me?" he shouted.

"Loud and clear!" the Irishman's voice replied from the invisible carrier.

"We're going up the wadi. Cover us. Tell Mazzari to use the cannon: two rounds at the tower; two in the village. No more. Then he can fire the machine gun. The rest of you take the Armalites. Tell Abe to show us what he can do!"

"Willco," Hammer yelled back. "Starting when?"

114

"Now!"

Dean motioned his men to get ready. They crouched behind the overturned carrier, dry-mouthed, wiping the sweat from their hands on the seams of their pants. Firing had broken out again during Dean's exchange with Hammer; they could hear the thwack of slugs into the bank, and an occasional ricochet. "How the hell can we make that fort, even if there is a dead area beneath the wall?" Molony said hoarsely. "The rock of that butte would crumble to hell, even if—"

"Don't be a jerk!" Dean snapped. "I'm not crazy enough to try to scale a fifty-foot bluff under fire! We're using the dead area of the wadi as a trench—to fire on the village across the road!"

Before Molony could reply, there was a sharp, flat explosion from the other MICV's turret gun. The 73mm shell burst against the rock just below the tower, temporarily obscuring the fort in black smoke and sending a cascade of debris into the wadi. At the same time, they heard the coughing crack of the Armalites over the deeper boom of the ambushers' guns. Mazzari must have corrected the elevation of the cannon. A vivid orange flash, and a mushroom of smoke erupted halfway up the watchtower facade. The mud walls shivered, cracked, and then slowly toppled outward. Fragments of the wall were still showering down onto the trail when the echoes of the explosion had died away. "Okay!" Dean shouted. "Let's go!" With his Uzi SMG at the ready, he ran out from behind the carrier and led the way up the wadi toward the butte.

Boots scrabbling on the rounded stones of the dried-up riverbed, they raced after him. Over the pounding of his feet and the labored gasps of his breath, each man was aware of the sounds of battle, the death that could smash into him invisibly out of every lungful of the hot and dangerous air. From behind, they heard the whiplash detonations of Furneux's Kalashnikov. Two more cannon shells burst out of sight on the far side of the trail, followed by the menacing rattle of the machine gun.

Mazzari's second shot had torn away the outer wall of the watchtower, and there had been bodies among the rubble plummeting to the ground. But there were still figures moving amid the dust veiling the exposed galleries. Bullets whined among the mercs dashing up the wadi, stinging their arms and faces with chips of rock. One of the men fell, rose to his knees in an attempt to claw his way up the stony bank, and then rolled to the bottom and lay still.

From the turret of the second carrier, Wassermann fired his Armalite coolly at selected targets. A robed shape jerked upright on the parapet linking the two nearest towers of the fort, and then folded forward to fall out and down like a great white bird.

Dean reached the dead ground at the foot of the butte and crawled up to the lip of the wadi. Raising himself above the level of the track, he waved an arm to signal the carrier to advance. As the dust-covered caterpillars jerked into movement, a man appeared above one of the ruined walls high up on the far side of the roadway, his long-barreled rifle aimed straight at Dean. Before he could fire, Wassermann's Armalite coughed once from the turret and the marksman spun around and slumped to the ground.

With a whine of gears the carrier crept forward, spitting fire from the slits in the armored hatches. Mazzari was loosing off short bursts at the fort above.

Dean motioned his men to join him at the top of the slope. "We'll blast off a magazine across the trail," he called. "No special target: psychological effect." He closed his hand around the grip-safety projecting from the rear of the Uzi's pistol butt, squeezing it inward so that rounds could be fed into the breech. His forefinger curled around the trigger. He looked along the line of mercs spread out on either side of him and nodded.

Flame belched from the muzzle of the stubby weapon
116

as it kicked and bucked in his hands. At the same time the six Kalashnikovs sent a stream of lead hosing in among the tumbledown walls and arcades of the casbah. Together with the fire from the carrier, the noise of a submachine gun and six automatic rifles, all shooting at a rate of six-hundred rounds per minute, made an alarming and deafening racket.

Cracks and pockmarks and ragged scars appeared along the mud walls. A man screamed. A pall of dust hung over the hillside. Then, as abruptly as it had started, the appalling clamor ceased.

In the silence that followed, with their ears still ringing from the effect of the shots, the men became aware of the smallest sound. Somebody coughed. A boot scraped on rock. Across the road, a fragment of stone fell, sending a miniature avalanche of pebbles down the slope.

"Marc!" Hammer's excited voice from inside the carrier, which had stopped on the edge of the dead ground. *"They're quitting the fort! I can see them runnin' down the far side of the bluff! . . . They got horses there; they're pullin' out!"*

Dean heaved a sigh of relief. Whether it was a true retreat or not, this was a tactical error on the part of the ambushers. While there were guns still firing in the old fort, he and his men were pinned down in the wadi: to cross the road would be to invite a shot in the back. Now they could advance on to the trail and clean up the casbah, shielding themselves behind the hull of the MICV. The shooting from the hillside was only sporadic now in any case; from the sound of the reports and the intensity of the fire, he judged that at least some of the Arabs were using slow-loading .44 Winchester repeaters, or even nineteenth-century single-shot Mauser rifles.

Suddenly he was aware again of the sun's heat. The bank of the wadi was bright with ejected shells. He slammed a fresh magazine into the Uzi and beckoned

117

his men to follow him. *"We're coming on up!"* he called to Hammer.

A fresh fusillade from the casbah greeted their appearance on the trail, though it lacked the concentration of the original attack. Daler spun around and sat down in the dust, cursing, his right hand clasped over his left arm. The rest of them leaned on the track guard of the carrier and poured a steady stream of fire into the arches and alleys of the ruined village. It was Dean who saw the confused movements among the shadows that told him the enemy were in retreat. "Come on, we're going in to finish it!" he yelled.

Firing the Uzi from the hip, he stepped out from behind the carrier and ran for the nearest stretch of mud wall. The five mercs followed him, treading warily and letting off an occasional shot to left and right as he advanced up the hillside. From the open hatches of the MICV, Mazzari and Hammer covered them, ready to shoot at the first sign of hostile movement. Schneider and Wassermann jumped to the ground and joined Dean's advance, each of them armed with a Uzi.

In fact there was very little opposition left. Furneux flushed an Arab out from an alcove in back of an outer wall of the casbah, but he was too eager to fire and the man got away, leaping frenziedly from wall to wall as the Kalashnikov drilled rock chips from the ground behind his feet. Schneider downed another with a single staccato burst from his Uzi. After that there was a lull, broken only by the sound of galloping hooves from around a shoulder of the hill. For the moment at any rate, the battle was over.

Some minutes later Dean was exploring the farther recesses of the old village, holding his gun loosely by the sling, when he heard a stealthy footfall behind him. He swung around . . . and froze. A tall Arab in blue-and-yellow robes was standing at the entrance to one of the arcades. The Walther automatic in his hand was trained on Dean's chest.

118

Dean remained rooted to the spot. The forty-round magazine of his Uzi was spent, and in any case he could never have gotten the gun up into a shooting position in time. It was equally useless to turn and run: the man was less than fifteen feet away; he couldn't miss. Dean was back in a boyhood nightmare, legs caught in a swamp as the tiger leaped. His eyes took in the Arab's fierce, proud face, the hawklike nose beneath the burnoose, the drooping mustache, and the brown finger around the pistol's trigger.

The flesh of the finger paled as the muscles tightened.

The trigger was pulled.

The gun's hammer clicked on an empty chamber.

For a timeless instant the two men stared at each other, then, with a furious exclamation, the Arab stuffed the pistol into his waistband and turned to run. Dean let him go. He had no way of knowing what lay at the far end of the dark, twisting alley. Seconds later, he heard for the last time that day the muted thunder of a horse in flight.

The cold sweat was still trickling between his shoulder blades as he walked out into the sunlight and rejoined his men around the carrier. Hammer and Mazzari were dressing Daler's arm with the help of the emergency first-aid kit: the slug had grazed the bicep, fortunately without damaging bone or muscle. Dennis had been removed from the wrecked MICV and laid down in the shade. Apart from the blow on the head which had knocked him out, he appeared to have suffered no injury. But the man who had fallen as they advanced up the wadi was dead. It was Kent, one of the two Vietnam veterans. A heavy-caliber slug had torn its way through his belly and smashed his spine on its way out.

"Oh, shit!" Hammer said wretchedly. "It would have to be bloody Kent, wouldn't it? What a place to croak for a guy who loved the sea! He and his old lady had just bought a dandy little house on Cape Cod. You

119

know?" He sighed. "He was the only one of us who had kids—a boy and a girl, aged six and eight."

"That's life, sure," Molony said, but nobody laughed.

"They'll be looked after," Dean said, laying his hand on Hammer's shoulder. "I'll make myself personally responsible."

The Arabs had evidently taken their wounded away with them, but there were seven dead among the ruins of the village and the fort. Together with Alphand and Kent, the mercs buried them as best they could beneath the stones of the wadi. They transferred weapons and supplies from Alphand's machine, plus the two ten-gallon jerricans of fuel that were stored in back. The carriers had a range of 310 miles on a full tank, which was more than enough to get them to their target. But with this extra ration, plus the diesel in their own jerricans, those in the remaining one would now have a good chance of getting back to the coast as well. The only problem was transport of the men themselves.

The MICV's were designed to take a commander, a driver, and a gunner, with eight men beneath the hatches in back. There were now thirteen of them, plus a sizable amount of supplies, to ride in the same vehicle. To complicate matters further, the wounded Dutchman had to sit with his splinted leg straight out in front of him, which reduced space still more. "We'll do it this way," Dean decided. "Mazzari can drive, and I'll sit beside him. You, Sean, and Kurt Schneider, you're the smallest—you can squeeze up together in the turret. That leaves nine . . . and there's room for no more than five in among all that gear. So we'll ride with the hatches down and four guys lying along the hull behind the turret, okay?"

"Jesus, we'll be *roastin'* in there with all them hatches shut," Furneux complained. "How much longer we got to go, for fuck's sake?"

"If we get no more ambushes, we should reach the rain forest by nightfall," Dean said. "Until then, we'll stop every hour, and the guys inside can spell the men on the roof. No more questions. We're on our way."

The overloaded MICV moved slowly off along the dusty trail, with Furneux, Wassermann, Goldsmith, and Novotny stretched out along the hot armor plate, their weapons by their sides. Molony and Weisenberger took the first turn inside, with the three men who had been hurt.

"Do you expect another ambush?" Mazzari asked as they jolted up a rough track leading farther into the hills. "And who the devil staged that one, anyway? Surely it's too far from home for the tribe we're after— even if they knew we were coming."

Dean didn't reply at once. Something about the Arab who had so nearly killed him had been familiar. A recollection, half-submerged, had been trying to surface. He was sure that somewhere, sometime, they had met before. He visualized for the tenth time the pistol, the blue-and-yellow stripes, the fierce expression, and the hawk nose above . . . And suddenly he had it: the man had been coming out of the car-rental office back in Halakaz when he had returned the Renault.

"I don't aim to waste time thinking about another ambush," he said at last. "We'll keep our eyes peeled this time and deal with it if it happens. What gets me worried is who organized the last one, and why. It certainly wasn't the Nya Nyerere: they're not Arabs; they're African." He paused and then added slowly, "No . . . the characters lying in wait for us back there were Berbers—the guys we're supposed to be here to help."

IV

Dead Reckoning

11

Toward the end of that afternoon, the character of the terrain changed dramatically. From the site of the ambush their route had climbed to one of the *hamadya*— barren plateaus which surround the western fringes of the Sahara. Here, in a landscape with no vegetation to knit the surface together, weather erosion had desiccated the bare rock, and prevailing winds blowing in from the ocean had then sifted the smaller particles, carrying the finest of all the greatest distance to form dune deserts and abandoning the rest in wildernesses of shale and coarse gravel. According to the composition of the bedrock, the appearance of the denuded *hamadya* could be anything from a wasteland strewn with a chaos of boulders to something resembling a cobbled street for giants—a nightmare geometry of huge flat slabs of stone swept clean by some science-fiction broom.

They passed flatlands where the monotony was broken only by grotesque pillars and towers of sandstone; they saw salt lakes with no outlet and rushing streams that disappeared into the sand. Once, swerving to avoid a broad river that suddenly appeared on the far side of a rock buttress, Mazzari realized that what he was seeing was a mirage caused by the effect of sunlight on the dried salt left at the edge of a vanished lake. And throughout the second half of the day, the heat grew steadily worse—an intolerable assault that thundered behind the eyeballs, drying the mouth and shriveling the skin. Their shirts, clinging and black with sweat at the beginning of the day, now stood away stiff as boards as their bodies progressively dried out.

Around four o'clock, morale was at its lowest. Dean would gladly have set his whole timetable back by a day and halted so that they could rest in the shade—if there had been any shade to find. But their route, insofar as there was a discernible track at all, continued to snake through the interminable badlands that shimmered and trembled in bald desolation beneath the blazing sun.

If conditions were impossible in the open air, the furnace heat inside the MICV threatened to suffocate the occupants. Since the men riding outside were unable to bear the touch of the blistering metal if they lay along the hull, they perched on the track guards or walked when the rough ground slowed the carrier to a crawl. This meant they could travel with all hatches open wide; even so, it was necessary to spell the insiders every fifteen minutes and change drivers each half-hour. They propped Van der Lee up against the turret from time to time, but despite frequent shots of antibiotic, he was suffering intensely and his leg had begun to smell bad.

Daler's arm had stiffened, and that was now painful too. "Bloody hell," he muttered as the carrier topped a stony ridge to reveal yet another waste of shale, "I thought I'd already been in the asshole of the world, fighting in eastern fuckin' Arabia! But this is the shittiest of all: it really takes the biscuit!"

"Worse'n the motherfuckin' Congo in the rainy season?" one of the men asked.

"Or 'Nam when you're up to your balls in mud?" Goldsmith said.

"Jesus, yes!" Daler said.

"Where *are* we, anyway, for Chrissake?"

"Around eight degrees west and twenty-seven north," Dean said shortly. "And you can thank your lucky stars we're that far from the goddamn equator. We're still 280 miles north of the Tropic of Cancer, for God's sake. Farther south, you'd get yourselves a taste of real heat!"

"Oh, listen to the man!" groaned Dennis. "Talking of

126

degrees—what *is* the damned temperature, would you say?"

"Around a hundred and forty out of the sun, I would think," Dean replied. "Christ knows in full sunlight. Twenty degrees more? Thirty?"

"And how much bloody longer before it lets up?" Daler asked. "What's the sodding time, for fuck's sake?"

"Four-thirty-five. Another couple of hours and we should be okay."

"Past four-thirty?" Wassermann said. "That's swell. Who's for tennis, yet?"

It was soon after five that Dean saw the landmark he had been waiting for: penetrating a farther range of hills, two converging valleys joined at the eastern extremity of the plateau. "We take the right-hand gulch," Dean said. "It curves away to the south, at right angles to our present course, and leads to the forest this side of Gabotomi."

"Och, that's too bad—just as we was gettin' acclimatized to this interestin' stretch of country," Hammer said with a rare attempt at levity. "And where would a person be findin' himself if he carried straight on and took th' other gorge?"

"If he could stay alive another seventy miles," Dean replied, "he'd find himself on the highway from—"

"The *highway*?"

"Sure. There's a twenty-five-hundred-mile turnpike that goes all the way from Algiers to Dakar, skirting the edge of the Sahara. Tindouf, the nearest town in Algeria, is about a hundred miles from here."

"But why the *hell* . . . ?" Hammer's astonishment was mirrored on his battered face. "For what reason in God's name would folks be constructin' a proper road in a hell-hole like this?"

"Oil," said Dean.

Thirty minutes later, when they were still three or four miles from the entrance to the valley, Dean saw a cloud of dust above the rocks. "You'd better climb up to the top of that spur, Edmond," he said. "Christ knows if there was a connection between the chopper and the ambush we ran into . . . or whether there's a connection between either of them and that dust cloud. But I sure don't aim to run our heads into another noose today!"

As Mazzari picked his way slowly up to the crest of the low ridge, Novotny, who was driving, switched off the motor of the carrier. The sun was low enough now to cast an appreciable shadow. While the contracting metal of the overheated diesel ticked slowly into the silence, the mercs crammed themselves into the narrow patch of shade at the side of the vehicle and leaned their backs against the wheels. They could see the big Congolese sergeant lying flat between two boulders, so that the light would not reflect from the lenses of his binoculars. It was ten minutes before he rose upright and hurried down toward them, leaping from rock to rock with an agility surprising in a man of his size and weight.

"Jolly good guess, Colonel," he said breathlessly, dropping to the ground in the lee of the carrier. "Couple of half-tracks full of soldiery . . . a dozen Arab horsemen . . . taking up position on the hillside above the entrance to our valley. I don't know if they're the same johnnies we tangled with back there, but they could be."

"Okay," Dean said grimly, "that settles it. We'll quit the trail, take the high ground, and come into the valley farther up, after we've bypassed the bastards."

"Jesus," Furneux began, "didn't we have enough already—"

"Shut up!" Dean snapped. "I said we'll take the high ground, and that's the way we'll play it."

He settled himself behind the controls, waited until they had all piled aboard, and then turned the MICV southward off the trail. Here, between piles of boulders and jagged outcrops of rock, the going was tougher still. Without the distinctive outline of the mountain at the valley entrance to guide them, they could have lost

128

themselves or taken the wrong direction every few hundred yards. There was less risk of raising dust on such stony ground than there had been on the trail, but Dean was taking no chances, and they advanced at a crawl. In many places it was impossible to do otherwise: the ten-foot-wide carrier was obliged to sidle between the large boulders strewn in its path or negotiate giant steps cut in the bedrock. Once the machine almost capsized, tipping suddenly over the edge of a near-precipitous slope; another time, the underside of the hull fouled a thin basalt dike running through the baked and contorted strata, and it took the combined efforts of ten men to lift it off the iron-hard ridge of rock.

Gradually, however, the distant mountain slid behind them and to the left, and then advanced again as Dean turned eastward to bypass the ambush. The sun began its plunge toward the western horizon; the smoky haze above the wilderness they had crossed turned purplish and then orange. When at last the MICV arrived at the lip of the gorge some four or five miles from the entrance, an extraordinary sight met the eyes of the exhausted mercs.

In the shadowed depths below them, they could see a geographical metamorphosis. The entrance to the valley was like a continuation of the *hamadya*—a wasteland of boulders and rocks between bare cliff faces. But farther up there was a change in the structure of the land and the barren sandstone ledges tilted upward to reveal a lower layer of craggy limestone. Already, at the junction of the two formations a sparse vegetation of cactus and thorn bushes clothed the hillsides flanking the dried-up riverbed. This was supplanted by an area of dune grasses and reeds, and then—so unexpected it was like a mirage—a belt of tamarisk surrounding a pool of water that must have been a hundred yards wide. The pool was fed by a cascade sliding over a shelf in the rock—and from there the water had worn over the ages a passage through the soluble limestone, so that instead of

129

continuing down the valley, it flowed away through some primeval channel buried beneath the surface of the earth.

The cascade fell sixty or seventy feet; from where they stood high above the valley floor, Dean and his men could hear the roar and thunder of the stream as it plummeted into the foaming pool. Upstream the vegetation grew more dense. Creepers clung to the rock on either side of the watercourse, and then, as the gorge widened again, spreading out from each bank were thickets of tropical trees that gradually became thicker and closer until the whole valley brimmed with woods as far as they could see.

Not far from the pool, plastered to the rugged hillside like a swallow's nest beneath a gable, there was a Berber village. Between the palmeries and squares of cultivation outside the walls, goats browsed among the coarse grasses, and there were horsemen and Arabs leading pack camels up from the trail beside the river. Farther down, toward the mouth of the valley, some kind of truck was laboring toward the village.

Dean heaved a sigh of relief. "This is the beginning of the forest," he told Sean Hammer. "The trail peters out beyond that village, and there's only a narrow footpath leading to Gabotomi . . . unless you take the bridge another ten miles up the valley."

"That's the one we're goin' to blow?"

Dean nodded. "With luck. But we're too late to reconnoiter tonight, as I'd planned. We'll set back the attack twenty-four hours . . . and pull up as soon as we reach the nearest belt of trees."

"We couldn't get a wee bit nearer the viaduct first?"

"Not now." Dean looked at the sky. The sun had disappeared, and the short subtropical twilight was already thickening. "We'll be lucky to make the trees before it's dark, and I dare not risk the headlights with that village down there. It's probably home ground for the guys laying for us in that second ambush."

130

Slowly the carrier plowed on just behind the crest of the ridge, with Mazzari and Goldsmith scouting on the far side, ready to signal them over the moment there was cover enough to hide the machine. They were dim blurs against the night when at last Mazzari's great bulk showed above the rocks to guide them down beneath the low branches of the forest fringe.

12

It was soon after dawn that they saw the helicopter again. It flew along the winding length of the valley from the entrance to the waterfall and had clearly been following the trail they had left when Mazzari wised them up on the existence of a second ambush. The machine circled twice over the forest, made a second run above the trail, and then vanished beyond the dun ridges to the north.

"That settles it," Dean said to Hammer and Mazzari. "The chopper was acting as a spotter plane for the guys who tried to ambush us."

"The Berbers?"

"Yeah—and I still don't understand why Berbers should *want* to knock us off. After all, it's their goddamn city we'll be handing back to them if the mission succeeds!"

"You figure they came from that village?" Hammer nodded his head toward the mud walls on the far side of the ravine that were just visible through the outer fringe of trees.

"Could be. Some of them, anyway." Dean scratched his jaw. Shaving in cold water always played hell with his fair skin. "It must have fazed them when we didn't show for their second trap, so they called up the chopper to find out where the hell we'd gone."

"I guess we're fairly safe from observation here," Mazzari said, indicating the branches they had strewn over the MICV lest a stray gleam of metal should penetrate the trees and give away their position. "But I suppose they'll go on looking. I wonder if we left any spoor be-
132

tween here and the place we quit the trail. If we did, it wouldn't take a genius to work out where we were now: once they knew the direction, the distance could be computed easily enough."

"I don't think so," Dean said. "We were traveling over bedrock most of the time: there wasn't any ground soft enough for the caterpillars to leave tracks." He looked ahead along the slant of wooded hillside. The mercs were sitting around the carrier, talking in low tones as they chewed dried apricots and raisins. "In any case, we'd better get going. If we can't find some kind of trail through the forest, these trees will grow so thick farther up the valley that we won't be able to get the buggy through, and we'll have to make the last few miles on foot."

"You don't think the Berbers in that village will hear the sound of the motor?"

Dean shook his head. "The cascade's between us and the village. They'd hear nothing over the roar of those falls. Anyone deeper in the forest, of course—that's different; that's why I want to make a start."

Making a start wasn't as easy as he had hoped. It took a long time for the carrier's six-cylinder diesel to fire; and then, as they made their way slowly along the sun-dappled arcades between the trees, Mazzari had great difficulty maintaining engine speed: the motor kept stalling on him, and when it did turn, the timing seemed very rough. Finally, with a screech of tortured steel, the vehicle shuddered to a halt in a cloud of steam.

Mazzari pressed the starter. There was a click from the armature and no reaction from the motor at all. The other electrics worked perfectly; there was nothing wrong with the battery. The water in the radiator header was boiling, but there was plenty of it. "It's almost as though the bloody thing's seized up," he said with a puzzled frown. He climbed out of the cab. There was a throat-gripping stench of overheated metal. "I

133

think we'll have to take a look below decks," Mazzari said.

Once the underneath of the engine compartment was examined, the mystery was solved. A welded seam in the oil sump had sprung ("It must have been that goddamn basalt dike last night," Dean said disgustedly); little by little, splash by splash, although not quickly enough to leave a trail over the rough ground, they had been losing oil. The sump was now dry. As Mazzari had surmised, the overheated pistons, working without lubrication, had seized up solid in the crankcase. There was nothing they could do. The MICV was permanently disabled.

"It wouldn't be worth waiting? The pistons might free when she cooled down and the metal contracted," Novotny suggested. "Maybe we could get her going then."

"With no oil? She'd seize up again or throw a rod as soon as you fuckin' started," Hammer said.

"Jesus, what the fuck can we do?" This was Furneux.

"Keep our cool for starters—even if the son-of-a-bitch motor can't!" Dean said acidly. He was studying his maps. After a little he broke into the murmurs of dismay and anxiety with a crisp: "Okay, that's enough. Quit bellyaching. So we got no more transport. All right, we carry on without transport, is all."

"But how can we do the job . . . how do we *get* there without the bloody carrier?" Daler asked.

"We keep going . . . on foot."

Amid the groans of discouragement that this decision provoked, the inevitable grumble from Furneux could be heard: "Jesus . . . but how will we get back to the coast afterward?"

"There'll be transport at Gabotomi that we can liberate," Dean replied.

"How far's the damned place from here?" someone demanded.

"It's hard to say with maps like these: the details are kind of sketchy. As far as I can see, the viaduct's around
134

ten miles farther up the valley. Gabotomi's more like fifteen—but on a diagonal, north and east of the river."

"How do you want us to handle it, Cap?" Mazzari said.

Dean was pensive. "I don't like to change my plans once they're fixed, but this time I guess I have to make an exception. We were going to make the bridge first and then go on to the town, remember? Okay. Well, we got too much gear to hump all the way now that we're on foot, so I'm going back to something like the original scheme we had before we lost the boats."

"You mean a simultaneous attack? One party for the viaduct and another for the town?" Hammer looked mystified. "But surely . . . ?"

"Kind of. But not a simultaneous *attack*. We don't have the strength for that, of course. But I figure on dividing you into two parties now." Dean tapped one of the maps. "The main road to Gabotomi crosses the bridge. But there's a trail—just a footpath, I guess—leading there from a ford a couple of miles farther on. We'll stash the heavier gear somewhere near the beginning of that path. Then one small scouting party can go on up and case the city, and the rest of us can take out the bridge. Both parties can be lightly armed—and we'll meet up later by the hideout where we left the rest of the weapons and take them on for the final assault. That way we avoid being lumbered with all of the gear the whole of the way."

An hour later they were at the bottom of the valley, treading warily beneath interlaced branches as they followed the course of the river upstream. As Dean had predicted, the woods grew more dense as they advanced. Gnarled roots of acajou and chestnut and baobab and even mangrove overhung the muddied banks. Later there were creepers and parasite growths like mistletoe hanging down to impede their progress with the cumbersome armaments they were carrying.

135

Sometimes the water ran through a miniature gorge in the limestone, forcing them to detour farther up the slope to bypass the obstacle.

It was curiously quiet under the trees. No forest creatures scurried away as they approached, and there were no birds singing. There was a change, too, in the climate: the sun still shone as fiercely above, splashing occasional pools of gold between the riverbanks, but the heat was now humid and close, with clouds of insects hovering like smoke above the water.

They saw no sign of life until they reached the ford, although once Dean thought he heard the beat of a motor in the distance. It could have been a truck, some kind of rough-country jeep, or even the helicopter again: it was impossible to say, because they were passing a stretch of rapids and the rushing of the stream drowned the noise almost as soon as it occurred. By the time they had put the broken water behind them, it was no longer audible.

Flat, smooth stones rose above the surface at the ford, and roughly hewn logs had been split and pegged down on either side to shore up the bank and make a revetment for the trail that crossed their path here at right angles and climbed the far hillside on the way to Gabotomi. There were signs of a crude attempt at fishing around a pool fifty yards upstream. They were now, clearly, in Nya Nyérere territory.

"Redoubled precautions from now on," Dean told them. "We'll find a hiding place for the gear on the other side of the river, up the hill a ways. Jaap, you figure you could hang in there and act as watchman while the rest of us play soldier?"

Van der Lee was a tall, large-boned man with a ruddy complexion that had gradually paled in the time since they left the coast. He sat now on the ground by the two men who had been carrying him, with sweat dewing the ridges between lines of fatigue and suffering etched into the pallor of his face. "Sure, I do all I can," he said weakly. "Already I am too much a difficulty for you all, making space and transporting and the medicaments. Plus I know the leg smells bad: I think perhaps in spite of your care he is gangrene, isn't it?"

"You don't want to talk that way," Dean said with an optimism he was far from feeling. "That leg has been set good: poor Alphand knew what he was at. It'll be okay as soon as those damned antibiotics get a chance to work on it; you'll be walking again in a coupla weeks, you'll see."

The Dutchman gave a wan smile. "You are kind, but you do not say what you are thinking. Maybe I better can save everybody the trouble and make an exit?" He tapped the pistol holstered at his side.

"Don't give us that crap," Hammer said roughly. "We need you, Van, an' we need you bad. Sure we couldn't spare anybody else to stand guard over the supplies. You'll be doin' us a favor and earnin' your money here."

"Well . . . is a good feeling to be part of a good team," Van der Lee said.

They found a suitable cache thirty yards off the trail, a little way up the hill on the far side of the stream. There was thick undergrowth beneath the trees now, and a narrow rivulet running into the pool had worn away the topsoil and hollowed a shallow cave from the rock where this ground cover was at its most dense. The cave faced away from the trail and the entrance was behind a screen of creeper hanging from a giant acajou. "You'll be safe as a baby here," Dean said. "We'll leave you one of the Uzis, but it doesn't look like there's a hell of a lot of traffic over the ford. Those lines and nets have been there for weeks. In any case, we should be back from the bridge to relieve you sometime this evening."

Once Van der Lee was installed and as comfortable as possible, they carried across the arms and the stores—first the heavy boxes of ammunition and explosives, then the grenades, the mortar and the bazookas, and last the small arms and the remaining sacks of dried fruits. Reluctantly Dean had left the camp stoves and the less portable supplies in the stranded MICV. They had concealed it as best they could with branches and brushwood, but anyone patrolling the fringe of the forest would see the tracks it had left in the softer ground there, after which they could hardly fail to find the machine. It was a risk they had to take.

"We're going to split up into three groups of four men each," Dean said when everything had been stowed in the cave. "Hammer and me will take two squads to blow the bridge, one on each side of the stream; Mazzari will take the third and go on up this trail and case the town's defenses." Novotny, Kurt Schneider, and the veteran, Dennis, would form his own team, Dean decided. Wassermann, Goldsmith, and Furneux would go with Hammer. "That leaves you Daler, Weisenberger, and Molony, Edmond. Now, I want you to . . ." Dean stopped in mid-sentence. "Where the hell *is* Molony?" He looked around the tiny clearing outside the cave. The Irishman was nowhere to be seen.

"Now you mention it, I haven't seen him for some time . . . at least not to notice," Mazzari said slowly.

"And the son of a bitch is carrying two of the boxes," said Hammer. "I *thought* we were kind of short on the ammo, but I hadn't gotten around to runnin' a check yet." He looked at the other mercs. "Where was Molony when we saw him last? Who did see him last?"

"Dunno," Weisenberger said. "He was behind me. Like last in the line. I was, you know, not paying too much attention. Too much to think about, balancing those damned bazookas. Come to think of it, I can't remember *when* I last noticed the guy. I mean, you know, actually registered the fact that he was there behind me."

"Maybe he stepped aside to take a leak?" somebody suggested.

"Ah, be your age! We are here a half-hour already. So who needs that long to take—?"

138

"P'raps he was taken short! With the chow we been fed . . . all them dried fruits . . . figs an' all . . ."

"You want I should, you know, step back a ways and shout for him?"

"No!" Dean said sharply. "We're making quite enough noise already. A couple of you can take an Uzi each and go back . . ."

For the second time he stopped short in the middle of a sentence. Molony, still hefting his two boxes of ammunition, was treading over the stones at the ford. "Where the fuck have you been?" Dean demanded angrily.

The Irishman looked up with a surprised expression. "Been? Sure I've been no place at all. Just followin' you fellers down the trail."

"What the hell kept you? We've been here quite a while."

"Oh, that. Tell you the truth . . ." He nodded toward the boxes, which he had lowered to the ground. "Heavy as bloody lead, these buggers are. I got a cramp in me arm. Very painful. Couldn't clench the fingers at all. I sat down to wait until the circulation returned. I knew I'd not miss you, and you on your way to the ford."

"Why didn't you alert the guy in front—Weisenberger—to let him know you were falling out?" Hammer snapped.

"I was already some way behind. I didn't want to call out. To shout, you know. To yell. That would be a bad thing to do, I thought, givin' the game away to anyone who might be listenin'."

"Well, don't let it happen again. From now on, any man steps out of line, for *whatever* reason, he tells the next guy first . . . and he don't move until that guy acknowledges that he's receivin' loud an' clear, okay? Jesus, I thought I was leadin' a group of professionals, not actin' as a fuckin' nursemaid!" Hammer said bitterly.

Before they moved off on their separate missions, Dean rationed out the weapons. They would go lightly armed on these two preliminary sorties, he decided. The leader of each squad would take a Uzi. Wassermann and the other two men in Hammer's group would carry the Armalites; the rest of them would tote Kalashnikovs. Each of them would start out with a full magazine and a 250-round cartridge belt. Everything else would remain in Van der Lee's care at the cave.

"Hammer and me will take five pounds of plastic each. Apart from the fuses and suchlike, that'll be the only extras carried," Dean said. "Okay. Now, like at last we're gonna get to grips with the action, I reckon we owe ourselves a celebration shot . . . so we can drink to the success of the mission!" He produced one of the precious liquor bottles, unwrapped the foil, twisted out the cork, and passed the bottle around.

"Stock 84!" Dennis said. "What the hell's that, for Chrissake?"

"Italian brandy," Hammer replied. "Straight to your balls, man. An' I figure maybe you're goin' to need it, but!"

When Mazzari and his trio had vanished up the steep path that would eventually bring them at last within sight of Gabotomi, Hammer and Dean took their squads back to the river, leaving the last half-inch of liquor to solace Van der Lee. At first the two parties marched within sight of each other, one on either side of the stream, which was in places no more than eight or ten yards wide. Then, as the valley narrowed, the cascades and rapids became more frequent, the rock cuts deeper, and they were obliged more often to make detours taking them into the belt of forest that still covered the slopes of the ravine. Finally they became completely separated, each group making its own way upstream.

As the morning wore on, the damp heat grew more oppressive and the attacks of insects more infuriating. By noon they were in near-jungle conditions, up to their waists in swirling water or hacking at the overhanging growth with the bowie knives they carried. Later, after he had rested his men and given them time to take in another ration of dried fruits, Dean saw that the walls of the gorge ahead became so steep that they could no longer support the forest trees: beyond the lip, the jungle spread out on either side, but between there and the water there was now nothing but dense undergrowth clinging to near-vertical banks and outcrops of limestone. By the time the bridge came into view around three o'clock, the sweat-sodden mercs were toiling up-country beneath cliffs that rose almost sheer for several hundred feet.

The last tree on the valley floor was a giant baobab growing on a spit of land projecting into the river. It was no more than twenty-five feet high, but the loaded branches radiating from its huge trunk covered an area sixty to seventy feet wide where they curved down to touch the ground. Dean rested his men here again while they waited for Hammer's squad to catch up to them on the far side of the stream. From the tentlike interior of the tree, he peered through a screen of chestnut-shaped leaves into the sunlight. The bridge was a mile and a half away—a slender, flat-topped crescent spanning the river of blue between the clifftops.

"How the *hell* did they build that bastard?" Dennis asked at Dean's elbow. "Those cliffs there must be seven, eight hundred feet high!"

"Ask the engineers," Dean said. "But they didn't build it up from the bottom of the canyon, that's for sure!"

Soon afterward, Hammer arrived. One of the great branches arched over the stream, which was deep and fast-running here, and it was not difficult for the mercs to swing themselves over and join Dean's party in the shade of the baobab. "We'll have to go back some, then climb to the lip of the ravine," Dean said. "Stake her out from the top, somewhere nearer the place she's at. I don't see too much point continuing down here, now we've located her. What do you say, Sean?"

"Oh, I'm with you, sure," Hammer replied. "There'd

141

be no sense making an attack from below. No sense at all. We will be much better off advancin' on that ould bridge along the trail—carefully, mind, in case they have posted some sentry there—and then settin' off a wee charge at either end."

"Okay," Dean said. "Like the song says, we'll take the high road. Come on, you guys, let's make our way to the top!"

They had to retire several hundred yards along the watercourse before they found a slope that was less severe, and even then it took them one hour and twenty minutes of hard slogging to reach the lip of the ravine. Up above, the forest was dense, with no visible trail between the trees, and a thick carpet of undergrowth barring their progress at every step. It was not until they were within half a mile of the viaduct that Dean found a rock outcrop standing far enough away from the wall of the canyon for them to see both ends of the arch at once. Together with Hammer, he scrambled down a rough slope and then climbed to the top of the crag. He lay flat on his face, focusing his field glasses on the bridge.

It was built of roughly dressed limestone blocks, the two roots of the arch springing from revetments reaching no more than forty or fifty feet down the near-vertical cliff. "They must have felled some of the taller trees," Dean said, "and laid them across the ravine so that they could work from cradles slung beneath them."

Hammer was staring down into the chasm. Almost a thousand feet below, the sinuous silver thread of the river was already deep in shadow. "It's not a job I would want at all," he said.

Sweeping the binoculars left and right, Dean gave a sudden exclamation. "What the hell . . . ?" He made a fine adjustment to the focus wheel. "For Jesus Christ's sake! Not *again*!"

"What's up?" Hammer said. "Is something wrong now?"

142

Without a word, Dean handed him the glasses. The stocky Ulsterman refocused and gazed at the bridge. He gave a long, low whistle. In the circle of magnified vision, he could see that clearings had been made on either side of the ravine where the trail emerged from the forest. In each clearing there were men working around two structures placed hard by the entrance to the bridge. They were flat-topped, with slit windows, and they seemed to be made of concrete. "Pillboxes," Dean said bitterly. "Guardhouses. With enough men to fight off an infantry regiment, goddammit!"

"I can see," Hammer said. A platoon of soldiers in steel helmets was marching across the bridge. There were two army trucks drawn up by the buildings on the far side.

"They weren't there when the photos we have were taken," Dean said. "And those pictures were shot only a couple of weeks ago. They're still working on the things, for God's sake! If you look to the right of the nearest one, you can see a cement mixer and guys lugging sandbags around."

"Sure. Machine-gun nests. How d'you read that, Marc?"

"The way I see it, it looks like we're expected. Again. And what that means, I'm damned if I know. A leak, a spy, some kind of cross somewhere along the line? You tell me."

"You figure we can make it—blowing the bridge, I mean—with those guys in there?"

"Not on your life," Dean said decidedly. "Not against those odds! We'd need to bring up every man and every weapon we had . . . and even if we made it then, we'd have nothing left for shooting up the town."

"There'll be more guys than that—an' more weapons—in the town when we attack it."

"Sure there will. But there *we* shall choose the time and the place and the way to make the assault. Here we have no choice. We'd have to rush fortified pillboxes

143

across open ground, and there's only one way we can come: out of the forest. And if I'm right and they *have* been tipped off some way to our plans, that's just what they're geared to deal with."

"So what do we do?"

"We attack the bridge in a way they *don't* expect."

"But you just said . . . ?"

"I said we can't attack the bridge, against those odds, from *up here*."

"Meaning?"

"Meaning we have to attack it from below."

"From *below*?" Hammer sounded scandalized. "You mean . . . fire mortar shells, or rockets from the bazookas, into the air? Man, at that height you'd never even make a hit, let alone—"

"I didn't say fire at it," Dean interrupted. "We'll still use explosives, but we'll place them under the arch, not on top."

Hammer lowered the binoculars. "How the hell would you get 'em there? Sure the risks'd be the same. The guys in them blockhouses—"

"The guys in the blockhouses won't see us."

"How come?"

"Because," Dean explained, "like I said, we'll be attacking from below. Up the face of the cliff."

Hammer stared. "Marc, you have to be joking."

"I was never more serious, Sean."

"But . . . For Chrissake! You mean . . . like *climb* up that fuckin' cliff, all eight hundred feet of it, and place charges?"

"That's what I mean."

"Two squads of four men? One each side? And you say the guys in the blockhouses . . . ? Now I know you're crazy!"

"No, no!" Dean sounded impatient. "Of course we can't do it that way. Of course they'd be rumbled. No, just a couple of guys. Me and one other. Novotny, I guess. We only have to blow one end, after all: once a

144

bridge is down, it's down. The big drag is, we'll have to put the whole damned operation back another twenty-four hours, that's all."

"Oh, really? You don't want to do it now—in the last fifty minutes before the sun sets?" Hammer inquired sarcastically.

His leader grinned. "Furneux is the guy most likely to show a yellow streak," he said. "We'll send him back to the cache to warn Van der Lee, Mazzari, and the others that they'll have to sit tight for a day. We'll stay somewhere around here. Then, tomorrow afternoon—as you say, just before the sun sets—we'll make our play."

"Why late in the afternoon?"

"When the sun's dropped a certain distance, the far side of the gorge will be in shadow. All the way up. The way it is now." Dean jerked his head at the dark cliff face opposite them. "Two guys should be able to make that climb, without being seen, in those conditions. After all, it's not sheer: there's handholds and footholds and occasional clumps of brushwood and scrub here and there."

"An' while you and the Pole is doing your two-man circus act, what's with the rest of us? We're sittin' on our asses countin' each other's mosquito bites? Or shooting pool with the guys in the guardhouse maybe?"

"You," Dean said gently, "will be off in the forest—the far side of the gulch from Gabotomi—creating a diversion to draw off some of the troops . . . and stop the guys in the guardhouse watching our act."

"It's the craziest idea I ever heard of," Hammer said again. "But I like it, Marc, I like it."

13

Mazzari lay in the shadow of a cork oak and surveyed the domain of the Nya Nyerere. It was rugged country. Below him, the trail they had followed from the river dropped down between huge boulders and then lost itself among a series of graveled terraces on which nothing grew. The terraces overlooked a saucer-shaped depression perhaps five miles across, on the far side of which rose three bluffs, one behind the other, like giant steps carved from the sky. The summits of these rock faces were flat and even, but the multicolored beds of which they were composed were buckled and distorted into whorls and loops and arches so tortured and convoluted that in places the strata dipped vertically into the ground. Somewhere beneath those cliffs, Mazzari guessed, must be the rich mineral-bearing lodes coveted by the people who had hired them.

There was no river or watercourse visible at the bottom of the depression, but there were patches of cultivation here and there—corn and sweet potatoes, with several flocks of goats tethered around small tented encampments. The granite boss on which Gabotomi was built towered over the eastern end of the depression, a craggy eminence rose-red in the vivid sunlight, with the ancient fortress town spilled over the ledges and slopes like melted caramel over a fruitcake. Below the complex of dun-colored battlements, walls, domes, and watchtowers, a trickle of brown water, later to become a tributary of the river, slid among the rocks at the bottom of a ravine.

Mazzari looked over his shoulder. There was a mile

and a half of savannah between him and the fringe of the forest; the three men in his squad were still hidden in the head-high scorched grasses. He stared more carefully at the town. He could see armed sentries above a fortified gateway pierced by an arch, but there seemed to be no guards at the entrance itself: robed men and women, with mules or camels or on foot, were passing in and out, apparently without being challenged. On the flat ground below the boss, trucks stood beside a line of concrete buildings flanked by what looked like a gasoline depot. Nearer still, a jeep carrying steel-helmeted soldiers raised a cloud of dust from one of the trails leading out over the depression. The jeep's windshield flashed in the sun.

The main road dipped down over the three bluffs, ran up to the main gate, and then curled away around the granite spur. The old silver mine, Mazzari knew, was on the far side of the rock. He had no idea if it was being worked again, and, more important, he could get no idea, at this distance, of how the place was guarded, or what armaments the defenders possessed. Moving slowly on elbows and knees, he wormed his way back to the shelter of the savannah. "Absolutely hopeless," he told the three mercs waiting for him. "Can't see a thing really—at least, nothing of military interest. There's nothing for it: I shall bloody well have to go on into town and take a shufti."

"Take a . . . ? You must be mad!" Molony exclaimed.

"You can't, you know, just walk in there as if . . . I mean, they're like on the lookout. Leery of strangers," Weisenberger said.

"I'm not going in there as a stranger," Mazzari said.

They stared at him. "Come on over here . . . but keep down," Mazzari said, beckoning them to follow him. At the edge of the prairie he parted the last clump of grass and pointed down below the gravel terraces. Now that the fiercest of the heat was over, men and women were emerging from the tents of the nearest encampment,

147

busy with various domestic tasks. Goats were being milked; work had resumed in some of the patches of cultivation; one man was heading for the ravine below the town, carrying a yoke and two goatskins, evidently to be filled with water; another had climbed to the first terrace and was digging gravel. "All right, chum," Daler said. "The buggers are all playing busy bees. So what?"

"Those chaps are recognized more by what they wear than by the way they actually look," Mazzari said. "Like the Arabs. Bedouins wear one kind of robe, Tuaregs and Berbers another. Different djellabas, different burnooses, some with a tarboosh, some without. It's almost like uniforms in the army. These fellows aren't Arabs, but the principle's the same."

"I still don't see . . ." Molony began.

"Look at the gate into the town, old chap. No questions asked. No passes to be shown. If you're wearing the right kind of clobber, you get in—or out. I shall make sure I'm wearing the right kind of clobber."

"Sure, and how the divil would you go about getting that?"

Mazzari gestured at the encampment below. "I shall take it off one of those coves down there. Simple as falling off a log."

"Yeah, but . . ." Weisenberger looked worried. "I mean, the clothes . . . okay. But, shit, they're gonna, you know, take a look at your phiz. Some of them, anyway. And you ain't exactly a dwarf, Ed!"

"There's a pattern," Mazzari said. "Nomads come in from the desert. Warriors. They fight the people living in some region where farming's a possibility, beat the shit out of them, chuck them out. They take the place over and start farming themselves. Then they get soft with the good life, another lot of nomads come in from the desert—and the whole thing starts over." He paused, and then added, "The Nya Nyerere were nomads. They're supposed to have come here from the southern Sudan sometime around the turn of the century. They

148

chucked out the Berbers. But they haven't gone soft yet; they're still warriors and still big men, most of them. That takes care of the size bit. But, more important, like I said, they're not Arabs." He gestured below again. "As you can see, they're black."

"Shit!" Daler breathed. "And you think you could pass ...?"

"I'll have a bloody good try, old man," Mazzari said.

Twenty minutes later, creeping from boulder to boulder, Mazzari was approaching the level on which the tribesman was digging gravel. He peered around the edge of the rock. A big man in white robes with green and yellow panels. A thick-lipped face almost blue-black in the shadow of the burnoose. He was wielding a long-handled shovel with an iron blade.

Mazzari watched him filling hemp sacks with the fine pebbles and then sliding them to a lower level down a wooden chute. Later, he supposed, they would be carried to the encampment for some improvement to the bases beneath the goatskin tents. When he was certain that the man was working alone, that there was no assistant at the foot of the chute, he scraped a stick along the surface of the rock and contrived a coughing grunt that he hoped could be mistaken for that of some animal. The tribesman paused in his shoveling and looked up. Mazzari repeated the noises, a little louder. The tribesman left hold of the sack, rose upright, and strode forward to investigate. He was still holding the shovel.

Mazzari was waiting behind the boulder. He leaped forward as the man rounded the corner, his right hand held flat, ready for a chop at the throat. But the tribesman's reflexes were good. He gave an exclamation of astonishment, stepped back, and swung the shovel in a murderous arc at Mazzari's head. Mazzari was obliged to drop to his knees; the metal blade whistled over his head and struck sparks from the rock. Before he could rise, the shovel was hurtling toward him again—brought

149

down this time from above the man's head. Mazzari came up inside the swing, but the haft of the tool nevertheless struck him a numbing blow on the shoulder. He cannoned into the man, big hands reaching for the wrist so that he could exert a judo lock and shake the spade free. The tribesman wrapped his other arm around Mazzari's chest in a bear hug. For a moment they swayed, locked together, in the shadow of the boulder. The tribesman had bad teeth and his putrid breath played hotly on Mazzari's face. Then suddenly he gave a strangled cry and went limp in the Congolese sergeant's arms. Behind him, Daler nodded, wiped his palm across the heavy butt of his Dardick pistol, and shoved it back in its holster.

"Nice work, Daler," Mazzari panted. "As I said, there's still a touch of the warrior about these chaps!"

When they had verified that there was nobody at the foot of the chute who would notice the man's absence, they dragged his unconscious body back into the shelter of the savannah and stripped the robes from it. He was wearing a white shift underneath, and they tore this into strips so that he could be securely bound and gagged. "He should be out for a couple of hours," Mazzari said. "But I'll be away longer than that. Molony, you stand guard over him and make bloody sure that he doesn't kick up a row when he wakes. We'll set him free later if he's a good boy. Daler, you take Weisenberger and work around as far as you can toward that ravine. Note down everything you see—especially anything to do with the defenses. Then go back to Van der Lee and tell the Colonel that we'll have to postpone the assault twenty-four hours: I simply can't find out enough in time for us to plan an attack for dawn tomorrow. Molony can wait for me here. Right?"

Toward the end of the afternoon, Mazzari strode out from a thicket of desiccated trees on the edge of the ravine and headed for Gabotomi's main gate. Curiously— he saw as he drew nearer to the fortified structure—the

150

gatehouse and the watchtowers on that side of the town were built of massive sandstone blocks, evidently quarried from the bluffs on the far side of the depression, while most of the ramparts and the houses behind them were of the usual Berber mud-walled composition. Perhaps, long ago, the Berbers themselves had displaced another people—a more sophisticated tribe building in stone, more civilized and less military than the Arabs. Perhaps, Mazzari thought, it was they who had originally started the silver mine behind the town. He wondered how many times in its history the place—so isolated, yet so self-sufficient—had changed hands.

The stolen robes fitted him tolerably well, although, being taller and heavier than their owner, he found that the hems floated six inches clear of the ground. This meant that he was obliged to go barefoot: the rubber-soled combat boots that he customarily wore would scarcely have fitted in with the costume. It was this more than anything else—the pain of rough ground beneath his nonhardened feet—that made him fear discovery. An inadvertent exclamation or a sudden hop occasioned by the pressure of a sharp stone would give him away more surely than any scrutiny of his form or the dark face beneath the burnoose. If he was questioned, of course, if he was obliged by some inquisitive guard to speak . . . well, that was something else!

Reaching the granite-paved slope leading to the gate, he joined the trickle of tribesmen approaching the town. Their walk, he noticed, was an upright heel-and-toe affair rather than the splay-footed shuffle of the Arabs. So far as he could judge, the language resembled one of the Hauser or Yoruba dialects from northern Nigeria.

There were Arabs there too, of course: white-gowned desert Bedouin, Tuaregs leading restive horses, merchants with camels laden with merchandise from the equatorial states south of the Sahara. Only the Berbers were conspicuous by their absence.

From a distance, Gabotomi looked more like a

medieval castle than an open community, but as he approached the arched gateway, Mazzari watched the fortress unfold until the course of its narrow streets and lanes could be charted by the bands of shadow splashing the age-old walls in the setting sun. The sentries behind the battlements surmounting the gatehouse appeared to be surveying the far side of the depression through binoculars. Perhaps they were expecting the jeep to return. At any rate they were paying no attention to the tide of humanity that was now flooding in below them. Beneath the weathered stone arch, steel-helmeted black soldiers in camouflage-daubed battle dress stood chatting outside an armory door, but they too gave no more than a cursory glance at the passersby. Mazzari strode inside the city.

He was faced with a number of narrow streets radiating like spokes of a wheel from the entrance *place*. Not daring to hesitate lest it should tag him as a stranger, he turned right and walked briskly up a flight of steps leading to a belvedere overlooking the ravine. As he mounted, a man wearing identical robes to Mazzari's own hurried down. Passing the black mercenary, he paused in his stride and made some unintelligible remark. It could have been a greeting, a warning, a question, anything. Mazzari grunted something that he hoped would sound convincingly guttural, half-raised an arm in salute, and went on up. From the belvedere, he saw that the man had turned around at the foot of the staircase and was gazing after him. He hastened to the far side of the stone platform.

Below the parapet was another platform, and this one was clearly closed to the public, for the soldiers there in combat kit surrounded a twenty-five-pounder light field gun and two old German MG-42 machine guns—probably salvaged from the western desert after World War II, Mazzari thought. The ammunition belts ready to feed into them, however, were strictly 1980s, and the guns commanded the approach to the town.

One of the soldiers looked up and saw Mazzari staring. He shouted angrily and waved his arm. Mazzari swiftly retired and went toward a network of alleys honeycombing the buildings farther up the hill. The narrow streets were crowded, thronged by townsfolk on their way to the *souks* and workers from the fields returning home. Mazzari walked quickly, in no particular direction: the less he was noticed by soldiers or addressed by tribesmen whose robes he was wearing, the better! He passed a dense mass of people milling around the entrance to the covered way that led to the *souks*, and found himself in a wider street that seemed to lead in the direction of some central square. In the distance now he could hear the plaintive quarter-tones of Arab pipes and strings over an insistent beat of hand drums and the roar of the crowd.

Twice the people jamming the thoroughfare from wall to wall had to shrink back to allow the passage of an armored jeep carrying what seemed to Mazzari to be TOW antitank missiles.* The square itself, when he reached it, looked a little like an army camp, with tented booths set around a giant fig tree—but these were just stalls where merchants squatted behind mountains of nuts, neat pyramids of herbs and spices, and quantities of dried fruits and dates piled on open counters. The crowd was at its densest here, circling around snake charmers and storytellers, drifting among kiosks housing barbers, doctors, and scribes offering to write letters for a fee. Above the music and the hubbub, the shrill bells of water boys chimed as they threaded their way from group to group, festooned with brass goblets.

Mazzari walked around the ruins of a mosque and

---

*TOW—Tube-launched/Optically tracked/Wire-guided. Designed as an antitank weapon, the missile has a two-stage rocket motor. Once the crossed hairs of the sight home on a moving target, sensors translate the movement into electrical impulses that are fed to a computer which determines the range and trajectory. TOW missiles remain connected to the launcher by two fine wires along which the computer transmits further instructions as the target changes position during flight.

headed for the far side of town. The Nya Nyerere, he recalled, were non-Muslims; he wondered what the Arabs who still came to Gabotomi thought of the desecration of their former place of worship. He passed an open space in which three army trucks were parked. There was another jeep at the far end, and the four-man crew, he saw with dismay, were armed with Russian-made rocket launchers: RPG-7V's, more recent than their own. He hurried down a flight of steps leading to the outer wall.

Beyond the battlements, the western sky drained through vermilion to limpid green behind the sandstone bluffs. And just above the battlements was a firing platform with another twenty-five pounder and two machine guns. Mazzari turned to go.

Four soldiers with submachine guns barred the entrance to the alley. An officer holding a Colt automatic stood off to one side. "Sergeant Mazzari, I believe?" he said in heavily accented French. "I will ask you to accompany us and explain the reasons for this masquerade."

14

Twenty-four hours later, Marc Dean and the Pole, Novotny, were at the foot of the eight-hundred-foot bluff
beneath the viaduct. Hammer had taken Wassermann,
Dennis, and Kurt Schneider deep into the forest to
prepare the diversion that Dean had asked for. At noon,
having already learned from Furneux that Dean's operation too had to be postponed for a day, Daler arrived
with Mazzari's message. Dean had ordered him to find
his way back to the stranded carrier and salvage the remaining cannon shells from its magazine.

"As you say, Cap," Daler had replied. "But—no offense!—what the fuck use will they be without the
bloody gun?"

"They can be detonated," Dean said. "I have special
plans for those babies. Goldsmith can go with you and
help carry them back to our arms dump."

Now, relieved that their plans had coincided even if
the long wait had irked him, Dean reached for the root
of a stunted fig tree and hauled himself up on the first
stage of his perilous climb. The sun had sunk toward
the forest far enough for the shadow of the opposite cliff
to move halfway up the face of the bluff. They dared
not wait any longer or it would be dark before they
made the top.

They carried nothing but the plastic explosive, detonators, Primacord fuse, a coil of rope, and short-handled
mountaineer's picks, for it was essential that each man
should be as free and as lightly burdened as possible.
Their pistols were holstered at the hip, fully loaded, but
even for these they carried no extra ammunition. The

155

Dardick's "trounds" would in any case not fit in to a regular bandolier.*

The first hundred feet were relatively easy. Stunted bushes and an occasional small sapling provided plenty of hand- and footholds; the bluff was inclined away from them at a slight angle, and there was earth and sometimes a clump of coarse grass packed between the rock outcrops. After that the going became tougher.

About halfway up, there was a massive overhang in the limestone which obscured their view of the bridge's nearer end and would probably mask them from any watchers at the guardhouse more effectively than the dense shadow which hid them from the guards on the far side of the ravine. But to get past the overhang they would have to make a traverse and then return on a diagonal course to the face below the viaduct arch. At that time—Dean calculated it as forty minutes after they started—they would be at their most vulnerable, visually. And it was precisely then, therefore, that Hammer's diversion was due to start.

A light wind blew up the valley from the west, carrying the rank odor of creepers spiced every now and then by the scent of aromatic herbs growing in spidery clumps among the rock fissures. As they climbed higher, the breeze stiffened, accelerated by the temperature change between the sunlit clifftop and the shadowed depths below. When they were still a hundred feet short of the overhang, it started to moan through the grasses and rattle the dry stems of thorn bushes. Otherwise, apart from the scrape of their boots and the laboring of

*Invented by an American, David Dardick, in 1949, this gun was for some time considered as a possible weapon for the U.S. Army but was later discontinued. A mixture of revolver and automatic, the Dardick is a .38 caliber pistol with a fifteen-round magazine held in the butt in the normal way—but each cartridge case is surrounded by a triangular-section polycarbonate plastic sleeve. There is a cylindrical chamber with three triangular cutouts each shaped to receive one of these trounds (as Dardick called them). Pressure on the trigger rotates the chamber, ejecting a spent cartridge, firing the next, and locating the third cutout above the magazine, where it will be fed by the magazine spring with a further tround.

their breath, the late-afternoon air was silent. They could hear no sound from the bridge that curved across the blue sky above.

The shadow creeping up the canyon wall was gaining on them. Its upper edge had driven the sun from the top of the overhang. Dean paused to look down. Dusk dulled the light at the bottom of the valley as a sediment dulls wine; the river swirled heavy as lead among the blurred outlines of rocks. So far, the climb had taxed their strength but had not been frightening; a slip or a fall would have been unnerving but not fatal, for there were plenty of roots projecting from the pockets of soil to grab at, or brushwood clumps to act as a brake. But from now on it would be rugged. Rather than a near-vertical hillside, they were faced with a regular cliff almost five hundred feet high, most of it dropping sheer from the lip of the gorge. From now on they would be seeking footholds and handholds in the crumbling limestone, testing every crevice before they dared transfer their weight, taking advantage of each tiny ledge, pitting their skill and determination and physical condition against vertigo and the pull of gravity. Wordlessly Dean uncoiled the rope from around his waist and lowered the free end to Novotny, who was standing ten feet below and a little to one side of him.

When the Pole had made fast the line, they started on up once more, clawing at the friable rock, wedging toes into the interstices while they stretched out again. Dean hesitated to use the pick, lest the noise alert the guards above, but he was forced to drive it in twice during the next phase of the climb, when smooth areas of rock offered no handholds in any direction. On a ledge beneath the overhang, he rested again and looked upward. Both sides of the ravine were in shadow now; only the treetops and the guardhouse roof snared the last rays of sunshine. He glanced at his watch. They had been climbing for forty-three minutes.

A sudden muffled detonation, followed by three more,

157

sounded from the forest behind the far guardhouse.
Soon afterward a column of black smoke rose into the
air above the trees. As the wind teased it out toward the
east, Dean heard shouting from each end of the bridge.
A jeep started and careered across to the far side. He
looked down at Novotny and raised his eyebrows. Novotny held up a thumb. Hammer's diversion was evidently starting as planned.

The traverse was difficult: it required all their powers
of concentration to work their way successfully along
the slanting crack in the rock that Dean discovered. By
the time they had circumvented the great bulge in the
cliff face, they were a hundred yards wide of the bridge,
with a long steep diagonal to climb before they were
once more beneath the shelter of the arch. Dean looked
over his shoulder. Crimson reflections now flickered on
the underside of the smoke cloud, which stretched some
distance above the forest. The shouting from the far side
of the ravine was louder. Several vehicles racing up from
the direction of Gabotomi roared across the viaduct.

Three hundred feet below the arch, Novotny and his
leader toiled upward—ten yards of ice-smooth rock,
planed down by the wind; a ledge white with bird drop-
pings, supporting a sparse vegetation of thistle and cactus; a section of hollows and curves, sculptured by
tropical rains from the softer strata; a fault in the
limestone giving them greater purchase. With raw fingers and aching toes, shoulder and calf muscles crying
out for respite, the two men had reached a point where
they no longer dared to look down: below the vast swell
of the overhang, white mist already veiled the pale
curves of river at the bottom of the abyss.

Below the mechanical level of concentration, Dean's
mind roved over the chain of events linking his initial
meetings with Jarvys and the Belgian gunsmith to this
desolate cliff face on the fringe of the Sahara. His unknown employers had furnished him with a suitable
ship—an obsolete French cross-Channel ferry, with stern

158

ramps that could be lowered to facilitate the launching of LCT and LCI's in the calm seas off the Canaries. He had picked her up at the Polish port of Gdynia, on the Baltic, for it was here that the arms coming north from Omnipol in Czechoslovakia could be shipped with the least trouble and formalities. An end-user certificate, supplied by an obliging army general in Tchad, had been all that was needed to clear the beautifully packed weapons through the communist customs. Jammot had arranged for the vehicles to be loaded in Antwerp, and the forty mercenaries had been embarked off Cherbourg and La Rochelle. Dean had known neither the captain nor the crew; he imagined they were Cypriots or Greeks, though the ship flew the Liberian flag. Once his private army had been disembarked, the ferry had put about and vanished over the horizon without so much as a farewell signal. Officially, no doubt, the voyage had never taken place. It would figure in no log, and the various port records would conveniently have been fudged.

Since then, Dean recalled grimly, the operation had been nothing but a catalog of disasters: the unexpected storm and the loss of most of his men and supplies; the "surprise" attack on the army depot that *was* expected; the ambush and the loss of their carriers—there were still a hell of a lot of things that needed to be explained. For the moment, however, he was concerned to make this son-of-a-bitch climb the first hundred-percent success of the mission!

Clearly Hammer—tough, indomitable, reliable, wiry little Hammer—had once again justified Dean's faith in him. He had taken four incendiary grenades a couple of miles into the forest to the south and east of the viaduct, with orders to collect as much dried brushwood as his squad could gather, pile it in four places several hundred yards apart, and then set off the grenades. Ordinarily the big jungle evergreens would be too damp in the humid atmosphere to burn easily. But if Hammer's four small blazes could be persuaded to coalesce into a

159

single big one, the heat should be fierce enough to dry out the nearer trees to the point that their resin would ignite spontaneously. They, in turn, in a kind of firecracker effect, would then set fire to the next row, and once a fire front was established, aided by a following wind, there was no telling where it would stop. Certainly, although the bridge would never be left unguarded, the fire would serve to draw away the surplus members of each gatehouse and retain the attention of the sentries that remained. The fact that this was working out was proved by the fact that nobody had spotted Dean and Novotny while they were exposed at the limit of their traverse. To confuse things further, Hammer's men were to take cover and shoot at the first firefighters to arrive. If an attack *was* in fact expected, Dean hoped, this might fool the defenders into thinking it was coming from the forest.

Since he had now heard several army trucks approaching from the north, he figured that maybe this part of the plan was working too. If only they could manage to maroon a sizable part of the garrison on the wrong side of the ravine before they attacked the town!

They had now reached the final, most critical stage of the climb. A chimney, or vertical shaft between two unscalable rock faces, led to a tiny shelf that would bring them within reach of the stone revetment supporting the root of the arch.

Novotny was in the lead now. Dean was halfway up the shaft, his back pressed against one wall and his heels thrusting against the other, when a sudden shower of small stones, followed by several larger chunks of rock, pattered against his legs. An instant later, there was a choked exclamation and Novotny fell. His body plummeted past Dean's; the rope linking the two men together tightened and yanked at Dean's middle. Unable to withstand the abrupt wrench with all of the Pole's weight dragging on the rope, Dean jackknifed and dropped in his turn. His arms and legs threshed wildly, scrabbling painfully at the jagged limestone, but it was not until Novotny had fallen clear of the chimney that the point of Dean's pick caught in a deep crevice . . . and held.

His fingers closed frenziedly around the haft as his hand slid down to the thicker end; the weight of his own big body plus that of Novotny jerking in space at the end of the rope almost pulled his arm from its socket. But miraculously he held on. For what seemed an eternity, pressure from the muscles of his right hand was the only thing that prevented him and his companion plunging into the chasm. Then one of his feet, groping in desperation for a solid surface, found a minute toehold in the rock and he was able to ease fractionally the excruciating traction on his arm. Slowly he brought up his left hand and closed it too around the shaft of the pick.

Ten feet below him, the Pole was swinging to and fro like a pendulum across the cliff face. Each time the rope plucked—left . . . right . . . left . . . right—at Dean's waist, it threatened to dislodge the precarious hold he had on the rock. "For Crissake!" he panted. "Don't . . ."

But suddenly Dean realized what Novotny was doing: off to one side or the other, there must be a cleft or a projection, just out of reach, that he hoped to grab, so that he could ease the intolerable drag on Dean's waist. He was swinging wider each time in the hope of making that place.

Small particles of limestone dribbled over Dean's hands. He looked up—and saw that the edge of the crevice in which the point of his pick was wedged was slowly crumbling away under their combined weight. "Quick!" he gasped. "Hurry! . . . For God's sake!"

The metal pick shifted, jolting them another inch and a half lower down the precipice. The trickle of particles became a stream. Dean opened his mouth to call out again . . . and then all at once the pull on the rope eased. Novotny had gained the hand- or foothold that he was aiming for.

161

Sobbing with relief, Dean clenched raw fingers on the rock, lifted the pick and drove it in farther, and then with infinite and agonizing care raised one leg so that he could drag himself up to safety. Planting his heels in the crevice, he leaned back against the chimney and hauled Novotny up beside him. The Pole's face was deathly white. "Jesus," he said. "Oh, Holy Mary, Mother of God . . ."

Dean gazed across the ravine, fighting to regain his breath. A red glow pulsed against the thickening dusk. Above it, black smoke now blotted out the sky. "C'mon," he said. "We're losing time. Up you go."

Novotny was trembling. He shook his head. "No," he whispered. "You go first. I'd hate to bring down—"

"Get up there!" Dean cut in roughly. "You hit a piece of rock that had rotted. It could happen to anyone: it wasn't your fault. Go on—I'm relying on you."

Novotny shrugged. "Whatever you say, Colonel." He tested the rope around his waist, rested his back and the lacerated palms of his hands against the rock wall, took a deep breath, and then raised his feet and began pushing himself upward. A moment later, Dean followed.

This time both men reached the top of the chimney without incident. Now they had almost reached their goal. Immediately above them, the stone blocks of the viaduct arched out over their heads. To each side, the revetments sloped steeply up to the edge of the ravine. And just below, on the left, a three-inch ledge snaked away along the face of the cliff.

Novotny was the explosives expert. While he placed the charges, the plan was for Dean to inch away along this ledge, paying out the Primacord fuse as far as he could. He was then to climb to the lip of the gorge and return to help Novotny up under cover of a clump of bushes at the edge of the revetment. After that they would explode the plastic and get the hell out. It was, however, useless laying the charges at the root of the arch, Novotny had said: they might not be strong

162

enough to destroy the bridge. They would have to be packed into the angle between arch and revetment, high up near the roadway, if the job was to be done properly.

He untied the rope from around his waist and recoiled it around Dean's. Dean handed over detonators and his packet of explosive. Novotny spread-eagled himself facedown against the revetment and began working his way up against the angle of the arch, feeling for the gaps between the dressed stones with his toes.

Dean stepped out with a foot braced against the narrow ledge, still grasping the last block of the revetment with one hand. The stonework trembled slightly as two more trucks roared over the bridge toward the fire. From beyond the parapet he could hear the sound of voices and tramping feet.

He looked to his right. Novotny was a dark shape high up against the side wall of the arch. He couldn't be more than nine or ten feet below the parapet. He was crouched down, wadding the plastic into the angle of the stonework, the white Primacord looped down against the darkness between them.

Dean slid his foot farther out along the ledge. Warily he transferred his other foot to the narrow rock shelf. He let go of the limestone block and stood on his toes, facing the cliff with his arms spread. Gingerly, inch by inch, he began moving away from the revetment, the Primacord separating itself from a spool at his waist as he moved.

Theoretically, a three-inch strip of stone should be wide enough for a man to traverse. But when the ledge projects from a sheer wall, the bulk of the body becomes critical, for if the center of gravity shifts too far away from the median line of the ledge, it will overbalance and fall. To succeed, a man must either face the wall and move on the balls of his feet, with his heels jutting out into space; or rest on his heels with his back to the wall, in which case he is desperately conscious of his exposed position and will probably—if the ledge is high up—suffer from vertigo and fall. In either case, the center of gravity will be farther out than the edge of the shelf, so the body must be flattened against the wall as much as possible and prevented from toppling outward by the tension and thrust of muscles in the legs and feet.

With his arms flung wide and every available square inch of his rugged form pressed to the rock, Dean advanced his foot a short distance, shifted his weight, brought up the other foot, moved the first one again . . . thrusting furiously upward and inward with his calf muscles at every instant. His cheek lay against the limestone—becoming moist now with the approaching night—and his eyes were fixed on a point ten yards away where the ledge slanted up to join the lip of the gorge. He knew that if he looked down and saw the space yawning between his heels he would fall. Even to turn his head and stare directly at the cliff face would displace his weight enough to overbalance him. He felt as though the shuddering of the blood in his veins was sufficient to shake him from his perch and hurl him eight hundred feet into oblivion.

The sounds around him became exceptionally important as he moved. They were invested with a special significance; loud enough to drown the world, they became his lonely universe. The slither of his soles along the ledge . . . the rasp of his bush jacket against the rock . . . a tread of sentries' feet on the bridge . . . the hoarse, shallow gasps of his breath (for the deep lungful he needed so badly could expand his chest enough to push him away from the cliff face). Somewhere in the darkening sky behind him, he thought he could hear a distant roar and crackle of flames.

At one moment during the traverse of that interminable thirty feet, Dean's iron nerve almost gave out. Fleetingly he suffered the reaction said to be common to drowning men—the desire to stop fighting, to let go, to be carried away. But enough of his determination remained to spur him on. Biting his lip, he set out on the

164

last few perilous feet. And somehow they were the worst of all.

He was bathed in an icy sweat. The breeze freshened again and plucked at his clothes. He was more than ever conscious of the abyss beneath him, of the hairline separating his life from his death. His calf and thigh muscles were on fire.

But at last it was over. He had negotiated the final sloping section of the ledge and the lip of the ravine was within reach. As he raised his arms to grasp the roots of a *pistache*, a fragment of the limestone shelf crumbled under his weight and broke away.

Dean fell.

His legs dropped away into the void. His flailing arms struck the rock sill with an impact that shocked the remaining breath from his body . . . and miraculously, for the second time that day, one of them hooked over it and held. For a dizzy moment he hung suspended over the drop with all his weight tearing at that arm. Then he managed to reach up with the other hand and slam the pick into the inner section of the ledge. But it was only at the fourth attempt that he was able to will his muscles to haul him back up to a position where he could stumble the last few feet and collapse over the lip of the gorge.

Dean lay on the hard, solid, and wonderful flat ground, his face pressed to the dry earth, waiting for the hammering of his heart to die down. He was sick to his stomach, he was shuddering all over, and he was suffering from shock—the intolerable tension of these last two hours of ferocious concentration and near-disaster. But he dared not let up for a moment: Novotny would be waiting; the bridge must be blown; they must find their way back to the arms dump in the dark and plan the assault on the town.

He rose groggily to his feet. The short southern twilight was almost over. It would be night in a few minutes. But he could still make out the details of the

165

guardhouse and the road that emerged from the forest to cross the bridge. Beyond the trees on the far side of the ravine, a long line of angry flames licked the sky. The wind was in the wrong direction, but he thought he could hear shots over the menacing roar of the fire.

Dean removed the last few inches of Primacord from the spool at his waist and weighted the end down with a stone. Pulling the fuse up over the edge of the drop as he went, he returned to the screen of bushes masking the clearing above the revetment. Novotny was a huddled blur at the foot of the stone slope. They had been right to play it this way, Dean thought: the Pole could never have made it along that ledge in the dark. He uncoiled the rope once more and lowered the free end for Novotny to grab.

"What kept you?" Novotny whispered when he had been hauled up beside his chief.

"I went back down again to check that we'd left nothing at the bottom of the gulch!" Dean muttered furiously.

Novotny stared at him in the gloom and said nothing.

"Okay?" Dean asked in a low voice. "Detonators in place?" He picked up the white cord where it dipped over the revetment. "Fuse location checked?"

Novotny nodded.

"Okay. Let's go."

On hands and knees, they scurried back to the far end of the Primacord fuse. Novotny pushed the stone aside with his foot and closed a small plastic box over the end of the cord. He fitted a miniature flashlight battery inside the box and twisted out two short lengths of insulated wire with naked ends.

The stone rolled to the edge of the ravine and dropped over. It bounced off the cliff face, landed on the ledge, and clattered along that.

There was a shout from the guardhouse. Another from the parapet of the bridge.

The stone fell from the ledge, crashed into a limestone

outcrop once, twice, three times, then vanished into the depths.

"Down!" Dean hissed. "Christ!"

Flame stabbed the dark from the end of the bridge. The two mercenaries heard the ripping detonations of machine pistols as they flattened themselves to the ground. Slugs smashed through the leaves above their heads.

Novotny still held the plastic box in his hand. "Now!" Dean said.

The Pole touched the two naked wires together.

The double explosion almost cracked their eardrums. A livid sheet of flame flashed into the night. For an instant smoke and fire boiled out from the nearer end of the viaduct, to send blazing debris spiraling through the air.

Then, in the reflected glow of the conflagration on the far side of the ravine, they saw the whole structure buckle and sway. The explosion had blown away a segment of the arch and sheared a supporting girder. Stones from the parapet dropped into the gorge. The roadway cracked, split open, tilted sideways, and slid into the void. And suddenly the whole bridge collapsed in the center: for a timeless moment, stones, steel, macadam, planking, seemed to hang in midair; then slowly they separated, to shower down into the darkness below. Seconds later, as the dull roar of the disaster subsided, a vast cloud of dust billowed up from the depths.

Dean punched Novotny on the shoulder. "Gabotomi," he cried exultantly, "here we come!"

15

Anya-Kutu was a large and powerful man. He was not especially tall, but he was very wide, deep-chested, long-armed, and packed with hard muscle. He weighed, Mazzari reckoned, close to two hundred pounds.

The confrontation took place in a bizarre setting. Evidently the original Berber pasha had been both rich and influential; like all good Muslims, he had followed the Koran, which instructs the faithful to keep the exterior of their dwellings simple so as not to excite the envy of the less fortunate. The facade of the town's most important building was therefore no more than a line of sandstone blocks pierced by a central gateway and a number of arrowhead windows at the upper level. But inside—as Mazzari found when his captors dragged him in front of their chief—it was an exotic palace.

A twisting, high-ceilinged corridor still hung with priceless rugs led past ornate reception rooms to a kind of cloister flanked by delicate, richly chased Moorish arches on slender pillars. Beyond this was a courtyard. The leader of the Nya Nyerere was seated on a low divan covered in furs. He was wearing a pale cotton suit with a high-buttoned neck in the style favored by Jawaharlal Nehru and Chairman Mao, with five gold stars on each shoulder strap and no other sign of rank. The sunlight had long ago withdrawn from the courtyard, but jeweled colors still glowed softly across the mosaic floor, and the tiled surround of a fountain shone silver in the dusk.

Mazzari, still in his stolen costume, stood between an orange tree and a pomegranate with two armed guards
168

on either side. The officer who had arrested him lounged against a wall beside the archway through which they had entered. "I wonder, Sergeant Mazzari, what brings a renegade mercenary from Zaire into the new People's Republic of Gabotomi?" Anya-Kutu said. He was speaking in French, but his deep voice was accentless and assured.

"Since you seem to know so much, laddie," Mazzari answered, "you tell me." He had spent almost exactly twenty-four hours in a dungeon beneath the palace and his brain was teeming with questions. How had they known there was an intruder in town? How had they known which man to arrest? How on earth had they known his name? Even if the man he had knocked out with Daler had somehow bested Molony and gotten away to report the theft of his robes, that wouldn't explain the fact that his identity was known. Unless Molony had been captured too and they had tortured the truth from him. But no—there simply hadn't been time: he himself had been in town less than an hour when he was taken. And even if there had been time, the biggest question mark of all still remained: how come they had allowed a whole day and night to pass before he was brought before the rebel leader, before he was even interrogated?

There could be only two reasons. One—and this seemed likely—Anya-Kutu was an autocrat: he wished to be present himself at any interrogation and he had been out of town until now; two, they already knew everything there was to know, so that questioning him became a formality rather than a necessity. Mazzari could scarcely bring himself to believe this. Nevertheless, if he could needle the man enough, maybe he could sting him into providing answers to at least some of the questions puzzling him. It was with this in mind that he had replied in English, adopting a deliberately patronizing tone that was only just short of insulting.

But that particular ploy didn't work. "Speak English if
169

you wish," Anya-Kutu replied in that language. "We know all about you and your gang of jailbirds—in any language you like." He paused and smiled. His skin was darker than Mazzari's own. The whites of his eyes were in fact yellow flecked with red. "Perhaps that is singularly suitable for a conspiracy of . . . multinationals," he said.

"I think you've got hold of the wrong end of the stick somehow," Mazzari drawled. "If you're talking about the mineral—"

"Don't give me that! I tell you we know all about the capitalist lackey Dean and his . . ." Anya-Kutu snapped his fingers. "The paper, Major."

The officer pushed himself languidly upright and clicked his heels. "Yes, sir, General. Right here." He opened the flap of his breast pocket and produced a folded sheet covered with lines of typescript.

"*General?*" Mazzari laughed aloud. "I wouldn't even have given you a lance-jack's stripe if you'd been under me in the Congo," he jeered. "You're about as much a general as Idi Amin!"

"In democratic countries, officers are *elected* according to merit rather than appointed through nepotism," Anya-Kutu said calmly. "That is why the democratic People's Republics of Black Africa will always outgeneral and outfight the press-ganged conscripts of the imperialist powers. That is why in the end they must win."

"Like the People's Republic of Uganda, where all the children are starving to death? Like the failed People's Republic of Katanga? Like the oh-so-democratic Central African People's Republic with that nice liberal emperor and his golden throne? Don't make me laugh," Mazzari said. "I don't seem to remember the People's Republic of Angola—or Tanzania or Chad or Cameroon, for that matter—among the top-ten economic miracles recently."

"If certain states have yet to gain their maturity, that is because they were erroneously modeled on the Western capitalist system that has since proved itself a

170

corrupt and decadent failure." The rebel leader unfolded the paper the officer had handed him. "Yes . . . as I was saying . . . the hopeless task of this multinational lick-spittle, Dean: you have already lost three vehicles, three vessels, almost thirty men, and a substantial quantity of arms. You have been ambushed and the material you stole destroyed. There cannot be many of you left. And yet you presume . . . you have the audacity . . ." Anya-Kutu stood up and Mazzari saw with a quickening pulse that he must somewhere have touched a raw spot. "You dare to hope that this puny handful of hired jackals can best *me*! You have the effrontery to pit your rented skills against the natural talents of the chosen leader of the Nya Nyerere!"

Mazzari looked around him at the dark faces of the soldiers. He smiled superciliously. "It's perhaps not the best time to remind you, old boy," he said, "but the English have a little saying about the pot calling the kettle . . . er . . . black. Rude words about mercenaries hardly become the gang boss of a mongrel tribe from the Sudan who are trying to cash in on someone else's mineral resources, don't you agree?"

The insult struck home, he saw with glee. Anya-Kutu's face became suffused with blood. His eyeballs bulged. "The Nya Nyerere are racially untainted!" he shouted. "They are of pure West African blood! Centuries ago, my ancestors ruled this part of the world; they were the masters of the common Yoruba and Hauser dogs. It was only through the machinations of white European imperialist profiteers in the sixteenth century that they were exiled to the Sudan! We are the lost tribe of Benin, the true aristocrats of the Southern Atlas, and we are here to claim our heritage—"

"Hardly the party line, I should have thought," Mazzari observed. "Very poor Marx, as far as the comrades are concerned—Karl *or* Groucho. More like Adolf, if you ask me. Hitler, not Menjou."

"Silence! You are wasting my time with your stupid and puerile neologisms."

"And you," Mazzari said deliberately and insolently, "are wasting *my* time with all this crack-brained talk of domination by some upstart tribe of illiterate nomads. Why don't you face up to a bit of jolly old socialist realism for once—and go back down to the bottom of the pile, where you belong?"

Anya-Kutu reached up and struck him backhanded across the face. Mazzari was astonished by the power of the blow. His head rocked on his shoulders and his lower lip split as it was mashed against his teeth. He could feel the warm blood running down his chin. "Felicitations," he said thickly. "General."

"Hold him," Anya-Kutu said to the two nearest soldiers. They moved in and grabbed Mazzari's arms. Anya-Kutu bunched his right fist and hit the sergeant in the solar plexus. The punch traveled less than eighteen inches but it drove all the breath from Mazzari's body and paralyzed the muscles of his lungs for seconds. While he was still choking for air, Anya-Kutu slammed a murderous blow to the pit of his stomach. The soldiers relaxed their grasp. Big as he was, Mazzari dropped to the floor like a sack of coals, retching and squirming.

At a signal from the rebel leader, the soldiers kicked the fallen man's feet apart and the stood on his ankles to keep them spread. Anya-Kutu moved in, lifted his right leg, and launched the toe of his boot hard and accurately at Mazzari's groin. Mazzari's body arched up off the floor. Little whinnying sounds bubbled from his swollen lips.

Sometime later, through a red mist of pain, he looked up and saw the massively built tribal chieftain standing over him. There was white foam at the corners of the man's mouth. "I am not going to have you tortured," Anya-Kutu said. "There is nothing you could tell us that we don't know already. Later, I may hand you over to the women: they have interesting, traditional ways of

172

. . . amusing themselves. But first you must be taught to speak respectfully when you are addressing an officer of the Nya Nyerere. I think I will have you publicly flogged."

For the first time, despite the agony racking his body, Mazzari felt really afraid. The man was clearly a monomaniac and half-insane—but the voice rang with conviction. If all the details of the expedition really were an open secret, and Anya-Kutu had certainly given enough proof already that they might be, what hope could there be for any of them? What chance of success would Marc Dean have? What price would he himself have to pay for the information he had gained?

"There is also the matter of theft," Anya-Kutu was saying. "In a small community, it must be discouraged, it must be punished. The man whose robes you stole will make a complaint. His claim for retribution must be met." He nodded to the soldiers standing above Mazzari. "Take him away and cut off his hands."

As Mazzari was dragged to his feet, a black officer in leopard-spotted battle dress hurried into the courtyard. He spoke urgently to the major who had arrested Mazzari, and then the two of them approached Anya-Kutu. Mazzari was unable to hear what they said, but some of the chief's comments, spoken in explosive French, came to his ears. "*What!* . . . A fire? . . . On the *far* side of the ravine? . . . But I just got back from there . . . a conference with our friends down south: they promised to send reinforcements to deal with this mercenary trash. . . . Yes, tomorrow! . . . Send as many men as you can. The fire must be mastered."

There were more urgent gestures from the officers, more muttered explanations, and then: "Good God!" Anya-Kutu roared. "Shots, did you say? . . . Must I always be surrounded by imbeciles! Send *more* men: the bridge must be protected and the invaders annihilated! . . . That route *must* be kept open for the Polisario units."

Shaking with rage, he stamped off into the interior of the old palace, accompanied by the major. The officer who had brought the news looked across at Mazzari and his escort, rapping out some order in the local dialect. Two of the soldiers sprang to attention and marched over to join him; then the three of them wheeled about and left the courtyard. The two remaining men hustled Mazzari toward the passage that led to the cell where he had spent the night and all of that day.

There was one factor that nobody had allowed for. Despite the savage beating he had received, Mazzari's powers of recuperation were equal to his enormous strength. The stumbling walk that had him lurching against his jailers on the way to the passage was therefore contrived rather than a result of maltreatment. Just before they reached the courtyard wall, he fell to his knees. The two soldiers bent down and started to haul him back onto his feet. Mazzari's two great hands came up, one outside each black head, and cracked the temples together with such force that the men both dropped, temporarily stunned.

Mazzari sprang upright. There was no time for planning: he had to act intuitively, to play it by ear; the others could return at any moment. He picked up the nearest man by his heels, swung him around with vicious force, and cracked his head against the side of the fountain. The soldier went limp in Mazzari's grasp. He hurled him at the second man, who was trying to stagger to his feet, and the two of them crashed sprawling to the mosaic floor.

Mazzari hesitated. Should he take one of their guns? He decided not: an armed fugitive would be more noticeable than someone who could get lost in the crowd. Besides, the weapon would be an encumbrance. He had no desire to indulge in a show of force: only to get away. Kicking the machine pistols out of reach, he jumped up onto the rim of the basin surrounding the fountain. A canopy of tiles projected veranda-style from the walls around the courtyard. Mazzari leaped upward and grasped this half-roof, dragging himself up and then running across the flat sandstone surface beyond. Behind and below him he heard a shout—the racket of a machine pistol and a slug screeching off the sandstone into the dusk.

He raced across the roof and dropped to another at a lower level. Beyond the fortified walls he could see an orange glow in the sky above the forest. "Hah!" Mazzari's liquid, mellifluous laugh anointed the night air as he jumped down into a narrow alley at the back of the palace. Behind him he heard more shouts and the tramp of feet.

At the far end of the lane was the covered entrance to the *souks* that he had seen before. He was lost among the dense crowd thronging the street of shoemakers before the soldiers chasing him had reached the end of the alley. Mazzari ran across an open meat market loud with the buzzing of flies and took another long, narrow street thatched with palm fronds. Here were silversmiths sitting cross-legged in small booths, stamping out bracelets and collars and then filling the intricate inlays with molten metal poured from tiny iron crucibles suspended over braziers. Beyond, the alley forked left and right. Mazzari took the more crowded—a dark tunnel in which merchants displayed bales of silk and brightly colored cotton by the light of naphtha flares, for here in this warren of markets it was already night.

All around him there was a deafening jabber of voices speaking in alien tongues. Once he thought he heard the rough shouts of the soldiers, questioning. *A tall man, powerful . . . dressed thus-and-thus . . . he must have come this way. . . .* The press of townsfolk parted to allow the passage of a donkey loaded with piles of Moroccan rugs. Mazzari glanced over his shoulder. Before the crowd flowed together again he glimpsed the dull gleam of a helmet, the khaki of combat gear, but whether they

175

belonged to his pursuers or to soldiers simply marketing in their free time, he could not tell.

He plunged up a side alley, past brassware stalls and the workshops of men tooling leather. There were fewer people here. Around a corner he found a dark booth that was empty and ducked inside.

Mazzari sat panting below the sill of the deserted kiosk. Around him in the close, dark atmosphere was the sickly stench of half-cured hides. The search for an escaped prisoner, he reckoned, would be less intense than it might have been, now that Anya-Kutu and his officers were concerned with a forest fire and a possible attack from the far side of the ravine. Even so, it would be wise to wait until it was really night before he made another move. Over the noises of the crush in the markets he heard distant shouts of command, and then the roar of truck motors being gunned. Later, far away but unmistakable, there was the heavy thump of an explosion.

Mazzari's white teeth gleamed in the dark. If the first part of Dean's operation had been successfully concluded, it was time he was on his way.

Among the robed black tribesmen, the nomads and Arabs and veiled women in their brown gabardine djellabas, he had noticed a number of large blacks—they looked as if they might be Nubians—dressed only in white shifts, simple garments halfway between a loincloth and a sarong, that seemed the uniform of some servant class. Believing that nothing is more anonymous than near-nudity, Mazzari figured he would have a better chance of getting away disguised as one of these men than he would keeping the distinctive dress he had stolen. Stripping off the burnoose and djellaba and colored panels, he rolled them up and stuffed them beneath the sill, first ripping off enough white stuff to fashion himself a shift.

Once in the open, he felt himself as naked as though he had been undressed on stage in a spotlight. It took a great deal of determination for him to stride out through

176

the markets as unconcernedly as the other men as scant-
ily dressed as he. In fact none of the people still milling
around the stalls looked twice at him, and even a couple
of armed soldiers standing outside the entrance to the
souks gave him no more than a cursory glance.

Mazzari came to a wider street and paused to let a
boy on a bicycle swerve past, his bell trilling imperi-
ously. There were crowds here too, but they were all
moving toward the central square. He joined them, and
found that although most of the stalls were now closed,
there were still tumblers, snake charmers, and Arab
dancers working in the flickering naphtha light. Most of
the onlookers, however, were facing the outer wall of
the town, staring at the pulsating red glow illuminating
the sky to the south. Rumor and disquiet swept through
the crowd like wind in a field of wheat. When the words
were in Arabic, Mazzari caught some of the phrases.
*They say the bridge is down . . . infidels from the sea
. . . some kind of military attack. . . .*

A Land Rover moved slowly past the old mosque.
Beside the driver, Mazzari saw with surprise, there was
a beautiful European girl with short dark hair. Taking
advantage of the cover, he stepped to the far side of the
vehicle and walked with it as far as the corner. Then he
turned and hurried up a lane following the uphill curve
of the outer city wall. There were still sentries patrolling, he saw, but most of them, too, were gazing anx-
iously at the forest blaze. Toward the summit of the
granite boss on which the town was built, he found a
deserted stretch where the fortifications were not too
high. He scrambled up into the branches of a fig tree,
scurried across the battlements, and dropped a dozen
feet to the stony ground outside.

It took him two hours to work his way downhill to the
wadi, and then up through the scrub to the savannah
separating the town from the forest. His chest hurt, his
belly and genitals ached like hell, his ankles were
bruised and lacerated where the guards had stood on

177

them, and the soles of his feet were raw. But he had made it: he had obtained the information Dean wanted, and he had gotten away with it!

Moving warily through the dark, he rediscovered the trail that led to the ford, and returned to the fringe clearing where he had left the man whose robes he had taken.

He whistled and then called softly. There was no reply. Frowning, he made a circuit of the glade. Perhaps that careless bastard Molony had fallen asleep? Surely the Arab couldn't have died?

The glade was deserted. Draped over a thorn bush, he found the strips of cloth he had used to bind and gag the tribesman. But of the prisoner himself and the Irishman guarding him there was no sign: they had disappeared as completely as though they had never existed. And with them had gone his own clothes, his field glasses, and his gun.

V

End Game

16

Sean Hammer was astonished at the rapidity with which the fire he had started spread. Before the magnesium incendiary grenades had squandered their white-hot residue, all four piles of brushwood were blazing, and flames roared and crackled among the surrounding trees. Within minutes the fire had gathered speed and size, streaming eastward toward the desert, rolling towering columns of smoke away from the ravine; soon afterward the four separate centers coalesced into a single front. The smoke-filled air darkened. Trees in the path of the blaze swayed and threshed in a hot gale. Flocks of birds flew up into the sky, fighting for altitude above the billowing cloud.

By the time the first jeep appeared along the forest track leading from the viaduct, black-streaked flames were soaring into view high above the treetops. Hammer had withdrawn his men to a wooded gully which dipped down to the ravine. From here, beneath a dense screen of bushes, they watched the army trucks that followed, the squads of soldiers fruitlessly beating at the fringes of the conflagration with improvised brushwood flails, the attempts to fell enough trees in the distance to make a fire-break, and the eventual appearance of a water cannon. Before this could be used, Hammer gave the order to shoot. Half a dozen rounds from each of the automatic rifles was enough. The firefighters scattered in a panic, took cover behind their vehicles, fired blindly into the undergrowth. One of the Nya Nyerere lay dead in the center of the clearing; another dragged himself painfully to the far side of the jeep. The mercs crawled silently through the bushes. When they were a hundred yards from their original position, Hammer ordered another volley . . . and then sent Schneider and Wassermann halfway back to the first place to fire again. He himself advanced still farther and loosed off a magazine at the water cannon. Silver jets sprayed out from the punctured tank.

The officers in charge of the black tribesmen were in a quandary. Three more of their men had fallen. They appeared to be semisurrounded by hostile marksmen, and if they advanced in an attempt to flush out the snipers, they would be neglecting the fire they had been sent to suppress. It was in addition growing darker by the minute. The predusk light in the west had been overshadowed by smoke: the only illumination beneath the trees now was the pulsing glow of the fire itself, and this was diffused by a black rain of ash and burning embers trailing spirals of smoke as they drifted to the forest floor.

Even behind the receding blaze, the heat was becoming insupportable: a lung-choking assault that tightened an iron band around the chest and forced sweat from every pore. Two more truckloads of soldiers arrived, and almost immediately afterward, Hammer heard the thumping detonation of the bridge going up. Before the new arrivals had disembarked, he crawled along the floor of the gully, signaling his men to withdraw. They had done what they had come to do. A sizable proportion of Anya-Kutu's forces—and any reinforcements that might be coming from the south—were now marooned on the wrong side of the ravine. It was up to the mercs to rejoin Dean and help him storm the town before these troops could find another way back.

They reassembled at the head of the shallow valley. The fire was now a frightening thing. Even the unflappable Hammer was a little awed by what he had started. A hot wind bitter with the stench of charred vegetation plastered their clothes to their bodies. They had to shout to make themselves heard over the roar and growl of the inferno that was consuming the forest. "She sure is goin' good." Dennis chuckled. "That's one camp-fire don't need no songs to encourage her!"

"What's that?" Hammer was frowning.

"I said that fire took off real good," Dennis called.

"Maybe too good." The nut-faced little Ulsterman sniffed the air. He tilted back his head and looked at the sky. Through the black lacework of branches he could see that the mountain of smoke stretching from farther back in the forest had doubled its height, leaning out into the sulfurous glow above them. "I'm thinkin' maybe the wind is veerin'. Happens sometimes she follows the sun around. The met guys say it means good weather to-morrow."

"I like a man he should be optimistic," Wassermann said. "You are saying that if we get caught in our own trap maybe, the fire it could change direction and we would be in *shtook*: is that it?"

"Yea," Hammer said. "That's exactly what I mean."

"But just the same, if our bodies should be inciner-ated, it will be fine weather for the cremation?"

"We've got to get back to that trail, cross it, and split like greased bloody lightning," Hammer said.

"*Now* he tells us!" complained Wassermann.

The forest floor was not flat. Beyond the head of the gully it dipped again and then rose to a crest several hundred yards away. As they watched, the wall of smoke hanging over this rise leaned out from the slope and the fire front appeared suddenly over the ridge—a long wavering orange glare that silhouetted the tossing branches of jungle trees. "By Christ! She is changed direction! You are right!" Schneider shouted.

Following Hammer, they turned and began running through the woods toward the trail. The angry murmur of the fire had turned into a menacing and terrifying crackle that drowned the distant noises of the black troops and grew louder every moment. Behind them,

183

outriders of flame spilled downhill like a lava flow, spouting smoke and sparks above the swaying foliage.

They crossed the trail a quarter of a mile away from the Nya Nyerere trucks and plunged down a slant of land that led toward the ravine. The searing wind scorching the backs of their necks blew harder. Beside the trail a giant evergreen that had started to smoke burst abruptly into flame and burned like a torch. Ahead of the fleeing mercenaries, sparks and embers floated down, plunging through the branches like bright, exotic birds to replace the real birds that had flown in panic earlier.

There was a clearing above the lip of the ravine. Beyond it the land dropped away to a trail, dimly seen in the darkness, that sloped gently across the face of the bluff toward the ford several bends of the river away. Thankfully, they flung themselves over the edge and rolled down to the pathway as the blaze approached the open space.

The ruins of a stone building—perhaps an ancient lookout post—stood on the far side of the clearing. The fire was already there, bending around it like the fingers of a hand to squeeze black smoke and then flame from the empty windows. The walls crumbled and collapsed. As voracious as a cloud of white-hot locusts, the fire swept on, and the trees, like outnumbered soldiers on a battlefield, began to fall.

Hammer and his men arrived at the arms cache on the far side of the ford soon after Dean and Novotny and some time before Mazzari. The big Congolese sergeant was just completing his story—and the account of his amazement at the disappearance of Molony and the tribesman—when the two men who had been sent back to the stranded carrier for its cargo of cannon shells returned. They were exhausted by the difficulties of the journey, the last part of it in darkness, and by the weight of the clumsy 73mm shells.

"I guess you guys could do with a slug," Dean said. "Most of us could, at that. It's been kind of a rugged day!" He produced another bottle of their limited supply of liquor and handed it around. "At least you got the goddamn shells. I was afraid maybe some roving band of nomads would have picked the wagon clean!"

"They didn't take no shells," Goldsmith said. "But they sure as hell took a good look!"

Dean stared at him. "What are you saying?"

"Someone had been there before us," Daler said. "All the bloody branches had been pulled aside, hatches left open, that kind of thing."

"But what the hell for, if they didn't take . . . ?"

"It seems they used the radio," Goldsmith said. "Whoever they were."

"The *radio*?" Once more Dean stared at the two men. Each of the MICV's had been equipped with a short-wave radio, of the normal kind used by military commands, but since they had never lost sight of one another—and were in any case supposed to keep a low profile—he had paid them no mind, had in fact never considered them at all.

"Some character got into the carrier just for that," Daler said. "Someone in a hurry, I guess. Or that's the way it looked. The ant was still full-length. The batteries were flat, but the set was still switched on to 'Send.' "

"The aerial was extended? But what in . . . ?" Dean's eyes widened. He smashed a fist against his own thigh. "By Christ!" he said. "*Molony!*"

"Molony?"

"Yes, Molony!" Dean turned to Mazzari, huge and dark above his pale shift. "Edmond, you said this guy Anya-Kutu knew all about us, knew everything that had happened, how many we were, and all that jazz?"

"That's right," Mazzari said.

"And he also knew you were coming, and when? He even knew what gear you'd be wearing, right?"

"Absolutely."

"Then it's got to be Molony," Dean said.

"What has? I'm afraid I'm not with you, old boy."

"The leak, the spy, the lousy double-crossing bastard, the son of a bitch who's been selling us out all along the line!"

"I don't get it," Hammer said. "Why would a man—?"

"I don't know why," Dean interrupted, "but look at the evidence. Who's been picking holes in every plan we made, ever since we started? Who's been raising every goddamn difficulty he can, trying to put a spoke in the wheel at every turn? Fucking Molony."

"Okay, so the guy's a pain in the ass. But that don't—"

"Look," Dean cut in. "Details of the shipwrecks and stuff—the guy Mazzari saw could have been wised up on that by someone in Halakaz. But the ambush and the carrier snafu—nobody'd know about them until *after* they'd happened, okay? And they're so recent that the info could only have been relayed one way: by radio."

"Yeah. Okay. But what has that—?"

"That's what the carrier radio was used for. Obviously. But Mazzari's sightseeing trip wasn't planned: it was off the top of his head. Nobody could have known he was going—or what he was going to wear—until after the guy whose clothes he took was zapped. From then on down, any one of the three could have ratted: Daler, Molony, or Weisenberger. But only Molony could have done that *and* used the radio: only Molony had the opportunity to do both those things and release the tribesman. My guess is that he set him free and made it into Gabotomi the moment Mazzari had left and the other two had started back here."

"I guess so," Hammer still sounded dubious. "But I don't figure the radio bit. How could he . . . ?"

"Who was last in line when we made it here from the carrier? Who was missing and didn't show for a half-hour? Who came up with some damn fool story about cramp in his arm to explain his absence?"

"That's right," Mazzari said slowly. "And you think...?"

186

"I think he waited until the rest of us were out of sight among the trees, dumped the ammunition boxes right there, and hightailed it back to the carrier to make his lousy call. After that he left everything the way it was because he had to catch up as quick as he could. He never thought anyone would go back to the carrier and find out."

"And that's why we've been expected all along the line?"

"It figures too well not to be true," Dean said.

"The dirty, treacherous fucker!" Hammer exploded. "Now, why would a man do a thing like that? Would you tell me that?"

"We'll find out," Dean promised him grimly.

Before Mazzari's story and the report from Daler and Goldsmith had dovetailed to expose Molony's treachery, Dean had made his plans for the attack on Gabotomi the following day. But the moon didn't rise until almost midnight; it would be impossible to lug all the arms and equipment they had along the forest trail in total darkness; they would therefore have to take what rest they could during the first part of the night, transporting their supplies and deploying them around the city defenses in a single sustained operation culminating in the predawn assault Dean envisaged. "And don't think," he told them as they finished the last of the food ration they had carried, "that it's gonna be easy! You guys'll have to work your asses off even to get the gear in place in time. After that, the attack itself should be a piece of cake. Now, you got three hours before we move. I want every man resting and one-hundred-percent relaxed during those three hours. Get some shut-eye if you can . . . and we'll have a final drink before we go."

Van der Lee had offset the pain and the boredom of his lonely vigil during their absence by making an inventory of their armory. As the men settled down around the cave to try to sleep, Dean studied the scrap

187

of paper again in the feeble glow of his pocket flash-light. He read:

Kalashnikov AK-47 automatic 7.62mm rifles .... Eight
5,000 rounds ammunition in two boxes; also cartridge belts
Armalite automatic 5.56mm rifles .... Three
1 box containing approx. 280 rounds ammunition
only
Trilux telescopic night sights for rifles .... Six
Antitank rocket launcher RPG-7 .... Two
12 five-lb. rocket grenades; 2 NSP-2 infrared night
sights
Uzi 9mm submachine guns (limited ammunition) .. Six
One 3-inch mortar with 9 grenades
Twenty rounds 73mm cannon shells salvaged from
carriers; Primacord; detonators; Dardick handguns
(limited ammunition)

With that amount of offensive material, he reckoned—
even with the handful of men available—that he might
just be able to pull it off. It would be a gamble, it would
be tough, it would be damned dangerous . . . but by
Christ that was the way he liked it! Bucking the odds,
after all, was what made life worth living for Marc
Dean.

In theory, the plan he had worked out, audacious
though it was, should work—given that Mazzari's report
on what he had seen of the defenses was accurate and
that Dean's own estimation of the number of men marooned on the far side of the ravine was correct. Those
two factors were imponderables, as subject to variation
as the supplies cataloged by Van der Lee were finite.
Even less predictable, of course, was the human factor—
the way men would behave under fire, how they would
react to fear and pain and stress. If it wasn't for that . . .

He glanced at the Dutchman's list once more. How
much easier life would be if human qualities and human

emotions could be as precisely evaluated as that! How different his own life would have been if he could have ordered it the way he ordered a successful military operation! Switching off the flashlight, he crossed his arms behind his head and lay back, thinking of the wife who had left him.

17

The last time was at Christmas, only a few weeks before Dean met Saul Jarvys and started to plan the Gabotomi operation. It had been snowing in Boston. When Samantha met him at the airport, the field between the runways was unbroken white and the Mustang bumped over ruts of frozen slush maneuvering out of the parking lot. But between Plymouth and Barnstable, dark earth began to show through the drifts, and on the turnpike circling the south of Cape Cod Bay, the roadway was dry enough for her to switch off the windshield wipers.

Samantha lived in a clapboard cottage in the village of Bardfield, near Orleans, Massachusetts. It stood on a slight rise, looking through a line of trees across the thirty-mile sound to Sagamore and Plymouth. Beyond the elms in back of the big garden, the land dropped toward the wild Atlantic shoreline, where Dean loved to walk in winter, watching gannets and guillemots dive into the whitecaps while the wind rustled ghosts of sea pinks and goldenrod from the dead leaves at his feet. They had bought the place as a summer retreat, but since the divorce Samantha had chosen to live there the whole year around. Their son, Patrick, still went to kindergarten in Bardfield.

It was not quite dark when they arrived. Dean had legal access to the child one weekend every month, but since he was so seldom in the United States now, they had agreed that on his rare visits he should simply come to the cottage instead of taking Patrick away as he had a right to do. It would give the boy at least the illusion of some kind of family existence; the parents were still, after all, quite friendly.

It was crazy, Dean thought, studying her cool profile as she braked the car to a halt on the graveled driveway, that they should no longer be more than friends. What the hell had happened? Wasn't absence supposed to make the heart grow fonder? Not his kind of absence, he knew. She had told him often enough.

There was a holly wreath around the brass knocker on the front door. Inside, Christmas decorations gleamed silver, red, and blue around the tinseled tree beneath the oak beams in the hallway. After the ecstatic greetings had burned themselves out a little, Dean went into the garden. The sun, fiery and immense, was about to lower itself behind the distant Massachusetts coastline; from the low-lying tip of the cape to the north, a tide of gold flowed shoreward, silhouetting a fishing boat beyond the highway linking Orleans and Provincetown. As he watched, the color drained from the sea, leaving it steel-gray under a limpid green sky. Walking back up a stone-flagged path strewn with autumn leaves, he could hear the grumble of breakers along the Atlantic coast.

The sitting room was all chintz, with a log fire; the roses he had brought from Milan were reflected in the polished top of a bureau. Samantha stood by a table piled with gift-wrapped packages. She was wearing a purple jumpsuit with black patent boots, and her honey-colored hair was gathered at the nape of her neck by a wide black bow. She was, Dean thought, the most extraordinarily complex person. The garment she had chosen to wear, for instance, covered her to the wrist, the ankle, and the neck. It scarcely touched her anywhere. And yet, in its subtle emphasis on the swell of breast and hip, its hint of concave sculpturing elsewhere, it was sexier than all the strip shows in Europe put together. The suit epitomized her attitudes to physical love: she viewed the body and all its functions with a reserve and a delicacy that reminded him in its fastidiousness of a cat's—yet when she was aroused, and she turned on easily, she could be the most ardent, the most

191

wanton and abandoned and lascivious woman he had ever met. Perhaps that was why she had always appealed to the polarity in his own nature. He had known her since she was five years old, when her father, an Air Force colonel, and Dean Senior were buddies and neighbors; he had loved her since her sophomore year at Vassar.

He had thought she loved him, until the quarrels began. And they too were in a sense due to that same polarity in his nature . . . although to Dean the stinging words he would always remember applied to somebody else and were pronounced by a stranger. *An overgrown schoolkid romanticism . . . total inability to relate to the adult world . . . irresponsible and selfish . . . a restlessness derived from a sense of inadequacy and a banal need to prove . . . ruthless and cynical approach that killed any chance of a balanced and caring life* . . . He knew them all by heart. But he still couldn't see it. They had so much in common. They laughed at the same things. So if he was often away, shouldn't that make the time they did spend together more precious? Above all, they had made a baby together: they had Patrick. Wasn't he more important than either of them?

Precisely, Samantha had said. And it was because of that that she refused to bring him up with a permanent killer in the house . . . or at least a man whose income depended on killing and the means to kill.

The boy was now a sturdy four-year-old with pale blond hair and hazel eyes. "How is he getting along?" Dean asked that Christmas Eve when the excited child had at last been persuaded to go to bed.

"He's okay. He's bright, and he seems happy enough."

"And sports? Is he any good at games?"

"Matt, he isn't even five years old! There's plenty of time for that—"

"You want to get his hair cut," Dean said.

"Actually," Samantha said, "I *don't* want to get his hair cut. I like his hair the way it is."

192

"It's hell for a kid to be tagged as a sissy. You know that."

"Matt, be your *age*! They were wearing it shoulder-length ten years ago. It's not so exaggerated now, thank goodness, but—"

"I think you should get it cut."

"I don't want my son to look like a pint-size West Point cadet!" Samantha flashed.

"Like a soldier," Dean said. "Yes. I see." He walked stiffly to the drinks cabinet and poured himself a generous shot of bourbon.

There was embarrassment before the ritual unwrapping of gifts on Christmas morning. Dean slept in an annex at the rear of the cottage, where the sound of the ocean sighed in through the open window at night. He was drinking his second cup of coffee when Patrick said, "Mommy, why don't you and Daddy sleep in the same room? Gavin Ewart's mommy and daddy sleep in the same *bed*! Gavin told me."

"Your mommy and I both snore," Dean said gravely, "so we keep each other awake if we're in the same room."

Samantha repressed a smile. The boy buried his nose in a glass half full of milk. And then suddenly the pink face was lifted, the white mustache pouted. "But, *Daddy* . . . if you're *both* awake, how can you—?"

"Wipe your mouth and we'll see what Santa Claus has brought," Samantha said.

What Santa Claus had brought reflected accurately the differing attitudes of the two parents. Because the child showed signs of artistic interest, Samantha had given him watercolors, a bird book and a flower book, cassettes of *Peter and the Wolf* and a selection from Walt Whitman for his tape recorder, and a story about a cat from outer space with illustrations that stood up when you opened the pages. Dean's contribution was an elaborately modeled medieval castle, complete with turrets, drawbridge, and boxes of knights in armor. There was also a miniature baseball catcher's glove, a set of World War II pursuit planes, and a remote-controlled Centurion tank which could climb over cushions or books and emitted sparks from its turret gun as it moved.

The polarity in Dean's own makeup also showed in his choice of gifts for Samantha. Nothing personal, he had decided; no perfume or jewelry or blouses from Pucci. That might look as if he were trying to presume—cashing in on the fact that she allowed him to stay there. He was not a subtle man, but neither was he undiscriminating. He had bought her a Meissen conversation piece, a group of porcelain figures by Joachim Kändler the elder, dated 1752 and graced a hundred years later by the addition of an exquisite music box. The instrument, secreted beneath the flowered plinth supporting the group, played the first of the Handel variations known as *The Harmonious Blacksmith*. "It's beautiful, Matt," Samantha said. "Beautiful!"

And then, later: "Darling, you're sweet, but I do wish . . . I mean, *why* do you have to give Patrick all these macho war games? He loves you enough: you don't have to prove anything, you know."

"Boy's got to grow up to be a man, hasn't he?" Dean said. "It doesn't do to be too different from the other kids."

"But he *is* different; he's got talent. He has a terrific eye for color. He's painted the most unusual scenes—for his age, I mean. I must show you . . ."

Dean held up his hand. He was listening. From the next room they could hear the childish treble: "Wheeeeeeeel! Boom! *Boom!* . . . *POW!* . . . The tank's knocked over all the knights!"

"He doesn't sound as though he's a hundred percent into painting right now," Dean said dryly.

"Of course not. He's playing with those things, not because of what they are, but because *you* gave them to

194

him; they came from his adored father, his hero figure."

"Bullshit. He's playing with them because he likes them."

"If you'd given him a loom, he'd be weaving." Samantha sounded bitter.

"Look, honey, let's not make this thing into a melodrama. But Patrick mustn't turn into a softie: he has to grow up and compete, to take his place in a man's world."

"I'd rather think he was to take his place in a world of *people*," Samantha said.

Dean sighed. "Little boys always play bang-you're-dead. They always have and I guess they always will. The shrinks say it's a useful safety valve: it gets rid of a whole pile of aggression that would otherwise make them even more difficult to handle! In any case," he added, "they grow out of it."

"Some of them don't," Samantha said. "Not ever." She turned and left the room.

In the afternoon, Dean took the boy into the garden. There was damp in the air, and the waves on the Atlantic shore were louder. They were secret agents trying to steal Important Documents from the annex unseen. There was a chase, with a lot of shooting, through the shrubbery. After that Dean showed him how to catch with the glove. They wrestled, giggling, on the wet grass. Then Dean said, "Judo, karate, kung-fu—that's for the movies. It doesn't work out in real life. But a guy has to know how to defend himself, even to attack if necessary. He has to know how to use his fists. Get up now, son. I'm going to give you your first boxing lesson."

Five minutes later, Patrick ran into the kitchen, where his mother was carving slices of cold turkey. He was crying. "Daddy hit me!" he sobbed.

It was better in the evening. Patrick had gone to sleep, exhausted with excitement. The sitting room was comfortable and homey, with firelight playing on the drawn curtains and rain drifted in from the ocean now pattering against the windows. Dean nursed a highball and looked at his ex-wife. She was staring at the burning logs. Her lips were parted, and the wavering light cast shifting expressions over her features. If he was such bad news, Dean wondered why she had troubled to change into a long-sleeved black organza dress whose semitransparent top shadowed the slopes of her breasts so enticingly. He knew what her answer would be: she was doing it for herself, not for him; she felt good when she knew she looked good. All the same . . . she was wearing no bra. Dulled highlights slid across the satin slip beneath the organza as the soft flesh moved with her breathing. He could see her nipples outlined against the dark material. Dean thought he read the message right: as a mother, she rejected him because of what she considered his bad influence on their child, but as a woman, she still wanted him. He cleared his throat.

"Sam," he said. "Darling. What happened to us?"

"You know what happened," Samantha said. She was still staring into the fire. "You happened. Or rather, your job did."

"I am the way I am," Dean said. "I haven't changed. I can't change, and nobody can change me. Trying to alter folks—that's the quickest way to foul up a relationship. You know that."

"Yes," Samantha said sadly. "I know that."

"But you always knew the way I was, the way I felt. Why should it suddenly—?"

"Oh, Matt!" she interrupted. "You didn't have to change yourself, only the way you lived. Why couldn't you have stayed with Eastern Electronics? You had a good job there. You had prospects. With my father on the board and your own talents, you could have—"

"Oh, sure. All systems go, and the green light for automatic promotion. A raise every year, a vice-presidency at forty-five, weekends at the country club and golf to keep you amused when you retire. Not for me!"

"A lot of people might think that a better life than

being a traveling salesman," Samantha said. "A door-to-door apologist for the armaments industry. You didn't have to go back on the way you felt."

"Where do you think nine-tenths of Eastern Electronics' business comes from? Those rockets aren't designed to ferry businessmen between London and Paris and New York. No, it isn't that—there was no challenge at Eastern, don't you see, honey? There was no competition, nothing and nobody to beat. A guy has to have something in life that he must whip . . . or at any rate my kind of guy does. You used to play great tennis, Sam. Surely you understand about the challenge?"

She stood up and rested one hand on the chimneypiece. "Of course I understand. But, Matt . . . with me, tennis, it's the game itself that matters, not whether you win it or not."

"That's what I *mean*!" He moved closer to her. They had both drunk quite a lot. "Eastern was like tennis with nobody on the other side of the net, don't you see? There has to be an opponent; there must be a problem to solve."

Samantha turned toward him. Her eyes were in shadow but the firelight gleamed on her lower lip. "Some people think the toughest problem of all is to make a happy relationship, that the hardest opponent to beat is yourself. But of course, if you don't think your family is worth the effort . . ."

"Worth the effort?" Dean's voice was suddenly husky. "Sam, darling, you're the most . . . you're the only . . . Jesus, you're so lovely! So beautiful! You're the only woman for me in the whole damned world. You know that. You always have been: there's never been anybody else. I . . . Christ, I love you, honey. I'd give anything for us to be together again."

"But you wouldn't give *up* anything. Maybe you should try a little harder," she said in a low voice.

And then suddenly his arms were around her. He could feel the whole soft length of her against his own

197

lean hardness. Her fingers cradled the back of his neck, and her warm, winy breath played on his face. She closed her eyes. Their lips touched, opened, clung.

Dean could sense a muscle flickering, trembling, against the hand he had clamped around her waist. He moved the hand up to cup one of the breasts smashed against his chest. Through the filmy material he could feel the nipple hard against his thumb. "Oh, darling," he groaned.

She drew back her head and stared at him, wet-lipped. "Matt . . . ?"

With a wordless exclamation, Dean broke free. He stooped, plunging an arm behind her knees. With the other supporting her shoulders, he picked her up bodily and carried her upstairs to her bedroom. Wide-eyed, she stared up at him from the bedcovers. "Now," Dean panted, "we shall find out . . . about . . . good relations." He unbuckled the heavy leather belt at his waist.

The organza skirt was bunched around her hips. Like an iron bar clicking into place across the poles of a magnet, their bodies homed in on each other, his weight pinning her to the bed. His fingers clawed into the soft curves of flesh below her waist. Her hands were trapped between them, clenching on his loins. They kissed again.

Dean leaned his weight on his elbows, tearing open the fasteners at the top of the dress. And then his hands were on the warm, softly shifting mounds of her breasts, the nipples still now against his palms. His breath hissed in through his teeth as she unzipped his fly and he felt the cool grasp of her fingers wrap around him. The flesh was cool too beneath his knuckles, his hooked fingers tearing at the waistband of her nylon tights.

Samantha shifted her position and he slid down between her thighs. Small cries escaped from her throat. There was heat now and moisture and the graze of hair . . . and then all at once the tights had gone and as she guided him he was easily, scaldingly, wonderfully inside her.

198

Forceful and compulsive, his need drove him on with a savage tenderness, softly battering her against the mattress each time her strong young hips arched up to meet his thrusts.

For a timeless moment there was nothing but the hot clasp of flesh on flesh and the thundering of the blood. Then the pulse in the curve of her throat hammered wildly under his lips as she clutched him to her fiercely in the throes of her release and Dean felt his own climax shoot him up among the stars.

Later, lying side by side on the bed, she opened her eyes and there was a wetness glistening on her cheeks. "Oh, Matt," she whispered, "if only—"

Patrick ran noisly into the room. He had woken up. "Mommy! Daddy! You said I could get up and watch the late movie as a special treat! The man on television said it starts in just a minute."

Samantha sat up with an exclamation of annoyance. "Patrick! I already switched the set over to the right channel for *Dumbo*. In any case . . ." She glanced at the clock on the night table, smoothing her hair. "It doesn't start for another quarter of an hour. Be a good boy. Run along back to your—"

"I don't want to watch a silly old elephant!" the boy shouted. "I don't want to see *Dumbo*. Daddy promised we'd watch the war movie! He said he'd explain . . ." The small mouth crumpled and he began to cry. "I wanna watch the movie with Daddy."

"*Matt!*"

"I promised him," Dean said wretchedly. And that was the end of that reconciliation.

Lying on the forest floor in southeastern Morocco, Dean tried for the hundredth time to visualize his wife's outraged and furious face. Why was it that all he could see now were the features of the blond girl he had picked up outside the central station in Brussels?

18

Wassermann fired the first shot in Dean's attack on Gabotomi. He was lying beneath a thorn tree on a slope
above the wadi circling the boss on which the town was
built. The waning moon had sunk out of sight and it was
quite dark. He could just make out the road rising to the
main gate, a paler streak against the blackness of the
granite. But as soon as he raised the Armalite and
looked through the rubber eyepiece of the Trilux night
sight, his field of fire was dramatically illuminated. The
red Triphium light ray showed him the rough masonry
of the battlemented gatehouse and two men standing
guard behind the parapet. He estimated the range at 440
yards. Adjusting the sight, he eased himself into a more
comfortable position, elbows resting on a flat stone, and
drew a bead on the nearest guard. The crossed wires in
the sight settled between the shoulders of the magnified
image. Wassermann took up the first pressure and held
his breath. He moved the barrel of the rifle fractionally
and squeezed the trigger.

The coughing report of the Armalite sounded shock-
ingly loud in the predawn silence. The image jerked
abruptly out of sight. Wassermann heard a distant shout.
The gun was on single-shot. Unhurriedly he altered its
position until the crossed wires centered on the second
man, who stood in what seemed an attitude of petrified
astonishment. He squeezed the trigger again.

The second guard fell. And at once pandemonium
broke loose. From behind and above Wassermann, automatic fire from the two remaining Armalites and all
eight Kalashnikovs ripped out from the edge of the

savannah as Dean and his men opened hostilities in the first phase of the operation. Three hundred yards away, Novotny lay on his face on the far side of the wadi and touched off a length of Primacord. He had been creeping about beneath the walls since three o'clock, positioning the score of cannon shells salvaged from the carriers and arranging a cunning system of linked fuse and detonators. "It'll do nothing in terms of tactics," Dean had said. "But it may fool that son of a bitch Molony if he's advising them, because he won't know we have them and it'll sound like a goddamn artillery barrage!" As Novotny scrambled back to rejoin the others, the 73mm shells exploded one after the other in a crescendo of sound that cracked the ears and momentarily lit up the walls with flashes of yellow fire.

Inside the town, alarm bells were shrilling and a cacophony of frightened voices threatened to drown the military commands and the disciplined tramp of feet. Several sentries on the outer wall had been downed by the mercs using Trilux sights. Now they had taken cover and were beginning to return the fire. Dean shouted an order; his men hurried to their positions for the second phase of the assault.

This, in combination with the first, was designed to give the impression that the attacking force was much larger than it was, and perhaps, again, to gull the traitor Molony—who knew very well the strength of Dean's unit—into the belief that they had received some kind of reinforcement.

Phase One had been intended to eliminate the sentries, spread confusion, and make the defenders believe that they faced cannon fire and a sizable infantry attack. Phase Two, Dean hoped, would confirm that belief, widen the apparent sector of invasion, and—most important—mask the fact that the "cannon barrage" was a one-shot operation. Tactically, its aim was to smash down the heavy gates beneath the entrance arch and if possible silence the two twenty-five-pounder field guns

201

on the belvederes each side of the gatehouse. Only then could the third phase, actual penetration of the town, be attempted. Dean's plan was predicated on the hope that this point would be reached before daybreak.

Everything, therefore, depended on speed and surprise. Hammer and Dennis raced down to the topmost gravel terrace with one of the bazookas and took up position behind a boulder. Kurt Schneider and Wassermann ran a hundred yards wide of Dean's other flank with the second RPG-7. Behind them, Daler and Weisenberger set up the mortar among the trees on the fringe of the forest. Van der Lee, whom Dean and Mazzari had insisted on carrying up the trail from the ford, was seated on the ground beside them, ready to fuse the grenades. The rifles were wedged or lashed into place at the limit of the savannah. They were all set on semiautomatic, and Furneux and Goldsmith had been detailed to run up and down between them, firing sporadic bursts and recharging the ammunition belts to maintain the illusion that the men who had fired the original volley were still in place.

Mazzari and Dean himself slid down the stony slope to join Novotny at the lip of the wadi. They were carrying Uzi submachine guns, with an extra weapon for the Pole.

The signal for the start of Phase Two was a combined burst from the three of them, aimed at the gunners on the belvedere nearest the forest. "And when you get the signal, don't all open up at once," Dean had insisted at the final briefing. "Tease it out some, okay? One bazooka followed immediately by another, with a mortar shell bursting half a second later, is a hell of a lot more effective than a triple explosion at the same time. From the psychological point of view, I mean. Besides, it makes the little we have last longer!"

As the ripping detonations of the three Uzis split the air, the rifles above and behind began to fire again, and the machine-gunners on the belvedere started to reply,

202

hosing lead down into the ravine and then up toward the tropical grasses opposite the city wall. Hammer put his eye to the infrared night sight on the bazooka and aimed at the crack between the vast doors barring the city gateway. There was a shattering roar and a blast of flame from the rear of the tube as the five-pound rocket grenade took off. It streaked across the wadi at three hundred feet per second, increasing its speed three times as the rocket motor cut in and stabilizer fins opened. Hammer's aim was a trifle off—low and to the right. The grenade burst in the angle made by the ramp leading up to the gates and the wall of the arch. Fragments of rock were still clattering to the ground when the Schneider-Wassermann bazooka fired three hundred yards away to the right, followed almost at once by the flat thump of the mortar. Both were aiming at the platform below the belvedere where Mazzari had seen the first of the field guns. The rocket grenade exploded on the parapet, smashing a hole in the fortification and knocking out one of the machine guns; the mortar bomb overshot and pulverized the roof of a building behind.

Dennis had fixed a second grenade on Hammer's RPG-7. This time the Ulsterman's aim was correct. The flaming missile struck the center of the left-hand gate, blasting it to matchwood and blowing the other off its medieval hinges. Over the crackle of small-arms fire, Hammer heard the mortar and the second bazooka loose off their next rounds. He ducked out from behind the boulder and ran, followed by Dennis carrying the remaining grenades, to one of the lower terraces. For the flashes of fire in the darkness had now given the Nya Nyerere gunners a target to fire at. From the platforms two hundred feet on either side of the gatehouse, orange flame belched against the underside of a smoke pall hanging over the battlements. At a range of little more than a quarter-mile, the bellow of the twenty-five-pounders, the scream of the shells, and the crump of the explosions made a single continuous noise. Shells burst on the slope, in among the grasses, and perilously near the boulder where Hammer and Dennis had been sheltering, showering them with earth and rock chips on the terrace below.

From the center of the town, a green Verey light soared skyward, revealing the whole depression in its livid glow as the flare floated gently back to earth. Men were shouting above the gun platforms now. Whistles blew. The twenty-five pounders fired again. And again. And again. The slopes below the savannah became a temporary inferno of flame, concussion, and flying steel.

Dean had assumed they would have flares, and he had allowed for it. His men had been instructed to hold their fire immediately if the terrain was illuminated, to minimize the chance of the gunners sighting a target. The barrage in fact destroyed two of the Kalashnikovs that were jammed into tree forks—fortunately while Goldsmith and Furneux were at the far end of the line; the Canadian was blown off his feet by the blast, but apart from a gashed wrist, was uninjured; and Dean's own group was bruised and shaken by the flying chips of rock from a near-miss in the wadi.

The moment the green light wavered and died, the mercs opened fire again. They had precious little in the way of high explosive—nine mortar bombs and a dozen rocket grenades to be shared between the two bazookas. Dean's instructions to the bazooka crews allowed them to fire four only in the initial stage, keeping the final two for the actual assault. The mortar was to keep firing at the gun emplacements until all the grenades had been used.

A second Verey light spiraled up into the dark. Before the shell burst into brilliance, Hammer and Schneider had fired their third and fourth rockets and three more mortar shells had whined into the town. As the green flare brightened, they could see the damage the infrared sights had allowed them to inflict. Hammer had scored a direct hit on a personnel carrier full of soldiers that was

204

crawling over the shattered gates. Beyond the smoking mass of tangled metal, men scrambled in panic over slants of rubble brought down by the remaining grenades. A mud-walled building had collapsed, and there was a column of smoke, flame, and sparks whirling upward from the savaged interior. Most important, Daler and Weisenberger had gotten the elevation, range, and direction of the mortar right. The emplacement nearest the forest was in ruins; the field gun had been knocked out; and both machine-gun crews had been killed.

There were four mortar bombs left. Weisenberger tried for the emplacement on the far side of the wrecked gateway. But the platform was too far around the curve of the wall for him to get a good visual, and the grenade burst harmlessly on the granite below the fortifications. The next exploded somewhere beyond the gatehouse: they saw the flash reflected on the walls of buildings, but they couldn't see its effect. "Too bad they don't have night sights for these babies," Weisenberger said to Van der Lee. "We would be a fuckin' sight more efficient if we could get to see what we was doin'!" He turned to Daler. "We got two left. What say you hump 'em over to that outcrop? You know, where the trees come down to the edge of the bluff above Schneider's bazooka."

Daler nodded and scooped up the last two grenades. He ducked to avoid a shower of earth and splintered wood as a near-miss from the remaining twenty-five-pounder erupted among the trees, and then ran toward the bluff. "We should see the bastards direct from over there," Weisenberger said. They were the last words he ever uttered.

In his eagerness to score, he ignored Dean's instructions and began shifting the mortar tube before the light from the flare had died away. The movement, dimly seen among the trees, attracted the operator of the weapon that had caused Dean the most concern when he received Mazzari's report on the defenses. This was the jeep-mounted TOW missile. It was parked in a square high up on the hill behind the wall. As Weisenberger moved out from the trees clasping his mortar, the four-foot, forty-pound projectile streamed out from its launcher, spitting white-hot gases between its guiding wires.

It was fitted with a graze fuse and the high-explosive warhead went off as it plunged through the branches at the edge of the wood. Van der Lee was killed instantly by the concussive blast. Weisenberger was literally blown to pieces, and the mortar tube—mangled into an unrecognizable ball of buckled steel—lodged high up in a tree.

"Jesus!" Daler said as the echoes of the shattering detonation died away. "Oh, Jesus bloody Christ!" He dropped the useless grenades and ran back to the savannah to collect a rifle.

From below, a high-pitched whistle blew the World War II victory signal—three short and one long. Phase Three had started.

Daler slung the Kalashnikov over his shoulder and headed for the trail leading to the gravel terraces. He was to pick up the Hammer-Dennis bazooka and its two grenades and follow the two men down to the bridge over the wadi. From here the three of them could enfilade the remaining battery. Hammer and Dennis were already armed with Uzis for this purpose.

Three more of the Israeli submachine guns were in the hands of Dean, Mazzari, and Novotny, who were to make a frontal assault on the breached gateway from their temporary shelter in the ravine. The sixth and last was carried by Kurt Schneider. He and Wassermann, with his sharpshooting Armalite, had been entrusted with a specific task: to seek and destroy the jeep-mounted TOW. "The bastards have a maximum range of four thousand yards," Dean had told them, "but they're ineffective at much less than three hundred and unusable below seventy-five or a hundred. So the closer you get, the safer you are, okay? Furneux and Goldsmith can follow you down, pick up the second RPG-7 on the way, and keep the shells for the jeep when you locate it."

Panting and covered in dust, Daler slid down the last slope of gravel and joined Dennis and Hammer at the bridge. They were crouched behind the stone parapet, firing at the field-gun emplacement above them and to their left. Machine-gun fire sparkled from the dark wall alongside the twenty-five pounder and shells burst at regular intervals along the lip of the wadi. Yet another star shell—red this time—zigzagged into the sky and flooded the battlefield with a hellish brilliance. "Shit!" Hammer said between his teeth. "We have to get a fuckin' move on, but. If we ain't inside them walls by daybreak, we're bloody done for." Already, behind the granite spur on which Gabotomi was built, a faint grayness, a dilution of the darkness, was visible in the east. And the distant glow of the forest fire off to the south seemed less angry now.

While the bloodred Verey light lasted, Daler loosed off a whole magazine at the battlement shielding the field gun. He heard cries behind the stonework, and figured that at least one member of the crew must have been hit. There was yelling off to the right, where Dean and his companions were storming the gates, firing as they ran. The twenty-five-pounder and one of the machine guns above were concentrating their fire in that direction, but the second machine gun had clearly been ordered to cover the bridge. Daler ducked his head as chips of stone stung his face and the far parapet was scarred with slugs. The red light was flickering, fading. When the clamor of the Uzis ceased and Hammer and Dennis were reloading, he said, "The Colonel said to keep them for the final assault, but we need to get bloody in first. If we used the NSP-2 sight, maybe we could knock the buggers out while it's still dark. What do you say?" He gestured toward the bazooka and its last two grenades.

Hammer paused for only a moment. And then: "Right

207

you are," he said. "After all, gettin' in *is* part of the assault, wouldn't you think? Have a go, boyo!"

Dennis fitted a rocket as Daler lifted the bazooka to his shoulder and peered through the infrared sight. The field gun had been swung around to give it the tightest traverse toward Dean and his men; part of the breech and the shadowy figures toiling around it were now visible behind the steel shield. Daler supported his elbows on the parapet, heedless of the stream of lead that was still being poured into the dark. "*Now!*" he shouted.

Dennis dropped to the ground behind him. Daler squeezed the firing trigger inside the forward of the two handgrips, and flame streaked from the tail end of the tube. With a terrifying roar the rocket grenade arrowed toward the city wall. It struck the battlement immediately behind the breech of the twenty-five-pounder and the HEAT warhead exploded. The cracking detonation that accompanied the shell burst was immediately eclipsed by a louder, deeper explosion. A ball of fire erupted over the belvedere and streamed upward into the canopy of smoke obscuring the sky.

Hammer was dancing up and down in excitement. "Good on you, boyo! Good on you! You must have set off the shells on the ammo lift! That's great; that'll show the bastards!"

Daler and Dennis were already preparing the last rocket. Daler fired at the machine-gun nest, hit the wall just below the sandbagged emplacement, and brought a cascade of stonework down onto the rock. "Okay, let's go!" Hammer yelled. "We should be able to climb up into the town—over the stones and through the breach."

Firing his Uzi from the hip, he crossed the bridge and led them at a run up the slant of rock on the far side of the wadi. A moment later the bridge disappeared in a holocaust of flame as a TOW missile homed in on the abandoned bazooka.

Inside the main gate, Dean, Mazzari, and Novotny flattened themselves against the stones of the arch. Behind them, the wrecked personnel carrier steamed over its charnel-house interior. There were dead men on the ramp and there was one half in and half out of the empty guardhouse on the opposite side of the arch. But in front of them the small entrance *place* was deserted. Like the cultivators and goatherds outside the town, the inhabitants were keeping a very low profile. It wasn't their war. Most of the civilian population had either run for the old silver mine or simply stayed indoors, hoping the fighting would go away. Dean moved to the inner side of the arch. "Cover us," he said tersely to the Pole.

Novotny eased himself to the corner and hovered, raking his glance right and left. Nobody. Apart from the crackle of flames coming from the burning house, the *place* was silent. He fired two short bursts from the Uzi to discourage any would-be heroes as Mazzari and his chief sprinted for the alley leading to the central square. Then, as Mazzari in turn surveyed the open space from the far side, he ran across to join them.

The alley was as deserted as the *place*. So was the square. And now the day was definitely breaking: in the gray half-light, Dean could make out the empty stalls, the ruined mosque on the far side. He raised the whistle that hung from a lanyard around his neck and blew the same victory signal. It was answered from behind them, on both sides. The groups led by Hammer and Schneider were safely inside the town.

"We can't hope to eliminate the whole damned garrison," Dean had said at his final briefing. "We don't know the exact strength, for one thing—probably a couple of hundred, of whom seventy or eighty percent should be stymied on the far side of the blown viaduct. Even so, that leaves too many for us to take out man by man. Once we've battered our way through the outer defenses, therefore, we make straight for this palace or whatever it is—Mazzari's shown you the location. This bastard Anya-Kutu's gonna have his command post

209

there, that's for sure. And once we've taken that, we've taken the town."

Each group had been ordered to make its own way to the street leading to the palace entrance, cleaning up any resistance it met on the way. Dean would then decide what form the final assault would take, when he had weighed the situation.

Once they had clambered up and over the breached wall, Hammer and his men encountered no resistance at all. Skirting the *souks*, they found themselves in back of Anya-Kutu's headquarters and waited at the corner of the street for the others to appear.

Schneider and Wassermann had the most difficult job. Scaling the ruined fortification where the mortar had knocked out guns and gunners, they crossed the belvedere and took one of the steep stone staircases leading toward the highest part of the town. As the light grew brighter, the ascent became more hazardous: every wall, every roof, every twist in the alley could hide defenders ready to fire as the targets became clearer. Furneux and Goldsmith, who were bringing up the rear, were in addition encumbered with the bazooka and its shells; it would cost them vital seconds to unsling their rifles and fire in the event of an unexpected attack.

They had been climbing for some minutes when there was an outbreak of shooting behind and below them, somewhere near the central square. They heard the whipcrack of carbines, the distinctive pounding of several submachine guns, and then two separate shots that sounded as if they had been fired from a revolver. Soon afterward—they were crossing a courtyard separating two flights of steps—the boxy, garbled tones of a voice speaking through a walkie-talkie radio came to them from over the rooftops. Behind the distorted words was the sound of an idling automobile motor.

As they listened, the radio ceased and the motor was gunned. Slowly at first, and then more rapidly, the whine of gears rose up the scale, as if the vehicle was

210

running down a steep grade. Wassermann stopped and grabbed Schneider's arm, pointing along a lane that led off at right angles to their route. One short block away, parallel to the stairway they were climbing, a wider street sloped down toward the center. "The missile jeep?" Wassermann whispered. "Maybe they ordered it down to block the Colonel and the others already?"

Schneider cottoned on at once. He raced back to Goldsmith and Furneux, gesturing urgently. The three of them crouched down in the middle of the courtyard. Goldsmith lifted the bazooka to his shoulder, his hands closed around the two pistol grips. The whine of gears grew louder. And then, as inevitably as a cloud crossing the sun, the jeep appeared in the gap at the end of the lane. Goldsmith pressed the rocket-firing trigger and the grenade screeched away toward the intersection.

It hit the rear end of the jeep, below the tripod supporting the launching tube, just before the vehicle disappeared from sight. The cobbles trembled beneath their feet as the grenade and the missile above it exploded in a single blazing roar. Stones and fragments of adobe wall showered down from damaged buildings onto the bloody shambles of the jeep. Before the noise had died away, Wassermann swung his Armalite up to his shoulder, sighting, aiming, and firing in a single fluid movement. From the roof of a house farther down the stairway, a rifleman who had been about to open fire on the group around the bazooka toppled and fell into the alley.

"Good!" Schneider shouted. "Good! Come, now. We go to help the Colonel." Occasional shots still sounded from the square below.

Picking up the RPG-7 and its remaining grenade, they changed direction and raced down the lane. As they passed the smoking wreck of the jeep, a soldier stepped out of a doorway higher up the hill, the Schmeisser in his hands spitting flame. Wassermann dropped onto one knee; as before, he downed the gunman with a single shot. But Goldsmith had fallen under the hail of lead. He rolled over and over down the cobbled grade, came to rest against a curbstone, and lay still.

"*Gott in Himmel!*" Schneider raced after him, bent down, and gently lifted the fallen man's shoulders. Goldsmith's head hung limp as the head of a broken doll. Schneider looked up. "No chance." He drew a hand across his belly and shook his head. "All gone here."

"Oh, shit!" said Wassermann. "We'll have to come back for him later. Right now, it sounds as if the Colonel needs help." Schneider sighed and nodded. Furneux was already in the shelter of an alleyway on the far side of the street. Hefting the bazooka once more, they made their way as fast as they could back to the square.

Behind the mosque, Dean and his men had been surprised by a last-ditch squad of Anya-Kutu's personal guard. Mazzari had received a flesh wound in the leg that was painful but not incapacitating. Once it had been bound up and the flow of blood stanched, he was able to hobble after the others, giving them covering fire as they slowly forced the defenders back toward the palace.

Dean was keeping the fight at maximum distance, using the superiority of the Uzi over the old German MP-40 Schmeissers used by the Nya Nyerere. The Israeli weapon's sixty-four-round magazine was twice as big as the Schmeisser's; its rate of fire was marginally higher; and, decisively, it had a slightly longer range—225 yards against 200. Shooting at this distance, the mercs were able to use classic urban guerrilla tactics, flushing their opponents out from doorway to doorway, from wall to wall, while they themselves remained unscathed and virtually in the open because of the range differential. This advantage was greatly increased when Schneider, Wassermann, and Furneux joined them to supply covering fire with their automatic rifles.

The last squad of tribesmen fought well, using their knowledge of the town's rabbit-warren streets to the full.

There were about a dozen of them and they had lost only one man by the time their retreat had brought them back to the street outside the palace gates. But here disaster struck *them*. They darted across the roadway toward the entrance . . . and there were two Uzis and a Kalashnikov trained on the open gateway from the intersection at the corner of the palace wall. Hammer, Dennis, and Daler, arriving early at the rendezvous, had heard the fight coming their way and decided to make a surprise party for the retreating tribesmen. There was an appalling clamor as the three guns opened up at once. Five of the Nya Nyerere were cut apart by the stream of slugs from the submachine guns; two more fell to Daler's rifle; the remaining four, dragging a wounded comrade, dashed inside the palace. The great gates, of teak sheathed in armor plate, swung shut.

They heard the sound of bolts and locks and props being hammered into place. A jabber of voices. And then the same manic tones that Schneider had first noticed over the radio of the missile jeep: . . . *unprovoked and dastardly attack by neocolonialist mercenaries . . . fascist lackeys murdering innocent women and children . . . paid vultures of the imperialist powers . . . totally unjustified . . . peaceful democratic enclave . . . right to self-determination . . . call on our African brothers and nonracist comrades . . . not too late . . .*

Dean nodded at the bazooka. "How many shells you got left?"

"One," said Schneider.

"Okay. Use it. Let's get this over with—or it *will* be too late." The mercenary leader jerked his head toward the gates.

At point-blank range, the rocket grenade blew a four-foot hole in the armor plate, splintered one gate into ruins, and hurled the other through the Moorish arches into the courtyard. The mercs were through the gap, guns blazing, before the choking smoke had cleared. Two more soldiers lay dead beside the fountain. Seven

213

or eight men, unarmed but in uniform, cowered beneath the veranda.

Dean stopped at the edge of the courtyard. He was holding the bazooka. Behind him, the grim-faced members of his team stood with Uzis and rifles at the ready. "All right," he shouted. "Come out unarmed, with your hands in the air, or we'll blow the place to hell and set fire to it with you inside." He hefted the rocketless weapon menacingly between his hands.

The bluff worked. A dozen more men filed out of the chambers surrounding the courtyard. Last of all came Anya-Kutu. He was wearing a bush shirt with five rows of medal ribbons across his massive chest, and his face was suffused with rage. "This dastardly and cowardly attack will have to be paid for," he mouthed. "You will answer for it before the tribune of the United Nations. Such vile and unprovoked aggression, your masters will learn—"

"Save it for the Moroccan courts," Dean interrupted curtly. "They may disapprove of strangers trying to carve a slice of their country for themselves."

It was after the prisoners had been herded together in one of the reception areas inside the shattered gates that Dean heard the sound of the helicopter. The mercs were going through the palace room by room, searching for stragglers. The sun was up now and he saw the shadow of the machine flit across the courtyard before it sank down and hovered over a section of the outer wall farther up the hill. It was, Dean was certain, the same unmarked ship that had spotted them for the ambushers on the way up from Halakaz. That meant that it had in some way been associated with the Berbers. So what the hell was it doing here now?

He didn't have to wait long to find out. Somewhere at a lower level among the palace's honeycomb apartments, a starter whirred and a powerful motor burst into life. Immediately afterward, there were three long blasts on a klaxon. For the next few minutes, events moved with bewildering speed.

Anya-Kutu, who had been surreptitiously shifting position behind his men, made a sudden dash for a doorway. Beyond it were the stairs leading to the underground cells where Mazzari had been imprisoned. Somebody shouted a warning. Somebody else raised a gun. Mazzari himself, who was nearest the door, called, "All right, this one's mine!" With an immense hop, skip, and jump on his injured leg, he sprang to the head of the stairway, barring the rebel leader's passage. "Try it again without the hired help, old man," Mazzari said softly.

Anya-Kutu scarcely paused in his rush to escape. He charged at the big sergeant like an enraged bull, hamlike fists flailing, in the hope of knocking Mazzari aside with the sheer weight of his massive body. Despite the wound, Mazzari stood firm, as solid as a rock. Anya-Kutu staggered back, astonished at the man's strength. He came in again. Mazzari punched him, hard, in the solar plexus. "How does it feel on the receiving end . . . brother?" he said. He hit the rebel leader again, with all his huge strength.

Anya-Kutu went down, folding forward as the breath left his body. But he was tough. He came up again like a rubber ball, swinging a roundhouse left that caught Mazzari over the heart and knocked him sideways. Mazzari brought his laced hands savagely down on the back of Anya-Kutu's neck. He dropped for the second time, and as he scrambled back and up, he shot out his foot and kicked viciously and deliberately at the bloodstained bandage covering Mazzari's wound. With a bellow of rage, Mazzari picked him up bodily and threw him down the stairs.

Novotny started after him, his Uzi ready to fire, but Dean pulled him back. "Let him go," he said. And then: "*Edmond! Look out!*"

Mazzari swung around. Beneath the Moorish arches

215

bordering the courtyard, Molony stood with an expression of malevolent fury on his face. He was dressed in Nya Nyerere uniform, and the cocked revolver in his hand was aimed at Mazzari's heart. "Why, you dirty, treacherous little—" the African began. But before he could finish the sentence, Molony fired.

Because of its cumbersome breech and short, slender barrel, the foresight on the Dardick pistol is an oversize triangle shaped like a shark's fin. Dean didn't have time to bring the gun up into the classic two-handed position and use this aid to straight shooting. He shot from the hip, through the open end of the holster. The two reports seemed to crack out simultaneously, but Dean's was a hundredth of a second earlier. The heavy-caliber, steel-jacketed slug took Molony in the right side, just below his gun arm, plowing through both lungs and smashing an exit wound the size of a grapefruit beyond his heart. Spun around by the impact of the bullet, he crashed into the pillar of an arch and slid to the mosaic floor, spraying bright scarlet blood over the tiny blue-and-green tiles. His own shot whistled past Mazzari's head and drilled a hole in a Persian carpet hanging on the wall behind.

There was a sudden shout from Daler, who was on the flat roof Mazzari had used in his escape. Two floors below him, at the palace's lowest level, doors had opened onto a lane that twisted up toward the summit of the rock, inside the fortified wall. A Land Rover shot out backward, skidded around, and accelerated away. Dusty, bruised, and bloodied, his beribboned jacket ripped open, Anya-Kutu clung to the outside passenger seat. At the wheel was a dark girl, a European wearing riding breeches and a tight sweater.

The vehicle rocked to a halt beneath the hovering helicopter. A rope ladder snaked down, and the rebel leader, followed by the girl, climbed up and disappeared inside the machine. "I'll be damned!" Dean exploded, watching the helicopter fly away toward the northeast. The girl driving the Land Rover was Rada Hradec.

Before he could say any more, Daler was shouting again, more urgently, pointing away over the rooftops to the west. "Hey, Cap! . . . For Chrissake! Would you look at *that!*"

"What is it?" Dean called up.

"A fucking invasion! And we've nothing left to fight with. You better come up here quick!"

Followed by Wassermann and Novotny, Dean leaped for the tiled canopy surrounding the courtyard and pulled himself up onto the roof. He caught his breath. The depression that stretched between the savannah and the three sandstone bluffs was alive with movement. Surging around the huts and tents, a tide of horsemen raced toward the town. There were hundreds of them, brandishing rifles, muskets, carbines, submachine guns, bright robes flying above the streaming manes and tails of their mounts.

"My God!" Wassermann exclaimed. "*Indians*, yet!"

Dean shook his head. The riders reined in their horses, rearing and pawing, on the far side of the wadi. Before the dust cloud had settled, they were swarming down the stony slope and up the nearer side, uttering blood-curdling yells and firing as they came. In the lead was a tall dark man dressed in a burnoose and djellaba striped with citron and azure blue. "Berbers," Dean said.

"What the hell are we goin' to do?" Novotny asked.

"Nothing. We'll offer no resistance. It's their town, for God's sake! Or at least it was. Maybe they want it back." He turned and looked down into the courtyard. Stray slugs were already chipping fragments from the adobe buildings or whining off into the sky. "What we need . . ." Dean said. "A strip of white . . . Hey! Edmond! You speak Arab, don't you?"

Mazzari looked up and nodded.

"Come up here, then. You got yourself a job. You others—Dennis, Furneux, Sean—give the guy a hand so that we can pull him the rest of the way."

Half a minute later, Mazzari was on the roof. He was still dressed in nothing but the sarong-shift he had used for his escape the previous evening. He limped to the edge of the roof, unwound the improvised garment, and stood there, splendid in his ebony nudity, holding the cotton rectangle so that the wind teased it out into a long white flag.

The waiting mercs heard a shouted command from below. The firing stopped. There was more shouting, and then Mazzari began to speak, leaning down and cupping his hands around his mouth so that the words would carry. The interchange seemed to go on for a long time. Over Mazzari's shoulder, Dean watched a rolling cloud of dust approach along the trail leading toward the coast. A six-wheel command truck halted by the wrecked bridge on the far side of the wadi. A spruce figure, uniformed, neat, buckles and boots gleaming in the sunlight, strode toward the ranks of silent, waiting Arabs. Paul Ibanez, captain of gendarmerie.

Mazzari was still listening, talking, listening. Finally he turned around to face Dean. He was shaking with laughter—manic, liquid, gleeful. "You know what?" he choked. "Hah! Somebody had tipped these Berbers off. . . . Whee! Hoo! . . . They ambushed us because they'd been told . . . Hah! They'd been told we weren't coming to attack this town but to *reinforce* it!"

EPILOGUE ═══════

"I should have known, of course," Marc Dean said. "The explanation was so simple, so obvious, that it fooled me. The girl came from east of the Iron Curtain, all right—but not as a refugee. She was still working for them."

"Working for who?" Hammer said. "The Russkies?"

"No, not necessarily. Not for the Czechs, either. One of their international organizations, probably. Could even be the KGB, but more likely Comecon or one of the other bodies with an economic or industrial angle. After all, they could use silver and mineral concessions too."

"I still don't understand the role played by that girl," Mazzari said. "I mean to say, what was she trying to do?"

They were drinking again at the sidewalk café in the Place Glouai, Halakaz. It was breathlessly hot. It seemed like a lot more than six days had passed since they last looked out across that sun-drenched square. It seemed like more than a few hours since Captain Ibanez had brought them racing back to town in his command truck.

"What Rada Hradec was trying to do," Dean explained, "was quite simply to mix it. No specific aim to the operation—just to fuck up *our* operation in every way possible and preferably to make it self-destruct."

"But why?" Hammer objected. "What good would it do?"

"You know why we were hired . . . and who hired us," Dean said. "Once the Nya Nyerere were wiped out as an effective force and their half-assed independence

219

claim forgotten, our bosses could get around a confer-ence table with the three countries bordering Gabotomi and hammer out a deal on those mineral rights. But sup-pose we'd fouled up and left the Nya Nyerere in a *stronger* position—who d'you think would have gotten the concessions if they'd been dealing with Anya-Kutu? Don't forget, the guy was Moscow-trained."

"Yes, I see that, old chap." Mazzari was frowning. "But . . . I mean, there are still a couple of things that don't make sense."

"Very few things make sense in international rela-tions," Dean said. "That's one thing I've learned. That's why I do what I do and why I don't take sides."

"Those Berber johnnies were put onto us—and decided to ambush us—because they'd been told we were rein-forcements for Anya-Kutu, right? And you say it was the Hradec girl who tipped them off?"

"Sure it was. Dammit, I *saw* the Berber chief coming out of her office here in town!"

"And it was she who fixed for that chopper to act as a spotter plane for them?"

"That's the way it seems, yes."

"And the Berbers are enemies of the Nya Nyerere—were in fact probably planning to raid Gabotomi them-selves?"

"Right."

"Then how the *hell*"—Mazzari sounded indignant—"do you explain the fact that the same girl, and the same chopper, were on hand to *help* the Nya Nyerere, to res-cue their leader when we took the town?"

Dean said, "The Nya Nyerere were menaced by two separate forces: the Berbers and us. If we could be fooled into fighting one another, guess who'd be the bet-ter off for it?"

"You mean she was just using the Berbers? In that old Brit phrase, the comrades were playing both ends against the middle—and we were the bloody middle?"

"You got it. Once Molony had tipped her off—"

"Yeah—how about that southern son of a bitch?" Hammer cut in. "How'd you read that bastard, Marc?"

"Ibanez got a printout on him from the Interpol computer," Dean said. "He was a member of the workers' revolutionary wing of the IRA. Moscow-trained again. I guess the comrades' industrial spies got wind of the operation somehow—probably through a leak in one of the companies employing us. So they infiltrated Molony at the time we were recruiting, faked references and all. He must have been given the Hradec girl's name as a contact. Remember the day we planned the raid on the army depot? Molony was on the loose in town that day: he didn't get up to the ridge to join Edmond until late afternoon. He must have contacted her then, spilled all the beans he had, and received orders to make further reports on the radio."

"Bastard!" Hammer said.

Dean was silent. He was thinking of his own involvement with the Czech siren. Rudolph Valentino Dean, the Don Juan of Halakaz! No girl could resist his manly charms! He smiled wryly to himself. No wonder Rada had been so . . . accommodating! Thank Christ that their conversation, which would certainly have been taped, could have told the communist evaluators so little.

"Where d'you think the chopper came from?" Mazzari asked. "And where did it go? Algeria?"

"Maybe. They might have flown off in that direction to mislead us. Some left-wing organization for sure—but whether it was here, in Algeria or Mauritania, or even from the Polisario, we'll never know. They lost the battle but they saved their generals anyway."

Furneux and the other five mercs, who had been souvenir-hunting in the *souks* up on the casbah, had returned to the table and overheard Dean's last remark. "They lost the fuckin' battle, all right!" Furneux enthused. "You can say that again, Colonel. We sure

221

showed them black bastards where they got off, didn't we?"

Big-mouth, Dean thought. The first one to take cover when there's any shit flying around, and it has to be him shooting off his mouth about how brave we were! One thing's for sure, though: there won't be any Furneux on the list next time I organize a raid!

Captain Ibanez was crossing the square. The Mercedes was parked by the fireplug again. He was dressed in sandals, sky-blue jeans, and a beautifully pressed white shirt. Sunlight flashed fiercely from the lenses of his smoked glasses. He drew up a chair and sat down with Dean and his men. "I trust you gentlemen are enjoying your interrupted stay in our town?" he said politely.

"Very much," Dean replied. "I hope that you, for your part, were not too inconvenienced by any . . . interruptions . . . in the interior?"

"By no means." The policeman waved a languid hand. "Some local skirmish between rival factions among the more obscure tribes. I did not arrive in time to witness it myself. In any case, it is over." He raised a finger to summon a waiter, and added, "A border commission including UN observers and representatives of the three interested countries will arrive in two weeks to determine exactly where the frontiers lie. After that, I believe I heard that certain geologists and mining experts may be investigating the mineral prospects in the area. A company of *goums* have been sent to maintain public order."

"Talking of which . . ." Dean remained deadpan. "I believe there may have been some trouble at the army camp a week or so ago."

"Possibly." Ibanez flicked a speck of dust from one knee. "I was off duty myself at the time."

"It's greatly to be hoped that such . . . irregularities . . . do not in any way embarrass the local authorities. It is most regrettable when these things occur."

"The official view is that a small band of desperados

or terrorists—undoubtedly from some neighboring country—made an abortive raid in search of arms. Fortunately—most fortunately—nobody was killed." The policeman slid a blue Gitane packet from his breast pocket and lit a cigarette. A waiter was standing at his elbow. "Perhaps you gentlemen will permit me to offer you a farewell drink?"

"We should be delighted," Dean replied. "But . . . a farewell drink?"

"But yes. I think I warned you before that foreigners are allowed to stay only a week here. Unless a special visa is granted. In your case—although I myself would of course support your application—I am afraid that it might not be granted. And today is your last day in Halakaz. Perhaps you will be rejoining your ship?"

"Our ship?"

"The *Esmeralda*," Ibanez said suavely. "She had to put back for a minor repair. She sails for Rotterdam at dawn tomorrow. You did say you were merchant seamen, did you not?"

Dean coughed. "Of course. There was one other thing: I understand there was a forest fire in the interior. I hope not too much damage was done?"

"The wind changed and turned the flames back onto the area that was already destroyed," Ibanez said. "With nothing left to burn, the blaze soon died out. But what is a few hundred acres of jungle compared to peace in the region? Believe me . . ." He shook his head. Apparently inconsequentially, he added, "Pending the results of the commission, the administration of Gabotomi has been left in the hands of the Berbers. If only all administrative decisions were as simple as that. . . ."

"Like the story of the two psychiatrists," Wassermann said when the policeman had left them, "I wonder what he meant by that."

"I think he was trying to explain his position," Dean said.

"Meaning?"

223

Dean watched the sunlight flashing on the chrome of the Mercedes as it turned out of the square. "Meaning the guy's on the take, probably from the people hiring us; meaning some of his bosses probably are too, which is why everything was made so easy for us; but also meaning that there are different factions—there are *always* different factions—and that some of the bosses are on the other side, so he has to keep his nose clean. If he wants to keep his job, he has to report anything that comes to his notice *officially*."

"But wasn't it him tipped off the soldiers about our raid?"

"No. That was Molony." Dean pushed back his chair. "Well, if anyone wants a passage on that boat, I guess we'd better make it to the docks and fix it with the purser, huh?"

"Actually . . ." Mazzari cleared his throat. "We rather thought we'd take the train up to Fez and Tangier, and then cross over the strait and fool around in Spain a little. You wouldn't care to come with us, Cap?"

Dean smiled and shook his head. "No thanks, Edmond. I have to go on to the *souks* and find a pair of red leather slippers for my son. After that, there's a blond in Brussels I'd like to look up."

LOOKING FORWARD!

The following is the opening section
from the next novel in the exciting new
Marc Dean MERCENARY series from Signet:

THE SECRET OF SAN FELIPE
#2

The island batteries began firing when the leading assault
craft was still half a mile offshore. The attackers,
crouched behind steel gunwales in their netted and
camouflaged combat gear, saw flame belching from the
gun muzzles reflected on low cloud an instant before the
first shellbursts fountained from the dark water. Then
the tropical predawn blackness was split in a hundred
places as all hell broke loose around the tiny port and
along the cliffs on either side of the inlet.

It wasn't a very big raid—three World War II infantry
landing craft, each carrying twenty men, and a re-
modeled, converted LVT-6, modified to take a Saladin
armored car and a Büssing–NAG truck laden with arms
and explosives. The mother ship from which they had
been disembarked, an old Florida automobile ferry, lay
hove-to safely out of range of the guns.

The defense wasn't all that strong, either: it just
seemed alarmingly powerful after the dark silence of a
moonless Caribbean night. In fact, according to intelligence reports smuggled out of the island, the port com-

mander had at his disposal four Oerlikons; two 75mm tank guns; a dozen 105mm mortars; a quantity of heavy machine guns, bazookas, and 40mm cannon; and two self-propelled Ontos vehicles, each firing six 106mm recoilless rifles. "No radar, thank Christ, no sensors, and no computerized fields of fire!" the leader of the expedition said to the helmsman as the LVT plowed at eight knots through the swell. "I guess the bossman can't afford as much ironmongery as he would like to defend this neck of the woods."

The same wide-disk caterpillars that could rattle the tracked landing vehicle up to 20 mph on dry land also propelled it through the water, and it was the phosphorescence from the froth churned up by these rather than the whine of the 250-horsepower diesels in the stern that had alerted the islanders to the attack.

The night was alive with orange, scarlet, and crimson flashes crisscrossed by multicolored streams of tracer as the three LCI's, moving at more than twice the speed of the heavy transporter, forged ahead toward the port. The roar and thwack of 75's, the hammering of the Oerlikons, and the sharp stutter of automatic fire mingled with the sound of the invaders' weapons to compete with the shells exploding among the raiding vessels.

The men in the LCI's were mercenaries—Puerto Ricans, Cubans, expatriates from Nicaragua, Venezuela, and the former British West Indies, officered by a small group of Americans and Europeans. Their mission was neither to take the town nor to establish any kind of bridgehead, but simply to ensure the safe landing of the two vehicles in the LVT . . . and make sure that they were able to drive off into the interior unmolested.

They were armed with the latest Russian Kalashnikov AKM automatic rifles, Skorpion machine pistols from Czechoslovakia, Soviet RPG-7 rocket launchers, and a variety of mortars and grenades. But the weapons stacked to the canvas roof of the 4½-ton ex-Wehrmacht Büssing truck were all manufactured in the United States or at the FN arsenal near Liège, in Belgium. Destined for rebels whom certain powers wished to help but dared not openly support, they would be unloaded as soon as the convoy reached the mountains in the center of the island and dispersed among the guerrilla bands hiding there. It was the devout hope of the international businessmen who had, with government encouragement, financed the operation that these groups, spearheaded by the Saladin armored car, would eventually march on the capital and oust the dictator who was threatening to sequester the profitable mines in the interior.

"The idea is to make them think it's some kind of invasion raid," the spokesman for the business interests had told them. "Tie down the whole port defense until the two vehicles have gotten clear—then you can withdraw your men as if the attack had been beaten off." The native islanders crewing the truck and the armored car, he said, were familiar with dirt roads and trails that could lead them to the rebel headquarters without the risk of any interference from the dictator's patrols.

"The 75's are located on top of the bluff—one on either side of the creek mouth," the commander of the expedition had said at the final briefing. "The two mobile Ontos batteries—again one on either side—can maneuver between there and the port at head of the inlet. It's about three hundred yards in. The rest of the hardware is deployed around the basin."

A huge African who was in charge of the leading LCI said, "You mean we have to run a three-hundred gauntlet, Cap? Being shot at by 75's and a dozen 106mm pom-poms before we can get ashore?"

"Yeah. But we got the two best mortar teams in the islands aboard the LVT," the leader replied. He was a tall, muscular American with pale hair and blue eyes. "You got your RPG-7's on each of the landing craft. Between us, we concentrate all our firepower on the run-in on just *one* side of the creek. That way, if we knock out the two sets of guns there, we can sail on in the lee of the other bluff, knowing that our craft will be too close inshore to be touched: they'll be in dead water, safely below the traverse of the batteries above."

"Okay, Cap—but those Ontos bastards are tough weapons. Six 106mm barrels firing at once—that packs some punch!"

"Sure. But they're easy targets on direct aim: there's a hell of a back-blast visible from those eight-foot barrels . . . and one hit puts the whole half-dozen out of action."

The actual assault proved the commander right. In the sky, star shells wrapped red and green octopus arms around the dark as the flotilla approached the two small headlands framing the inlet. Soon the explosions from mortars and rocket launchers added vivid orange flashes to the twinkling points of fire along the right-hand clifftop. Then a parachute flare dissolved the night to silver the roofs of the port.

At once one of the mortars in the bows of the LVT scored a direct hit on the Ontos vehicle. Detonating rounds etched firecracker patterns against the dark bulk of the island as the stricken battery flared into oblivion. Soon afterward—perhaps because the streams of lead hosed shoreward from the LCI's had killed the crew—the 75mm gun on the right headland ceased firing.

The expedition leader barked instructions into the microphone of a hand-held radio. The three landing craft wheeled through a forty-five degree turn and headed for the opposite bluff. Two of them made it, but the third, a fraction slow answering to the helm, blew up in a spectacular eruption of flame and steam, victim of a concerted attack from the remaining Ontos and 75.

Steaming through the tower of white water still falling back into the sea, the cumbersome LVT was caught in a hail of crossfire from the clifftop and the port. Steel-jacketed slugs thrashed the upperworks; antitank grenades burst harmlessly against her heavily armored sides. "Mazzari!" the leader shouted into his mouthpiece. "Run ashore as soon as that goddamn bluff's low enough to scale. Send half your men to silence that shit on the headland. The rest can work their way inland and join Neilsen's team on the west of the basin."

"Willco!" the big African's voice crackled in the receiver.

Below the white-painted houses surrounding the basin, a dozen fishing boats rocked in the wash of the landing craft. Men from the second LCI waded ashore between them, firing submachine guns from the hip. Beneath the barnacle-encrusted piers of a wooden jetty, half of Mazzari's men stole behind the hulls of private powerboats to link up with them. But the main objective—the reason this small port had been chosen rather than another—was a stone slipway slanting down into the water from a boat-builder's yard at one side of the basin.

Two hundred yards away, the LVT maneuvered through 180 degrees in the center of the creek and then backed up toward the paved slope, its caterpillars churning.

The port area was now becoming an inferno. Flames from a tarred shack set alight by a grenade flickered redly on the underside of a pall of smoke hanging over the town. In the fiery light, invaders scrambled up banks of rubble spilling into the water where the RPG-7's rockets had breached the quay. They charged along the jetty, blasting the strongpoints from which Oerlikon and machine-gun volleys were sweeping the dock. Grenades and mortar shells exploding in the narrow lanes leading to the port punctuated the incessant rattle of small-arms fire. Voices shouted, boots clattered on cobbles, soldiers screamed and died. The oily surface of the harbor was strewn with planks and splintered spars, its crimson reflections pockmarked by the heads of survivors swimming away from the sunken assault craft.

As the parachute flare guttered and died, allowing darkness to settle again over the sea, the caterpillars of the LVT grounded on the submerged portion of the slipway. Steel links skidded on the weed-slimed surface, bit through to the stone, and slowly hauled the big amphibian out of the water.

Fierce hand-to-hand fighting had broken out on the headland, but the crew manning the remaining 75 managed to swing the gun around and fire two shots inland before they were overwhelmed by Mazzari's men. Their aim was good. The first round burst high up on the LVT's side, buckling the plates and reducing the mortar platform to a tangle of steel sliding with fragments of human flesh and brain. The second blew off the port caterpillar track and sheared a drive shaft.

It was no longer important. The target had been

reached. With a rattle of chains, the ramp at the stern of the vessel slammed down, and the truck, followed by the Saladin armored car, roared out onto the slipway. Two minutes later, screened by a line of smoke canisters launched from the Saladin, they were on a tarmac highway heading at 45 mph for the intersection where a dirt road led to the mountains.

As they passed through the outskirts of the tiny port, the gunner in the six-wheeled Saladin's turret blasted two of his 75mm shells into a blockhouse from which Oerlikons were firing. The rest of the vehicle's forty-three-round magazine was too valuable to the rebel cause to waste. Beneath the canvas top of the German truck there were crates of Armalite rifles, MP40 machine pistols, Belgian-made Uzi submachine guns, and a quantity of bazookas and mortar tubes. In addition to grenades, cases of plastic explosive and antipersonnel mines, the truck carried more than one hundred thousand rounds of 7.62, 5.56, and 9mm ammunition in magazines and belts.

The assault group's instructions had been to keep the port defenses tied down for a quarter of an hour after the convoy had left. In that time, the rebel islanders had told them, they could be in the foothills beyond any possibility of pursuit.

Promptly fifteen minutes after the LVT's ramp had grounded, the commander blew a whistle and then shouted instructions into his radio. With the helmsman and the remaining member of his crew, he quit the stricken amphibian, leaping from the slipway into the water and wading to Neilsen's assault craft among the fishing boats.

Dodging behind bollards and stacks of lobster pots, crouching in the shelter of an upturned dory, Neilsen's men fell back toward the jetty, firing as they retreated. Five houses were burning, the streets around the harbor were littered with rubble, and the quay was strewn with dead.

The two halves of Mazzari's team had joined up and reembarked in the second LCI. As soon as the wounded, under cover of the high dockside, had been loaded into

Neilsen's craft, the ramps were raised and the two vessels backed out into the creek and headed for the open sea.

Out of the seventy-odd mercenaries who took part in the raid, seventeen were killed or missing, a further thirteen were wounded, and three were taken prisoner. ("Any sense, and those poor bastards'll bite on their cyanide capsules," one of the survivors said sourly as they climbed back aboard the mother ship. " 'Less they wanna be gagged with their own balls and then strangled with their guts!")

On the way back to Florida, the go-between who had arranged the assault with the expedition leader paid out the end money in cash, with an agreed bonus to go to the dependents of those killed. "Where to now?" the leader asked Mazzari as the big African buttoned the wad of bills into his breast pocket.

Mazzari grinned. His thick lips puckered and he whistled the first few bars of "Kingston Market."

"Jamaica?"

"There's a torch singer in Montego Bay," Mazzari said. He shook his head. "Oh, *brother*!" And then: "What about you, Cap?"

"I feel like music too," the American replied. "Singing and dancing. You know. I figured on heading for Brazil and staying in Rio awhile."